When he saw her lying there, the first sensation that swept over Reese was relief.

He might resent Neely like hell, might wish she'd disappear from his life and his memory, but he didn't want her dead, hurt or in danger.

The second sensation was…hard to identify. Something weak. Soft. Damnably foolish…

She looked so fragile. Vulnerable. There was a part of him—the part that remembered loving her—that wanted to close the door and lock them inside this safe place, then gather her into his arms and simply hold her.

Thank God the rest of him knew better than to give in to such weakness.

Dear Reader,

Once again, we've rounded up six exciting romances to keep you reading all month, starting with the latest installment in Marilyn Pappano's HEARTBREAK CANYON miniseries. *The Sheriff's Surrender* is a reunion romance with lots of suspense, lots of passion—lots of *emotion*—to keep you turning the pages. Don't miss it.

And for all of you who've gotten hooked on A YEAR OF LOVING DANGEROUSLY, we've got *The Way We Wed*. Pat Warren does a great job telling this tale of a secret marriage between two SPEAR agents who couldn't be more different— or more right for each other. Merline Lovelace is back with *Twice in a Lifetime,* the latest saga in MEN OF THE BAR H. How she keeps coming up with such fabulous books, I'll never know—but I *do* know we're all glad she does. Return to the WIDE OPEN SPACES of Alberta, Canada, with Judith Duncan in *If Wishes Were Horses....* This is the kind of book that will have you tied up in emotional knots, so keep the tissues handy. Cheryl Biggs returns with *Hart's Last Stand,* a suspenseful romance that will keep you turning the pages at a furious clip. Finally, don't miss the debut of a fine new voice, Wendy Rosnau. *A Younger Woman* is one of those irresistible stories, and it's bound to establish her as a reader favorite right out of the starting gate.

Enjoy them all, then come back next month for more of the best and most exciting romance reading around—only in Silhouette Intimate Moments.

Yours,

Leslie J. Wainger
Executive Senior Editor

Please address questions and book requests to:
Silhouette Reader Service
U.S.: 3010 Walden Ave., P.O. Box 1325, Buffalo, NY 14269
Canadian: P.O. Box 609, Fort Erie, Ont. L2A 5X3

The Sheriff's Surrender

MARILYN PAPPANO

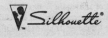

INTIMATE MOMENTS™

Published by Silhouette Books

America's Publisher of Contemporary Romance

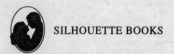

SILHOUETTE BOOKS

ISBN 0-373-27139-5

THE SHERIFF'S SURRENDER

Copyright © 2001 by Marilyn Pappano

Visit Silhouette at www.eHarlequin.com

Printed in U.S.A.

MARILYN PAPPANO

brings impeccable credentials to her writing career—a life-long habit of gazing out windows, not paying attention in class, daydreaming and spinning tales for her own entertainment. The sale of her first book brought great relief to her family, proving that she wasn't crazy but was, instead, creative. Since then she's sold more than forty books to various publishers and even a film production company.

She writes in an office nestled among the oaks that surround her country home. In winter she stays inside with her husband and their four dogs, and in summer she spends her free time mowing the yard that never stops growing and daydreams about grass that never gets taller than two inches.

You can write to her at P.O. Box 643, Sapulpa, OK, 74067-0643.

Chapter 1

Reese Barnett drove slowly down the main street of Killdeer, Kansas, his gaze sweeping side to side, across empty buildings and lots to empty parking spaces. The town was small, a nowhere place, and unremarkable except for the fact that it lay about halfway between Kansas City and Heartbreak, Oklahoma. Grass grew in cracks in the sidewalks, and the few buildings left standing were unoccupied—a grocery store, a gas station, a café. The place had never been prosperous, and these days, except for a combination gas station-grocery store-post office-restaurant on the edge of town and a handful of sorry houses, it was damn near a ghost town.

It was, according to his cousin Jace, a good place for a meeting.

Reese pulled into a parking lot that filled half the block and found a bit of shade underneath a blackjack oak. He parked facing the street, rolled down the windows, then shut off the engine. He was early for the meeting. Jace had asked him to show up first, to look around and make certain nothing seemed out of place. The only thing out of place was *him*, furtively scoping out a down-on-its-luck town with a population of maybe twenty, if he counted the stray cats and dogs.

Reaching for the cell phone, he dialed Jace's number. Jace answered on the third ring, skipped the greeting and went straight to business. "Where are you?"

"Sitting in front of what used to be a grocery store in the heart of what used to be a town."

"Everything okay?"

"No traffic, no people. Only the critters are out and about."

"Good. We'll be there in about ten minutes."

"I'll be waiting," Reese said dryly, then disconnected. He didn't have much of a clue about what was going on. All he knew was that he'd gotten a call from Jace that morning, asking for his help. Since he was in the help-giving business— his official title was Canyon County Sheriff—and since Barnetts never said no to family if they could help it, he'd taken a day off work. He'd followed Jace's instructions and left his uniform and badge at home. His black-and-white Blazer, complete with a shield on each door and a light bar on the roof, was parked at his house. He'd driven his own truck, worn jeans and a chambray shirt, boots and a straw Resistol.

Also per Jace's instructions, his Sig Sauer P-220 .45-caliber pistol was tucked between the seat and the console, his five-shot .38 was holstered at the small of his back, and his department-issue 12-gauge pump shotgun was within easy reach behind the seat. He was ready for damn near anything.

He did know one other detail—the favor Jace was asking of him involved baby-sitting. It would be for just a few days, his cousin had promised. All Reese had to do was keep this witness safe and breathing for a week, no more, while Jace wrapped up the case back in Kansas City, where he was a detective with the K.C. Police Department. Male or female, young, old, honest citizen or cowardly informant—Reese knew none of that. He didn't even know what crime the person had been a witness to.

But he was about to get a few answers.

The car that turned into the parking lot was a midsize sedan with heavily tinted side and back windows. He recognized Jace behind the wheel, but couldn't tell anything about the passenger. He stepped out of his truck as Jace parked beside it. Thanks to the window tint and the hat the passenger wore, Reese still couldn't tell much, although he presumed it was a woman. The hat was too fussy by far for a man.

Jace climbed out of the car and met Reese's gaze over the roof. Though they were the same age, the only sons of brothers who could have passed for twins, there was no family resemblance at all. Reese looked like their dads—brown hair, brown eyes—while Jace looked more like his Osage mother's family with black hair, bronzed skin and eyes so dark they seemed black.

"I appreciate your doing this," Jace said.

"Do I get an explanation, or do you plan to just drop her and run?"

"She's a lawyer who's been getting death threats. Last week someone tried to make good on them, so I put her in a safe house that turned out to be not so safe. Last night someone tried again."

"Which suggests that either your guy is damned lucky...or you've got a traitor in the department."

Jace nodded grimly.

"And no one knows where you've taken her now."

"She doesn't even have a clue herself. At this moment, only you and I know she'll be in Heartbreak."

"She have any bags?"

"Just one." Jace opened the trunk and lifted out a pricey leather suitcase. "If you have to get in touch with me, call my cell phone and leave a message for me to call, nothing more. And keep an eye on her. So far, she's been pretty cooperative, but that could change. And keep her safe. I really want to make this case."

While Jace opened the passenger door, Reese turned and stowed the suitcase in the cargo space at the rear of his truck. He turned back just in time to come face-to-face with the witness as she got out of the car. He stared, and she stared back. Even with the hat shadowing her face, he could see she was stunned—though no more than he.

Neely Madison. Criminal defense lawyer. Former friend. Former lover. And Reese's worst nightmare.

She looked as incredible as ever—tall, slender, perfect. Underneath the straw hat that sported a giant sunflower, a few strands of silky light brown hair parted across her forehead. Her eyes were brown, too, and too big for her face, giving her an innocent-waif look...but looks were often deceiving. There was nothing innocent or waifish about her. Nothing perfect about her, either.

Clenching his jaw, he pulled the suitcase out and dropped it to the ground with enough force to scuff the expensive leather. He slammed the door hard enough to rock the truck, then headed for the driver's side.

Before he reached the door, Jace grabbed his arm. "Come on, Reese, you agreed—"

"Only because I didn't know it was her. And you didn't tell me because you knew I'd say no."

"You can't walk away. Her life is in danger. Someone's trying to kill her!"

Reese jerked his arm free and faced his cousin. "Good! I wish him luck."

"You don't mean that."

Breathing in short, controlled puffs, Reese stared stonily at Jace. Did he wish Neely was dead? He wished he'd never met her, wished he'd never touched her, never wanted her, never needed her. Hell, he wished she'd never been born...but that was a whole different matter from wishing her dead.

And not wanting her dead was a whole different matter from risking his own life to keep her safe.

Well aware that she could hear him from the other side of the truck, Reese coldly, flatly said, "Don't bet on it." Then his anger surged again. "Why in hell didn't you tell me it was her this morning? It would have saved us all the trip. And why did you think I'd give a damn about keeping her safe? After everything that happened, everything she did—"

"Because I know you."

"Not well enough. Not if you think I'd agree to this."

For one long moment after another, they stared at each other. Reese was only faintly aware of a bee buzzing nearby, of the sun's heat beating down and the sweat that trickled down his spine. He was all too aware of Neely, seen from the corner of his eye, still standing at the sedan's door, one hand gripping the hot metal, that silly, floppy hat unmoving. He scowled at Jace, who scowled back just as fiercely.

It was Jace who broke the silence. His words were reasonable, his tone aggravated, his expression belligerent. "I asked you for help in protecting a witness, and you agreed. You can't back out now. It's not my fault you didn't ask the pertinent questions. We had an agreement, bubba. Now you have to honor it."

"I assumed you'd offered the pertinent information."

"You know what they say about assuming things," Jace said mildly. Then he sighed and lowered his voice. "You're right. I figured you'd try to say no if you knew up front that it was Neely. That's why I didn't tell you. But I also know you're professional enough to not let your personal feelings interfere with your job. Regardless of how you feel about her or what happened between you two in the past, she's the victim of a crime. And you're a cop, and you'll do your damnedest to keep her safe."

Reese shook his head. "Bring me a thief, a hooker or a murderer, and I'll do what I can. Bring me a *real* victim, and I'll do whatever it takes to protect 'em. But not her. She's not a victim—she turns other people into victims—and damned if I'll do anything that makes it possible for her to continue destroying lives."

"Get over it, Reese," Jace said scornfully. "It was nine years ago, and it wasn't her fault."

Nine years. He said it as if it were a lifetime, and in a way, to Reese it felt like one. In other ways, it seemed as if it were just last week. He'd never forgotten the anger, the bitterness, the hurt, the shame. He'd never quite gotten over the loss and the guilt. And it *was* her fault. If she hadn't been so stubborn, so convinced that she was right and everyone else was wrong, if she hadn't been so damned unreasonable...

"If she were living in Canyon County, you'd take her into protective custody without a second thought," Jace said accusingly.

"But she doesn't live there. She's not our problem."

"She became your problem the moment you said 'Sure, Jace, I'd be happy to help you out.'" Jace ran his fingers through his hair. "You've blamed her for what happened to Judy Miller for nine years. Well, bubba, if I take her back to the city and the next attempt on her life succeeds, you'll be far more responsible for that than she ever was for Miller. Do you want to live with that on your conscience?"

Reese wanted to shrug, to reply that it made no difference to him. He wanted to climb into his truck, drive away and never give this meeting—or Neely—another thought. He wanted to go back to the moment he'd answered the phone that morning and say "Sorry, Jace, don't have the manpower, don't have the budget, can't help you."

Well, he couldn't go back in time, but he could drive away and leave his cousin and Neely standing there. And what if he did? What if Jace took her back to the city and she was killed? He *would* be responsible, because he could have guaranteed her safety but had refused. It would prove he was no better, no more honorable, than she was.

And he needed to be better than she was.

But to have her back in his life, living temporarily in his house, bringing back all the bad memories and nightmares, making his present as damned impossible as his past.... Did he need *anything* that badly?

It was an effort to unclench his jaw, to force out words he didn't want to say. "Only until you find another place for her. Today and tomorrow. That's all you get. If she's still here then, she's going in the Canyon County jail."

Jace looked as if he wanted to argue, but knew better. Instead he nodded grimly. "I'll be in touch as soon as I have something set up. Thanks, bubba."

For a moment Reese simply stared at the hand his cousin offered, then grudgingly shook hands with him, then hugged him. "Today and tomorrow. And don't think I don't mean it." After releasing Jace, he climbed into the truck, started the engine and turned the air conditioner to high. He refused to look as Jace approached Neely, and he rolled up the window so he wouldn't have to hear their conversation. He couldn't believe his cousin—his best friend, the closest thing he had to a brother—had put him in this mess, couldn't believe he'd just agreed to take Neely Madison, of all people, into his home.

He was a better cousin and friend than Jace deserved.

Either that, or a damned fool.

As Jace picked up her suitcase, Neely stared at the dirty plate-glass windows that stretched across the front of the abandoned market. Sale prices were painted across the glass in faded white: Ground Beef, 3 Pounds/$1.00 and Bread, 5 Loaves/$1.00. Obviously the place had been empty a long, long time. In Kansas City, the windows would have been broken out by vandals years ago, the entire building either burned or torn down, but here in tiny Killdeer, not a single rock had been thrown.

At least, not the solid-in-your-hand mineral kind. Reese had gotten in a few good verbal tosses. He'd always been good with words, the sweet, tender kind as well as the cut-her-heart-out-and-leave-her-bleeding sort. This time she couldn't even blame him. Jace had played a dirty trick on them both, and she was no happier about it than Reese.

She was about to climb into the sedan for the long drive back home when Jace caught her hand. "Whoa, darlin', wrong vehicle. You're going with him, remember?"

She looked back at him. "You're kidding, right?"

"I don't kid about my job or your life. Reese has agreed to hide you out for a couple of days while I find someplace else for you. C'mon."

"I don't want to go with him, Jace. I'd feel safer in Kansas City."

"Neely—"

"You heard what he said. He doesn't give a damn whether Forbes kills me. He doesn't want me here." She managed to say the words evenly, without any hint of the hurt they caused deep inside. There had been a time when Reese had claimed to love her with all his heart, and she'd believed him with all her heart. But when she'd needed him desperately, he'd turned on her. He'd looked at her, lying in a pool of her own blood, and he'd walked away. And she'd never been the same again—not the same lawyer, the same woman or the same naive, trusting fool.

"You know he didn't mean that."

She wished she did, wished she could be certain of that, if nothing else. But she couldn't convince herself and made no effort to lie to Jace. "Take me to Tulsa or Oklahoma City. There are places I can go, people who will help me, people who wouldn't rather see me dead."

"What people? Your sisters? Your mother? Your old friends? Those are the first places Forbes is going to look for you. Do you want to put their lives in danger as well as your own?"

She felt the blood drain from her face. She already had Judy Miller's death on her conscience. She couldn't bear to be responsible for one more person's suffering. At least Reese was a cop. He knew the dangers and was prepared for them.

"I can stay to myself," she said hopefully. "I can dye my hair, change my name, dress differently, talk differently and take a leisurely tour of all the places I've never been. I can keep moving, never spend two nights in the same place, switch identities every time I cross a state line."

Jace shook his head as he pulled her away from the car and toward Reese's truck. "It's too risky. Hell, I don't even like you standing here in the parking lot this long. C'mon. It's just for a couple of days. You can endure anything for two days."

Maybe so. She'd survived the last nine years. But she'd still rather take her chances alone.

Before he could open the pickup door, she wrapped her arms around his neck and hugged him tightly. "In case I don't see you again, thanks for everything."

"You'll see me again. This is just for a few days. We'll get you someplace safe, make our case against Forbes and put the bastard away again—for good this time. Then you can go back to life as normal."

She wished she believed him, wished she was that optimistic, but the sick feeling in her stomach suggested otherwise.

He kissed her forehead, then pushed her back and opened the truck door. Swallowing hard, she climbed inside, fastened her seat belt, then raised her hand in a forlorn wave as Reese put the truck in motion.

The temperature inside the vehicle was frigid enough to raise goose bumps on her bare arms, but she suspected it had more to do with the driver than the air-conditioning. She didn't look at him and couldn't speak to him—couldn't do anything but sit stiffly in her seat, head turned to stare out the side window. They left Killdeer soon enough, leaving her nothing to look at but trees, pasture and an occasional house, but that was hands-down better than the hatred she knew she would see if she looked at him.

The miles passed in strained silence, and the muscles in her neck grew taut from holding her unnatural position so long. Gradually, an inch or two at a time, she turned to face forward, then risked the quickest of glances at Reese from the corner of her eye. He was gripping the steering wheel tightly enough to make his knuckles turn white, and his posture was rigid and unyielding. Just like his attitude.

Of course the past nine years that had been so difficult for her hadn't left a mark on him. He was older, handsomer, tougher. In denim and chambray, with the cream-colored cowboy hat, he looked like every woman's dream of a gorgeous, sexy cowboy. Put him astride a horse, and hearts would swoon all over the place. Even without the horse, he was more than capable of stirring wicked fantasies.

The first time she'd ever seen him, *she'd* swooned. He'd just recovered from the shoulder injury that had ended his pitching career with the Kansas City Royals, and had gone to work for the Keegan County Sheriff's Department. She'd been practicing law in the county seat of Thomasville. She couldn't have cared less that he was a former hot-shot baseball player. Sports didn't interest her much. But she'd been damned impressed with the man himself.

Too bad he'd never thought much of her.

Not even when he was claiming to love her.

With a shiver, she adjusted the vents so they blew away from her, then folded her arms across her chest. Feeling incredibly awkward, she locked her gaze on the road ahead and said, "I take it you're still a cop."

The silence that met her remark was oppressive. So this was what she had to look forward to for the next two days. Not a problem. She was experienced at being ignored by him—when she'd been shot, when she'd lain alone in the hospital, when she'd been harassed and threatened every single day until finally her tormentors had run her out of town. She could handle a couple of days of not being spoken to.

But as soon as she'd completed the thought, he did speak, in a voice as scornful and unforgiving as any she'd ever heard. "What did Jace tell you?"

"Nothing." It was an adequate answer that needed no elaboration, but that didn't stop her from adding it. "If he'd mentioned your name, I wouldn't have come."

"If he'd mentioned *your* name, I wouldn't have let you."

Fine. So they were agreed that neither wanted to spend even a moment together. The only problem was that the potential cost to him was merely a few days' discomfort, while the cost she paid might well be her life.

She returned to staring at the scenery. Jace had refused to tell her where she was going, presumably so he could hide who she was going with. All he'd said was that it was a quiet place where she would be safe.

Safe. With the one person who hated her most providing her only security. Gee, why didn't she feel safe?

Last night had been far from restful. She tried to doze along the way, but every time she was close to actually falling asleep, something brought her fully alert—some bump in the road, a honk from a passing vehicle, some little bit of fear deep inside her. She gave up her effort as they approached a sign that read Welcome to Heartbreak—Reese's hometown and, no doubt, their destination.

She smiled thinly. It seemed appropriate that she should wind up in a place whose name described her life so perfectly.

The real, physical Heartbreak didn't seem a much better place to spend her time than the intangible, emotional heartbreak where she'd spent much of her life. The businesses were on the shabby side, the houses nothing special, the town dusty and worn. They passed one grocery store, two gas stations and three restaurants, one hardware store, one five-and-dime, and a handful of other businesses before Reese turned off the main street into a tree-lined neighborhood.

Maybe the houses weren't big or fancy, she amended, but some of them, at least, had a certain charm. The trees in these yards were decades old, unlike her own neighborhood where every house had the same variety of very young saplings planted in the same location in the identical handkerchief-size yards. Additionally, there was nothing cookie-cutter about the houses—no identical plans for every fourth or fifth house, no homeowners association decreeing what to plant, when to mow and what colors to paint. There was a sidewalk on either side of the street for skating and playing jacks, front porches attached to every house for watching life pass by and mailboxes ranging from the purely functional to the eccentric to the just plain silly.

They were more like homes than her house could ever be.

After a half dozen blocks, the street ended in a driveway that ran long and straight through a stand of trees to a house some distance back. There were pastures on all four sides, a large yard in need of mowing and a barn out back that looked about a hundred years old with what must surely be its original paint. In contrast, the house gave every appearance of being brand-new. Its log walls, sandstone foundation and brick-red tin roof hadn't even collected a thorough coating of Oklahoma dust yet.

The garage was on the north end of the house. Reese pulled inside next to a black-and-white Blazer that said Sheriff on the driver's door beneath the department seal. Was that a general proclamation that all the sheriff's department vehicles carried, or did it signify that this particular truck belonged to *the* sheriff? Neely wondered, but she wasn't about to ask. He'd made it uncomfortably clear that he had no desire to talk to her, and she intended to make it easy for him to ignore her.

The door from the garage opened into a utility room. Straight ahead was the kitchen, and down a short hall to the right was a bedroom. She followed him through the kitchen and dining room and along another short hall to a bedroom diagonally opposite the first.

"You can use this room," he said brusquely. "Bathroom's next door." Then he pivoted and returned the way they'd come.

Neely hesitantly entered the room and set her suitcase on the bed. To say the room was decorated would be overly generous. There were no pictures on the walls, no knickknacks scattered across the furniture, no pretty pillows piled on the bed. At best, it was functional. The walls were pale green, the trim white, the carpet a serviceable hunter-green. There were only blinds, no curtains, at the windows. The furniture was antique oak—a bed, dresser, two night tables and an armoire, probably handed down through generations of the Barnett family.

The only antiques *she* had were handed down, too—just not from her own family. She doubted that a Madison had existed before her and her sisters who could afford or appreciate such treasures.

She didn't bother unpacking—why, when she would be leaving the next day?—but went to the bathroom next door, then headed back to the kitchen. She'd had only a doughnut and coffee for breakfast and had missed lunch completely. Though it wasn't long until dinnertime, she needed something to settle the queasiness in her stomach or she would have one more woe to add to her long list.

Reese was already in the kitchen, washing up at the sink. She stopped abruptly and considered sneaking back to the bedroom, then rejected the idea. She wasn't going to behave like a prisoner. She'd been willing to go back to Kansas City, or to strike out on her own, but no, they'd brought her here. If Reese hated having her there so much, he could damn well stay in the bedroom and go hungry himself.

Sparing her only the briefest of glances, he dried his hands, then took sandwich makings from the refrigerator. While she washed her own hands, he sliced a tomato, removed bread and chips from one cabinet, plates from another. He made his sandwich, emptied a ton of chips on the plate, then carried both the plate and a cold beer from the refrigerator to the corner table.

Neely made her own sandwich, filled a glass with water from the tap and settled for eating at the counter and staring at the horses in the pasture out back. When she was a kid, she'd wished every night for a horse to talk to, feed treats and ride a time or two. When she'd met Reese, she'd often wished for the chance to see where he'd come from, where he'd been shaped into the man he'd become, and at odd moments in the past nine years, she'd wished desperately, hopelessly, to see him just one more time.

Funny how wishes could come true in ways you most certainly didn't wish for.

From across the room came the sound of a glass bottle tapping against wood, followed by a hostile question. "What did you do to piss off this guy who's supposedly trying to kill you?"

Supposedly. Her smile was bitter. Last night someone had

fired fifty shots or more into the bedroom where she was sleeping, but Reese had no problem turning the incident into an allegation that might not have even happened. What kind of proof did he need before he could believe her? Seeing her get shot, falling to the ground, bleeding and in great pain? No, wait. Been there, done that…and he'd still walked away. Maybe if she died this time, he would believe her. Maybe then he could forgive her.

Her appetite gone, she dropped the rest of her sandwich onto the plate, then turned to face him. "I did my job," she said coolly. "A lot of people out there have a problem with attorneys who do what they're tasked to do under the law."

"And a lot of people have a problem with attorneys who use the law to let murderers, thieves and other criminals go free."

It was an old argument, one they'd had a hundred times, one that he'd refused to see from any viewpoint but his own. She wasn't going to be drawn into it again.

Pushing away from the counter, she walked to the broad doorway that led directly into the living room. It was more rustic than the other rooms, with log-and-stone walls, a big fireplace, wood plank floors and leather furniture. Rough cedar beams laid on the diagonal covered the peaked ceiling, and another beam served as mantel above the fireplace, supporting a collection of pottery. An entertainment system filled the corner on one side of the fireplace, and a computer and desk occupied the other. Great—TV, movies and Internet access. What more did she need?

"Nice house." Her glance in his direction was too brief to bring him into focus, but just enough to confirm that he was still there. "Small-town life suits you."

She could actually feel the sharpening of his glare as her mildly offered barb struck home. Small towns, small minds, he used to say about Thomasville. He'd gone there from Kansas City for the same reason she had—to make a start. Influenced by Jace, he'd been looking for an entrée into the law enforcement community. He'd planned to stay a year or two, get some experience, then start moving up into positions of more authority in larger departments.

She'd been fresh from passing the bar and had wanted a place where she could carefully build her practice. She'd had dreams back then of making a name for herself as a defender of the downtrodden, as the woman who would make good on that pledge she'd said every day through thirteen years of public school—*and justice for all.* Especially for the poor, the minorities, the people without a voice who couldn't afford hot-shot lawyers to protect them. She'd intended to be one of those rare hot-shot lawyers, with a price that was within everyone's reach.

She'd failed miserably. Apparently so had he.

She went into the living room, to the leather chair-and-a-half that was obviously Reese's favorite seat. The remote control and the TV schedule were on the side table, and the shade of the lamp there was tilted slightly to provide better light for reading. After kicking off her shoes, she sat and folded her legs on the seat beside her, turned on the television, then realized with a grimace that she still wore her flower-bedecked straw hat. She pulled it off and tossed it on the matching ottoman, then concentrated on finding something to watch on TV.

Reese came to an abrupt stop just through the doorway when she removed the hat to reveal her hair—or what was left of it. Nine years ago it had reached past her waist. For court she'd worn it in a prim-and-proper bun at her nape. One of his greatest pleasures had been removing every one of the pins that had held it in place, letting the cool silky strands fall over his hands, over her body, then kissing those strands back into some bit of order.

He doubted there was a single hair on her head longer than a few inches now.

Forcing himself to move naturally, he sat on the sofa. "Let's get the rules straight. You can't go outside. You can't answer the phone. You can't answer the door. If someone comes over, go to the guest room, close the door and stay there. If Jace doesn't have a new place for you by tomorrow, you're going to the Canyon County jail over in Buffalo Plains.''

Her gaze narrowed, and he felt a twinge of guilt. He wasn't in the habit of locking up crime victims, but these were special circumstances that required extraordinary measures. Besides, as jails went, Canyon County's wasn't bad. It was located in the basement of the county courthouse, which was about eighty years old, solidly built of sandstone and just about the safest place in town in tornado season. She would likely be the only woman in the section designated for female inmates, and she could have a few amenities such as TV and real food.

''I've taken the liberty of removing the phone from the kitchen so you won't be tempted to call anyone, and the alarm system is set, so don't try to sneak out. If you have any thoughts of using my computer, surfing the Internet or sending an e-mail to someone—'' he followed her gaze to the computer, its monitor displaying a brightly colored screen saver of tropical fish ''—just know that everything's password-protected. You won't get far.''

The chagrin that crossed her face left him with little doubt that using the computer had crossed her mind. Would she have been foolish enough to tell someone where she was—her sisters, her mother, whatever man she was seeing?

That last thought left him feeling decidedly annoyed—with her, with himself, with the mystery man. Of course there were men in her life. She was a beautiful woman with a healthy appreciation for sex and, as Jace had pointed out, it had been nine years. He'd had more than his share of women in those years, which was nobody's business but his and theirs, and her affairs were none of his business. Not worth caring about, sure as hell not worth getting annoyed about.

''Any questions?''

She shook her head, and did little more than ruffle her bangs.

He gave himself a silent command to stand up and walk out of the room, to say nothing else, to put her out of his mind for the moment. He managed the standing-up part, but not the rest. The question just popped out on its own. "What the hell happened to your hair?"

She didn't touch it self-consciously, which suggested that she'd worn it short a long time. She simply shrugged. "I went through a period a while back when I didn't have much use of my right shoulder and arm. Taking care of long hair was a problem, so I chopped it off."

Heat flooded his face and sent an edgy shudder down his spine. She was talking about the incident in Thomasville, when she'd gotten caught in the cross fire between an unstable client and a half dozen enraged deputies—the incident that had ended their relationship once and for all, that had haunted him for years afterward. He'd lost so much that day, and it was her fault. Yet she could talk about it so casually, as if it were no big deal. A woman had died, their affair had died—hell, sometimes he'd felt as if *he* were dying. But, hey, it was all in the past, over and done with.

She was waiting for him to say something, her fake-innocent brown gaze fixed on his face. He didn't know what she wanted—an acknowledgment of what had happened? An inquiry into her recovery? An explanation? An apology? Whatever she wanted, he offered nothing. He simply circled the couch and returned to the kitchen…but not before catching a glimpse of the disappointment that darkened her eyes.

As if he cared, after all that had happened, if she was disappointed in him.

After putting the dishes in the dishwasher, he used the cell phone to check in with his office. It had been an average day—a few arrests, a couple of burglaries, enough traffic stops to pay the department salaries for the day. He told the under-sheriff he wouldn't be in the next day, brushed off the questions about why, and ended the call.

It was barely four o'clock and he felt like a prisoner in his own home. The sounds of a daytime talk show came from the living room, one he wouldn't be caught dead watching. There was no cleaning to do, no groceries to buy, no laundry to wash. He'd been pretty damn industrious yesterday, which he wouldn't have been had he known he would be stuck at home baby-sitting Neely today. Other than mowing, there was nothing to do, and he wasn't sure he trusted her enough to leave her alone inside while he was outside.

Restlessly he gazed around the kitchen, then noticed the flashing light on the answering machine. He hit the playback button, then impatiently drummed his fingers on the counter until the first message started.

"Hi, Reese, it's Shay. I just wanted to remind you about dinner tonight. The dispatcher said you'd taken the day off unexpectedly. You'd better not be planning to stand me up, and if you do, you'd better have a real good excuse. See you."

He muttered a curse. He'd completely forgotten the invitation to have dinner with Shay Rafferty and her husband Easy tonight. They would be more than happy for him to bring Neely along, and she would be as safe at their place out in the country as she was here, but Shay knew him too well. She would want explanations he wasn't about to make, and when she couldn't get them from him, she would charm them out of Neely.

The next message was short and to the point—"Hi, Reese, it's Ginger. Call me sometime."—and the third was delivered in a hot sultry voice. "Hey, cowboy, I certainly enjoyed my riding lesson the other night. I figure this soreness will be gone in another day or two, so when can we saddle up for another go-round? Give me a call. You've got my number."

A snort drew his attention to the doorway, where Neely was leaning against the jamb. With her feet bare and the denim dress that exposed her arms and throat and reached almost to her ankles, she looked very country, very natural and right, as if he'd designed the room with her in mind.

But he hadn't. He may have given a thought or two to sharing this place with a woman someday—he didn't intend to stay single forever—but that dream woman had been faceless, nameless. She certainly hadn't been Neely Madison, whom he considered much more a nightmare than a dream.

When he turned his back on her, she padded across the cool stone floor to the sink to refill her water glass, he guessed from the sounds of it. He erased the messages, then called Shay at the Heartbreak Café. As soon as he said hello, she accusingly interrupted.

"You forgot, didn't you?"

"Sort of. Something came up at work. I'm not going to be able to make it."

"Oh, by all means, go on," Neely remarked on her way back into the living room. "I don't mind staying here alone."

Reese scowled at her back as a note of interest came into Shay's voice. "You have company—*female* company. Reese Barnett, are you seeing some woman that none of us knows about?"

"No. I told you, it's work."

"Uh-huh. I've never known you to take your work home with you. Is she a new deputy? A suspect? A suspect's lawyer?"

"Look, I really can't talk, Shay. I'm sorry about tonight."

"Not as sorry as you're about to become. Easy's buyer from Fort Worth is joining us for dinner."

She was right. He was sorrier now. Shay's husband was a rodeo champ turned horse trainer who boasted the best paints in Oklahoma. Victoria Morales, his Fort Worth buyer, was a regular customer, beautiful as an angel, rich as sin and as down-to-earth natural as any woman Reese had ever known. He'd met her a time or two before and liked her—a lot. "Tell her I'm sorry I missed her."

"This work you can't talk about...is she as pretty as Victoria?"

Though it was totally unnecessary, he couldn't stop his gaze from going to Neely, settled once again in his chair. She was beautiful, too, much as he wished he could deny it. But so much had gone wrong between them that couldn't be set right. He couldn't imagine ever getting beyond the past or reaching for a future, not with her.

Even though, for a long time, a future with Neely had been

all he'd ever wanted. Love. Marriage. Kids. Till-death-do-us-part.

Death had parted them, all right. Just not in the way he'd expected.

"I've got to go, Shay," he said abruptly. "Give my best to Easy and Victoria. We'll try again some other time."

Chapter 2

Neely stood at the living-room window, staring off to the west as the setting sun turned the sky pink, lavender, blue, and every shade imaginable in between. When the darkness began to gradually seep over the colors, she was tempted for one whimsical moment to applaud and call out, "Good job!" and "Do it again!" Of course, she did nothing of the sort. She smiled, though—to herself, for herself—and wished she could grab hold tight of this fleeting serenity and wrap it around her for a little longer. She had so few truly peaceful moments in her life that they'd become dear.

"Get away from the window. Someone might see you."

She didn't argue with the curt command—didn't point out that she stood in a darkened room on a dusky evening, or that the blackjack oaks that grew thick as weeds between the street and the yard made it impossible to see that there was even a house back here. She simply moved away from the window and toward Reese.

She'd offered her help with dinner and he'd turned her down. She'd said she would set the table and he'd told her to go away. Now she stood in the doorway of the brightly lit kitchen, hands clasped behind her back, and watched as he dished up steaks and baked sweet potatoes. If she could be reasonably certain that he wouldn't snarl or snap at her, she would make some lighthearted comment about how she liked having a man cook for her. But he *would* snarl or snap, and she wasn't up to it tonight.

And so she said nothing as he carried the plates to the table, then the glasses and a pitcher of tea, or as he gestured for her to take a seat. She didn't compliment him on the flavorful steak, grilled to just the right degree of doneness, and she certainly didn't speculate on how he'd remembered after all these years that she liked her beef medium-rare.

Halfway through the meal, she paused to refill her glass, then evenly asked, "Is there anything at all we can talk about that won't make you angry?"

He pretended to think about it for a moment, rubbing his jaw with one long, slender finger, then shrugged. "Not that I can think of."

The wise course would be to accept his answer, finish the meal in silence, and return to the living room, where the television would talk at her if not to her. Naturally she didn't go that route. "Aw, come on, Reese. You always prided yourself on being able to talk to anybody about anything, no matter how much you detested them."

"That was before I knew just how much I was capable of detesting someone."

She didn't wince, didn't give any indication that he'd scored a hit. She kept her expression bland, her voice level and empty of emotion. "Aren't you the least bit curious about what I've done the last nine years, how many people I've screwed and how many lives I've destroyed?"

She'd certainly screwed up her own life, and it wasn't fair. All she'd ever wanted was to be a good lawyer and to help people. She'd dedicated most of her thirty-five years to achieving those goals, and what had she accomplished? The only man she'd ever loved despised her. He'd taught her to despise erself. Her noble career was a joke. Judy Miller was dead, and if Eddie Forbes had his way, she would soon be dead herself.

"I am curious about one thing." Reese laid the steak knife aside as if he didn't trust himself to talk to her with it in hand. "How did you sucker Jace into believing that your life was worth saving?"

A faint tremor passed through her, making her pull her hands into her lap before he noticed. She summoned her best smile, her most casual shrug and her most intimate voice, and replied with her own question. "How do you think?"

Neely knew exactly what he thought, without needing to see the suspicion enter his gaze, or the tension that set his jaw and knotted his fingers. Keeping the smile in place through sheer will, she laid her napkin on the table and rose as gracefully as she could. "Dinner was wonderful. Hope you don't mind if I leave the cleanup to you." Still smiling, she left the room.

Her bedroom was dark once she closed the door, but she didn't need light to make it to the bed. She sat on the mattress and let the smile slip as a great shudder rocketed through her. She had never thought she would see the day when she would anticipate taking up residence in a jail cell, but as far as she was concerned, tomorrow couldn't come soon enough. Anything would be better than staying here one moment longer than necessary.

Well, anything besides a middle-of-the-night-wake-up call with fully automatic assault weapons.

She didn't know how long she sat there—long enough for the sounds of cleaning in the kitchen to stop, long enough to make her flinch when she turned on the bedside lamp—before she finally stood up. She removed a toiletries case and nightclothes from her suitcase, eased the door open enough to see that the lights were off in the kitchen and on in the living room, then padded next door to the bathroom.

Like the guest room, it was functional—all the necessary appointments, clean lines, nothing unusual or remarkable. Ev-

erything was white—counter, floor, walls, the plumbing and
light fixtures, even the towel rods and the towels they held.
The only spot of color in the room was her. She didn't know
whether she loved the pure starkness of it all or hated it. No
that her opinion mattered one bit to Reese.

After showering, she wrapped one white towel around he
body, another around her head. By the time she'd brushed and
flossed her teeth, dried her hair, smoothed three different mois
turizers over their appropriate body parts, added a dusting o
powder and put on her T-shirt and shorts, the pristine bath
room looked well-used. Though she was tempted to leave i
that way, she repacked everything and left the room almost a
spotless as she'd found it. She couldn't do anything about he
scents that lingered, but they would be gone before Reese eve
noticed them.

Kind of like her.

Suddenly weary, Neely returned to the bedroom, put the
toiletries back in the suitcase and folded her dirty clothes or
top of it, then stretched out on top of the covers. She felt more
alone in that instant than she'd ever felt before. Even he
toughest times—when her father had been taken away in hand
cuffs, when Reese had left her bleeding on the courthouse
steps, when she'd lain in the hospital praying that he would
come to see her, when she'd driven away from Thomasville
and known she would never return—hadn't felt quite like this
If she were a weaker woman, she would cry, but she'd learned
well that crying resolved nothing. It hadn't brought her fathe
back, or Reese. It hadn't made her feel any less betrayed o
helped her deal with her disappointments.

She'd had so many disappointments, and had caused so
many more.

When this was over—if she survived—she needed a new
life and a new job in a new place. She would forget abou
making a difference, about helping people or being importan
to someone, and she would concentrate on keeping to herself
not getting involved, not doing any harm or destroying any
lives. She could work as a waitress or get some dreary office

drone job where she would spend her days alone in a cubicle, having little contact with the outside world and zero chances to screw up.

As she turned onto her side to face the window, she smiled faintly. She didn't indulge in self-pity often, but when she did, she did it well. Anyone watching her now would think her life had gone to hell in a handbasket, when the truth was, she still had a lot. No one could take away her law degree and ten years of hard-learned experience. Her bank accounts were wealthy beyond her greediest dreams. She owned a beautiful house that would bring a small fortune in Kansas City's current market. She was alive and well, at least for the time being, and might actually manage to stay that way. She had a lot to live for.

Just not the sort of things she'd always imagined herself having by now. No family, but sisters with problems of their own and a mother who'd never been more than ineffectual. A house, but no home. Acquaintances, but no friends. Occasional sex partners, but no lovers.

No Reese.

She smiled again, but this time there was no self-mocking in it. Just enduring regret that she feared would never go away.

Waiting for sleep to overtake her, she stared out the window until her eyes grew gritty, until simple tiredness passed into fatigue. She watched the already-dark sky turn even blacker as a storm crept in, taking its sweet time in reaching Heartbreak. Lightning appeared first, far off on the horizon, then before long, distant thunder rumbled through the night—low, deep, unsettling. It seemed to vibrate through the cabin's thick log walls, through the wooden planks of the floor and the old oak bed, and right on through her body—long, relentless rumbles. She tossed restlessly, then gave up and went to the nearest window.

She loved thunderstorms—loved their primal edge, their cathartic fury. They were less impressive back home, where the lightning had to compete with millions of city lights, where the thunder was often just one more grumble in a clamor of city noise. But here there was only one man-made light—a flood lamp outside the barn—and the thunder was challenged only by the wind and the approaching rain. If she were free to do whatever she wanted, she would go outside on the front porch, curl up in one of the rockers and breathe deeply of the clean, sweet air. She would let the wind blow her hair and clothes every which way and when the driving rain arrived. she would let it drench her to the skin, and maybe, once the storm had passed, she would have been washed just a little bit cleaner.

But she wasn't free, and the way her luck was running, the first bolt of lightning that struck would be drawn unerringly to her soaked, superconductor body. Then everyone's problems would be solved—Eddie Forbes's, Jace's, Reese's and her own.

The flood lamp out back flickered, went off, came on and went off again as the power inside the house surged and ebbed. Next door the refrigerator cycled on and off, as did the central air, before finally shutting down in a silence that seemed eerie compared to the activity outside.

Now she could go outside. Without power, the security alarm would be worthless—unless Reese had installed some sort of backup power source, which he probably had. Besides. if she managed to get out without setting off the alarm, the electricity would surely come back on while she was outside and she would trigger it coming back in and, believing she was an intruder, Reese would blow her away—or, at least, that would be his story. And who would dispute him? Worse, who would care?

But staying inside didn't mean having to stay in her room. standing at one small window. Neely opened her door, listened, then carefully felt her way through the darkness to the living room. Flashes of lightning led her to a chair in front of the ten-foot-long window, where she curled up, head resting on one fist, and watched the show outside.

She'd been there five minutes, maybe less, when the power started flickering again. Sounding like the little engine that couldn't, the computer tried to boot up, shut down, then tried again. Finding her way by lightning and touch, she knelt under the desk to turn off the power strip and unplug it from the wall. She'd lost a computer once from just such activity, and though she was sure Reese wouldn't show the least bit of gratitude, she saw no reason to sit idly by while it happened to him.

She was resettled in the chair, watching as a curtain of rain moved through the blackjacks and across the yard, listening to its great thundering rush, when a thud sounded nearby, followed by a grunt of pain and a curse. She watched as a shadowy form pushed aside the wooden desk chair she'd pulled from its usual spot, then knelt in front of the desk—waited until he was half under, then quietly said, "I've already unplugged the computer."

The next thud was louder—the back of Reese's head connecting with the underside of the desk's center drawer—and the next curse was harsher. She didn't spare him any sympathy—he was hardheaded enough—but turned her attention back to the storm. The rain was pounding the metal roof now in a staccato rhythm that would wake the soundest sleeper...or perhaps lull the lightest off to sleep.

She was right about the gratitude. He sat in the chair that matched hers and fixed a weighty gaze on her that she couldn't see but could certainly feel. "What the hell are you doing up?"

"Am I restricted to my room at night? If so, you should have made that clear. Or maybe it would be best if you'd just reset the doorknob to the guest room so that it locks from the outside."

Lightning lit the night sky and the room, giving her an all-too-clear look at him. He wore a pair of jeans and nothing else, and he looked incredible. Broad-shouldered, muscular, smooth tanned skin, narrow waist, ridged belly, lean hips... In sudden need of a cool splash of water, she directed her gaze outside again.

"It's three in the morning." His voice was sullen, but surprisingly pleasant—low, deep, masculine—in spite of it. "Why aren't you asleep?"

"Why aren't you?" She wasn't about to admit that she couldn't sleep because she was feeling sorry for herself, because she found being thrown together with him again so unsettling. No way was she going to speculate that subconsciously she was afraid to sleep, because the last time she'd done it, someone had tried to kill her. Show him any sign of weakness and, just like other predators, he would use it against her.

"Do you always answer questions with questions?"

"No. Sometimes I don't answer them at all. On rare occasions, I actually answer with the truth. But not if I can avoid it."

A particularly loud clap of thunder rattled the windowpanes. In the relative quiet that followed, Reese asked, "What happened last night?"

"Last night?"

Impatience tightened his voice. "Jace said someone tried to kill you. What happened?"

Jace said… His best friend—family—had told him, and yet he sounded as if he wasn't at all convinced that she was truly in danger. What did he think—that she and Jace had concocted this plan to get the two of them together again? That she'd pined for him for nine years and was now making a desperate attempt to win him back?

He flattered himself…not that she hadn't been desperate a time or two. There had been times when she would have sold her soul, would have groveled and pleaded for his forgiveness. She wasn't proud of it, but then, she wasn't proud of a lot of things.

But to manufacture death threats… Did he think it was a bogus bomb that had scattered pieces of her car over a city block last week? Had those been bogus bullets tearing through the walls and windows of the safe house last night?

Feeling lost and alone, she managed a careless shrug. "Nothing happened."

"Jace said—"

"Then ask Jace." He sure as hell wouldn't believe anything she told him.

After another shuddering crack of thunder, he spoke again. "Why did he call me? Kansas City has a big department. He's got friends in other departments all over the area. Why me?"

She looked at him, in shadow one instant, brightly illuminated the next, then got to her feet. "He still has some illusions about you. He believes you're an honorable man." She walked as far as the kitchen door before turning back. "But you and I both know better, don't we?"

Tuesday morning was about as perfect a June day as Oklahoma ever saw. Except for the rain glistening on the grass and quickly evaporating from the porch, there was no sign of last night's storm. Of course, Reese thought sourly as he walked through the living room, there was no sign inside of his late-night run-in with Neely, but that didn't mean anything.

He'd smelled the coffee perking the instant he'd awakened and wondered if she'd developed a taste for it over the years. He saw the answer was no when he walked into the kitchen, where she sat at the table, bare feet propped on an empty chair, a magazine open in both hands and a glass of orange juice in front of her.

She wore another of those too summery, too feminine dresses, this one in a soft green that reminded him of his favorite sherbet. It was sleeveless, with a row of buttons from the point of a deep vee all the way to the hem, but she hadn't buttoned them all. The fabric fell away on either side, exposing ticklish knees, shapely calves and delicate ankles. Her pale brown hair was longer than he'd acknowledged yesterday, long enough to flip up in a tiny curl on the ends, and her glasses—

Apparently suspecting that he'd done a double take on the half-glasses that perched below the bridge of her nose, she peered at him over them. "Do I look like an old-maid school-marm?"

With that face? That body? That sleek, waifish hair and those brightly painted stars that decorated the glass frames? Not by a country mile.

She didn't seem to notice that he didn't reply but turned his attention instead to filling the biggest mug in his cabinet with steaming coffee.

"For vanity's sake, I resisted reading glasses for as long as I could, but I finally realized that I never saw anyone anyway, so what did it matter?"

"How do you practice law without seeing anyone?" He wasn't interested. He swore he wasn't. He was merely making small talk.

"Well, of course I see people in court, but I hardly ever read there. The rest of the time I'm usually alone."

Except for meetings in her office, he thought with a scowl. And lunches and dinners outside the office. Movies with friends. Dates. Sleepovers. Weekends away. She'd always been a very social person, more so than he would have liked when he'd been with her. He didn't believe for an instant that she'd changed.

How social was she with Jace? Intimately so, she'd hinted last night. Though he wouldn't admit it to anyone else to save his life, that hint was part of what had kept him awake last night. Every time he'd started to doze off, the image of the two of them together had jerked him awake again.

His first impulse was to write off her implication as a lie. She'd proven she wasn't above lying. Hell, she was a lawyer. One went hand in hand with the other. Besides, Jace knew everything that had happened—all that she'd put Reese through. He might like her, but his loyalty was to family first. He would never have an affair with her without telling Reese first.

His second impulse stopped him from following his first. It wouldn't be the first time it had happened. Barnett men shared a lot in common, including similar tastes in women. He and Jace had dated each other's exes in high school and again through college. And that would explain why his cousin cared so much about keeping her safe.

Of course, so would the fact that Jace was the best damn cop Reese had ever known. He had an unshakable sense of right and wrong. He hated injustice, hated to lose, and would give up his own life without hesitation to save the least worthy person out there. It was because of him that Reese had become a cop—because of him that Reese tried to be as good. He failed, though. He wasn't as selfless, and couldn't be as unbiased. He saw too many of the shades of gray that Jace simply didn't see.

The soft pad of bare feet on stone alerted Reese to the fact that Neely was coming closer—or was it the fine hairs on the back of his neck standing on end, or the unsettled twinge in the pit of his stomach? He moved to one side and watched as she took a bowl from the cabinet and a box of cereal from the pantry. Considering how little time she'd spent in his kitchen, she seemed very much at home there. She knew which drawer the silverware was in and which of four identical pottery jars held the sugar. What else had she snooped into while he'd slept, or tried to?

She settled at the table again, and for a moment there was only the sound of crunching. Of course the moment didn't last. "So...I realize you aren't married now, but have you been?"

"No." Marriage had never come high on his list of priorities. He'd more or less taken for granted that it was something he would do after he'd done everything else. He had assumed for a long time that he would do it with her, even though their relationship had come with its own built-in problems—namely, her nasty habit of helping crooks stay out of jail. Eventually, he'd figured, between him and the babies they would have, they would get her out of the criminal-defense business and who knew—maybe even make a full-time wife and mom out of her.

He'd been a fool.

"So you're playing the field." When he glanced at her curiously, she gestured to the answering machine. "Shay. Ginger.'' She lowered her voice into erotic-dream range. '''Hey, cowboy, come take me for a ride.'''

He tried to ignore the heat that seeped through him—did his damnedest to shut out long-repressed memories of him and Neely, naked and wicked and incredibly good. He'd always enjoyed sex. Even his first time, when he was seventeen and Joelle Barefoot's cousin had come up from Broken Bow for a week and shown him things he hadn't even imagined, had been pretty damn amazing. But it had been different with Neely. Not always-fireworks-seeing-stars-multiple-climax spectacular, but...special. Satisfying in ways that went much deeper than mere physical pleasure. Connecting in ways that had nothing to do with Part A sliding into Slot B.

He took a swallow of coffee to clear the hoarseness from his throat. It didn't work entirely. ''Shay's a friend. So is her husband. And Ginger would be too young to be my kid sister...if I had a kid sister.''

''What about 'Ride me, cowboy'?''

Her name was Isabella, she'd come to Heartbreak a month earlier to spend a weekend with her college roommate—Callie, the town's nurse-midwife—and hadn't left yet, and he wasn't sure he would ever look at her again without thinking of sex.

And Neely.

''Believe it or not, the riding lesson she was talking about was actually a riding lesson. She's never been around horses, so I taught her the basics.''

Studying him thoughtfully, she chewed a mouthful of cardboard-tasting wheat chaff and washed it down with juice. ''Why wouldn't I believe you?'' she asked evenly. ''As far as I know, the only thing you've ever lied to me about is the way you felt about me.''

''I never lied.'' He'd loved her dearly, even though they'd had some very different ideas on some very important subjects such as right, wrong and justice. Even though he'd taken a lot of flak on the job because of his relationship with her. He'd loved her more than he'd ever loved anyone.

Until the day he'd watched Judy Miller die.

"So your definition of always was just different from mine—as, apparently, was your definition of love."

"No. We'd simply reached the point where I could no longer overlook certain aspects of who you were and what you did. I couldn't continue a relationship with you and maintain any measure of self-respect."

She brought her dishes to the sink, rinsed them, dried her hands, then faced him. There were two spots of bright color on her cheeks, made more prominent by her unusual paleness. "I didn't kill that woman."

"You made it possible."

Stubbornly she shook her head side to side. "Feel guilty if you want, Reese, but don't try to put it on me. I didn't do anything wrong. My client was entitled to a proper defense, and I saw that he got it. I did my job, and I did it well. End of story."

"You did your job without regard for the truth, without the slightest concern for the reality of the situation. You wanted to win at any cost, and you succeeded—even though the cost was an innocent woman's life. You may not have pulled the trigger, Neely, but you put the gun in that bastard's hand. You put him back out on the streets. You made it possible for him to make good on his threats."

"I was just doing my job! I didn't do anything wrong!"

"Lie to yourself, but don't bother lying to me. I had to learn the hard way not to believe anything you say, but I did learn." He walked out then and left her standing there looking...shaken. Upset. Regretful. And guilty. She knew she wasn't as innocent in Judy's death as she pretended.

Just as he knew that he shared some responsibility, too, along with the rest of the Keegan County Sheriff's Department.

Refusing to follow that train of thought, he dropped down into his favorite chair and used the remote to turn on the television and surf through a hundred or so satellite channels before settling on a fifties-era Western. Though he'd seen the show before, he concentrated on it intensely so he wouldn't have to notice that Neely was still standing where he'd left her, that her head was bowed and her shoulders rounded, or that she looked as forlorn and alone as anyone he'd ever seen.

If she was forlorn, that was her own fault, and being alone was her choice. She'd never faced any shortage of male attention. When they were dating, men had often hit on her right in front of him. Not men in Thomasville, who knew what she did or what he did, but in the city—in restaurants, clubs or just walking down the street. From teenage boys to white-haired grandfathers, it had seemed that no stranger was immune to her charms.

He sure as hell hadn't been immune the first time he'd seen her. But he was now. He was older, tougher, less susceptible to women in general, to big brown eyes and delicate little smiles in particular. He knew there were things in life more important than great sex and that the price for getting mixed up with Neely was dearer than he could pay. Besides, after today, he wasn't going to see her again.

And now he'd learned one more lesson—he was never doing another favor for Jace as long as he lived. That was a promise.

In the kitchen Neely finally moved—he heard, felt but didn't see it—but she didn't come into the living room. Good. It was easier to keep her out of his mind when she was out of his sight.

She gave him a few hours of relative peace, with nothing but the television to disturb the quiet, before she came in and sat uncomfortably on the edge of the couch. He pretended to not notice her for as long as he could, but clearly there was something she wanted to say, and just as clearly she didn't intend to say it until he gave her his attention. He waited until the next commercial break, muted the TV and looked at her.

"What are the plans for today?"

His plans were to be rid of her by sundown. Other than that, he neither knew nor cared, and he shrugged to convey exactly that. "Either Jace will pick you up or you'll go to the jail over in Buffalo Plains."

"I understand that. But when?"

He shrugged again.

"Is there any reason I can't go now?"

"Beyond the fact that Jace isn't here?"

"You could take me to the jail."

He could do that, Reese acknowledged—could give her over into the custody of the jailer, then go to his office on the floor above. Get some work done. Forget that she was locked up below in a six-by-eight-foot cell with a metal cot, no windows and no privacy even for the bathroom. Forget that she preferred such accommodations over his company. And while he was forgetting that, he would also wipe the last twenty-four hours from his memory. Sure, not a problem.

"Jace can pick me up there."

But walking out of the jail with her would attract more attention than walking out of this house with her—more attention than his cousin would want. If she really was in danger, Reese wasn't about to do anything that might increase that danger for Jace.

Her voice grew taut. "I'd rather stay in your jail than in your house."

"I'd prefer that, too." But the words felt like a lie. Truth was, he found the prospect of Neely behind bars—an idea he'd once taken great satisfaction in—unsettling. Behind bars in his own jail... Not yet. Not until Jace's time ran out.

"I gave him until this evening," he said flatly. "Like it or not, you're stuck here until then."

For a long moment his gaze locked with hers, until he finally forced his back to the television. He turned the audio on again and watched from the corner of his eye as she stood and walked out of the room.

He was in the process of giving a small sigh of relief when the back door slammed. Jumping to his feet, he made it to the door in record time, crossed the deck in a half dozen strides, took the steps in one leap and grabbed her arm before she'd made it halfway across the yard. He was prepared for her instinctive jerk, holding tightly enough that she accomplished nothing more than pulling herself off balance. Before she could try again, he pulled her back toward the house.

At the steps, she grabbed hold of the railing and planted her feet. "I'm not your prisoner!"

"You're in my custody. What do you think that means?"

"I don't want to stay here!"

"Tough. Now I'd advise you to let go of the rail or risk taking a fistful of splinters with you."

At first she held on tighter, looking as if she'd like to sink her manicured nails into his hide, but after a moment she grudgingly released the rail and, making an effort at regaining some dignity, sedately climbed the steps. At the top, though, she dug in her heels again. "Let go of me."

"Once you're locked up inside."

Her eyes were dark with impotent anger and her lip was showing the slightest tremble as they stared at each other. There was no doubt he would get his way—he was bigger, stronger, and way too accustomed to being obeyed. The only question was whether she would enter the house under her own power or over his shoulder like a sack of grain.

There was no telling what the outcome would have been if they hadn't been interrupted by the surge of a powerful engine accelerating down the driveway. As if she weighed less than nothing, he dragged her across the deck and over the threshold, then gave her a shove toward the guest room. "Get in the bedroom, close the door and stay quiet," he ordered as he closed and locked the door.

There was a time to be obstructive and a time to obey without argument. As Neely watched Reese remove his pistol from the holster tucked at the small of his back, she had no doubt about which time this was. She beat a quick retreat into the guest room, nearly tripping over her suitcase. After locking the door, she leaned against it and gave the room a quick scan. As guest rooms went, for a man who probably shared his bed with most of his overnight guests, the room lacked nothing. As a safe place to hide from unexpected visitors, it lacked everything. There was no way she could fit in the few-inch clearance between the floor and the bed, no cover in the empty closet and, thanks to the shelves and drawers and her own long legs, no space large enough inside the oak armoire.

She was worrying for nothing, she counseled herself. The visitor was probably the mailman or a delivery man, bringing a package to leave on the porch. It might even be Jace, come to rescue her.

But what if it was cause for worry? What if somehow, some way, Eddie Forbes had tracked her down and he'd come to finish what he'd started? He was too big a coward to come alone, so his thugs would be with him. Would Reese be able to protect her?

Would he even try?

Without warning, the doorknob rattled. Neely clamped her hands over her mouth to muffle the startled gasp that slipped out and whirled away from the door, as if those few feet somehow offered more protection.

''Open the door, Neely.''

Even if she hadn't recognized Reese's voice, she would have known that scornful impatience anywhere. After taking a few deep breaths to ease her tremors, she twisted the lock, then hastily moved to the opposite side of the bed.

He opened the door but didn't come farther than a step into the room. ''That was one of my deputies. When the alarm's set off, it automatically dials into the dispatcher. Since I didn't answer the phone when the dispatcher called to clear it and Darren was in the area, he came by to check it out.'' His gaze shifted from her to the neatly made bed, then to her suitcase. For some reason she couldn't begin to guess at, he scowled. ''I told him I forgot about the alarm. Thanks for making me look like an idiot.''

He never looked like an idiot, even when he was being one, so she didn't feel too sorry for him. Back in Thomasville, they'd had some of the most ridiculous arguments, with him on the side of unreasonable, illogical, narrow-minded fools everywhere, but he'd managed to never look unreasonable, illogical or narrow-minded himself.

Though he'd eventually proven that he was all three.

Clasping her hands together tightly so they wouldn't tremble, she tried to look braver and calmer than she felt. "I'd really like to go to the jail now." Before he could turn her down flat again, she rushed on. "There's no safe place to hide here. If Forbes finds out I'm here, it's all over. I have no place to go."

He looked at her for a long still moment, then made a decision he apparently didn't like, followed by an impatient gesture. "Come on. I'll show you the safe room."

Chapter 3

Neely had heard of safe rooms—who in Tornado Alley hadn't?—but she'd never actually seen one. In her own house, the hall bathroom was her best bet in the event of disaster—an interior room, no windows, only one door—but a best bet was far from an honest-to-God, built-for-that-purpose safe room.

She followed Reese through the kitchen and down the other side hallway into his bedroom. The room was large, comfortable, messier than any other room in the house, but that was all she had the chance to notice before he opened a door in the corner. From the bedroom side, anyone would think it was a closet, which some safe rooms were. But not this one. It was small—six-by-eight, maybe eight-by-eight feet. The walls were painted white, the floor carpeted in beige. Much of the space was taken up by a twin bed. There was an electric light overhead, two wall sconces that held candles and a shelf filled with flashlights, a radio, batteries, matches and bottled water.

"Come over here and close the door," Reese commanded gruffly, and she returned from her examination of the room to do so. What had looked like a regular door from the other side was actually steel, she realized, and quite heavy. Fortunately, it didn't require significant effort to move it—at least, not until it was closed and secured. There was what appeared to be a heavy-duty dead bolt lock, along with a steel bar that fitted through brackets on the inside of the door.

"The structure isn't attached to the house, so the house can blow away without affecting this room at all. The walls and ceiling are reinforced concrete, more than a foot thick. This design has been proven to withstand winds up to three hundred miles per hour. It's also bulletproof."

A shiver danced down her spine, one she thought she controlled, but he noticed and frowned. "You're not claustrophobic, are you?"

"Oh, no. I'm learning to love small, enclosed, safe places."

They stood there a moment, the silence around them thick and unnatural. When he broke it, Neely wasn't prepared for the sound of his voice…or had she been anticipating it?

"Who is Forbes?"

A chill swept over her, and she rubbed her bare arms vigorously to generate some heat. After a halfhearted effort, she unfastened the two locks, pushed open the door and returned to the brighter, warmer environment of the bedroom. She thought about brushing him off, about flat-out lying that she didn't know anyone by that name or not answering at all. But as long as she was around, whether in his house or his jail, her problems were his problems.

Threats against her now included him.

A large bay window with a seat looked out onto the front porch and the yard. She sat there, folded her arms across her middle and replied, "Eddie Forbes is a convicted felon whose business interests range from trafficking in narcotics to money-laundering to murder-for-hire."

"Whose murder?"

"That of his primary rival in the drug trade. His wife's lover." She smiled tautly. "And mine."

"Why yours? You give him bad legal advice?"

Though her smile didn't waver, she felt a stab of hurt that he thought so little of her. She hadn't busted her butt all those years to become a lawyer to defend people like Forbes—career criminals, amoral scum who took what they wanted, destroyed countless lives and bought, manipulated and threatened their way out of trouble. Yes, she had defended some guilty people, and yes, she'd gotten some of them off when the cops or the D.A.'s office had screwed up. But that was justice. Even criminals had rights that couldn't be violated.

But justice was all she'd ever sought for any of her clients. She had never gone into court with the intention to free a client she knew was guilty. A fair trial. That was all she'd ever promised, all she'd ever delivered.

"No, I wasn't his lawyer," she replied carelessly. "That would have been a conflict of interest."

"Why?"

"Because I was working for the D.A.'s office at the time. I was Eddie's prosecutor. I sent him to prison."

She saw the surprise that flashed through his eyes, followed by a hint of bitterness. *Why don't you put that expensive degree to good use?* he'd asked her countless times back in Thomasville. *Why don't you go to work for the D.A., where you can do some real good?*

She'd never wanted to be on that side of the courtroom. Overzealous, ambitious or uncaring prosecutors were responsible, in her opinion, for much of the injustice in the justice system. They sent innocent people to jail, sometimes knowingly, sometimes not, but almost always without caring. But Judy Miller's murder and Reese's breaking her heart had convinced her that, just as in providing poor, uninformed clients with a chance for justice, there could be some noble purpose in providing that same justice to guilty people who so richly deserved to be in prison.

And so she'd gone to work for the Jackson County District Attorney's office. She'd been as good a prosecutor as she was a defense attorney. She'd built an impressive record and been rewarded with a heavier caseload and more pressure to perform. She'd had less attention to pay to the details, had had to rely on other people's information and opinions. Clearing her cases had become more important than justice.

The day she'd won a conviction against a man whom she honestly doubted was guilty, she'd turned in her resignation. In the years since she'd neither defended nor prosecuted anyone. She handled wills and trusts, product liability and medical malpractice, prenuptial agreements and divorces, custody cases and adoptions—a little bit of everything. She charged big fees of clients who could afford them and adjusted them accordingly for clients who couldn't, made damn good money and didn't care much about any of it.

"So you prosecuted this guy and got a conviction."

She nodded. "He served five years on a fifteen-to-twenty-year sentence. He warned me at the sentencing that he wouldn't forget me. He got out a few weeks ago, killed his wife, who'd divorced him while he was inside, then came looking for me." Her smile was thin and bitter. "So…thanks for the great advice. At least when I was on the defense side of the table, none of my clients ever tried to kill me."

"No, they killed innocent people instead."

She opened her mouth to argue, but what good would it do? He'd refused to see reason nine years ago, and he appeared even more rigid now. A decade of blaming her seemed to have set his opinions in stone.

When she didn't respond, he walked out of the room, his boots echoing on the wood floors. She didn't follow him, but sank back against the window. She was suddenly tired—of being alone, being afraid, being sorry. Of trying so hard and failing so miserably. Of being damned for doing her job, for obeying the law, for other people's mistakes. She wished she could run far away and never come back, but at the moment she'd be lucky to get within ten feet of a door.

Since that was out, she wished she could curl up in bed, pull the covers close around her and sleep deeply, peacefully, without dreams, until all this ugliness was done. There was a bed six feet in front of her, the navy-blue covers turned down on this side, the fat pillow with an indentation ready to cradle her head. She could kick off her shoes, leave her clothes in a pile on the floor and sink down into all that softness, with nothing showing but the top of her head. The sheets would smell of Reese, and the covers would create a warm, dark cocoon, and she would feel safe because Reese's bed had always been a wonderful place to be.

Had been. Until nine years ago. Wasn't anymore and never would be again.

Wearily she got to her feet, intending to return to the guest room and go quietly insane. She stopped beside the bed for a moment, picked up his pillow and lifted it to her face. It did smell of him, of the same cologne he'd favored years earlier, of the scent that was simply him, of the time when *she* had smelled of him. She breathed deeply, bringing back sweet memories of sweeter times, then, with a lump in her throat, hugged the pillow tightly to her chest.

When she finally walked away, it wasn't out of the bedroom, but into the safe room. She left the door open barely an inch, allowing a bit of weak light into the darkness, then sat on the bed and breathed deeply. There was nothing wrong with feeling melancholy as long as she didn't cry, and she wasn't going to do that. Crying served no purpose. It solved nothing and merely provided others with proof of her weakness. It didn't even make her feel better—her eyes got puffy and red, her head ached and she had trouble breathing—so she absolutely was *not* going to do it.

And then she lay down, snuggled close to Reese's pillow and cried.

Lunchtime came and went with no sign of Neely. Reese had spent the rest of the morning thinking about what she'd said, trying to imagine her working as an assistant D.A., wondering why she'd gone that route when her heart had always been set on defending crooks, not prosecuting them. Was it the Miller case that had pushed her to the other side? Had getting shot opened her eyes to the fact that there was more to justice than simple fairness?

He'd always thought her insistence that justice equaled fairness was naive. What was just about a man who'd beaten his wife half to death on numerous occasions going free because he hadn't been read his rights—rights he already knew by heart from the five other times he'd been arrested? Where was the justice in dropping charges against a drug dealer because the officers had lacked probable cause for searching his car? When their search had been justified, when drugs and money, both in great quantities, had been found, what did probable cause matter?

Why did acknowledged criminals even have any rights?

When his stomach started grumbling, he put a frozen casserole in the microwave oven, set the timer, then glanced at the wall that separated the guest room from the kitchen. What was she doing in there that kept her so quiet? Reading? Sleeping? Looking outside where she couldn't go and heaping silent curses on his head? He told himself it wasn't important. All that mattered was that she was keeping her distance from him. That was the only way they were going to get through the rest of the day. But when he kept wondering, he finally walked down the hall to check.

It was so quiet in the guest room because she wasn't there. He checked the bathroom—the door was open, the lights off—then his bedroom. It was empty, too. She couldn't possibly have left the house. The first thing he'd done after sending the deputy on his way was reset the alarm. Even if she'd managed to sneak out without his knowing it, the dispatcher would have called.

He made a quick check of the entire house, including the garage, then ended up once again in his own room. He was about to turn away and resort to searching closets when the door to the safe room caught his attention. Normally he kept it closed, but when he'd left Neely earlier, it had been wide open. Now it was only slightly ajar.

He pushed the door open and reached for the light switch,

then abruptly stopped. She was lying on her side on the bed, her knees drawn up, her sherbet-green skirt covering her legs and feet, and she was asleep.

The first sensation that swept over him was relief. He might resent her like hell, might wish she'd disappear from his life and his memory, but he didn't want her dead, hurt or in danger. Whatever wrongs she'd committed, whatever mistakes she'd made, she didn't deserve to die for them. She certainly didn't deserve to die for sending a drug dealer and murderer to prison.

The second sensation was…hard to identify. Something weak. Soft. Damnably foolish. For the first time he noticed the signs of unrelenting stress—the shadows under her eyes, the tension that wrinkled her forehead even in sleep, her fists clutching his pillow to her chest. She looked so fragile. Vulnerable. Pushed to the limits of her endurance and beyond. There was a part of him—the part that remembered loving her—that wanted to close the door and lock them inside this safe place, then gather her into his arms and simply hold her. That part knew instinctively that as long as he held her, she would sleep without dreams, without fear, until the fatigue was banished and she was rested enough to rely on her own strength.

Thank God the rest of him knew better than to give in to such weakness.

Minute after minute passed, and he simply stood there and looked at her. Nothing broke the silence but breathing—hers slow and even, his ragged and less than steady. Nothing existed but the two of them, no place but this room.

The timer beeping in the kitchen finally spurred him to move. He left the safe room, then, on impulse, returned with a chenille throw. Careful not to touch her, he spread it over her, pulled the door nearly shut and went back to the kitchen.

After lunch, he spent the next few hours on the Internet, searching for whatever he could find on Eddie Forbes. By the time he read the last archived newspaper article, he felt pretty damn grim. A lot of criminals accepted the risk of arrest and prison as part of the cost of doing business and bore no ill will toward either the cops or the D.A. Everybody—good guy or bad—was just doing his job.

Eddie Forbes wasn't one of them. He blamed his unfortunate incarceration on everyone but himself. He'd already killed his ex-wife and her lover and threatened to kill Neely next. Because he blamed them most? Or because they were women and more vulnerable than the cops, crooks and lawyers involved?

Reese had just signed off the computer and risen from his chair when the cell phone rang. He sat back down and answered, fully expecting to hear his cousin's voice. He wasn't disappointed.

"Hey, bubba. How's it going?"

Thinking about Neely's escape that morning and his dragging her back into the house, Reese ignored the heat rising up his neck and carelessly replied, "Everything's okay here. How about there?"

"Everybody's stirred up. Seems somebody disappeared from the department's protective custody and no one has a clue where she's gone."

"That's what you get for working in a big city. We couldn't lose a prisoner down here if we wanted to." Unless she just got up and walked out. If she had closed the door quietly instead of giving in to her temper and slamming it, who knew how far she could have gotten?

"Did you ever start locking the jail cells, or couldn't you find the key?"

"Funny, Jace. When are we going to see you again?"

There was a guilty silence, followed by a slow, "I don't know. I thought I was going to be able to get away sometime soon, but it didn't work out. There's too much going on here. I'm stuck."

Reese scowled. Jace had lied to him, conned him into taking Neely and accepted his deadline for getting her out by tonight, and now he was backing out of the deal, just like that. As if no one else had a say in the matter. And, really, how much say did they have? She was here. She had no place else to go, and he had only one place to take her—one place she certainly didn't belong. *They* were stuck, not Jace. "For how long?" he asked stiffly.

"I don't know, bubba."

"Listen, *bubba*—"

"Hey, I tried. There's just no way I can get away right now." After a pause, Jace's tone lightened. "But it's nice to know you miss me so much."

"Yeah, like a pain in the—" Reese broke off as Neely, looking very much like a small child awakened too soon from a nap, came into the room. "Hey, your mom says you never call."

"I call her every week."

"Yeah, well, call her twice this week." That would make Aunt Rozena happy, and all Barnetts had a stake in keeping Rozena happy. "You know, you owe me more favors than you'll ever be able to repay."

"I know, bubba. Thanks. And, hey, tell her… Tell her not to worry."

Reese glanced at Neely, standing in front of the fireplace and looking at the family photos there, and wondered yet again what was between her and Jace. It had better not be anything more than friendship, because if his cousin thought for one minute he was going to marry her, make her part of the family and subject Reese to her presence for the rest of their lives, he was crazy.

But Neely had been known to make men crazy before.

She'd sure as hell made *him* crazy.

"I will," he said quietly. "Keep in touch, will you?"

"When I can."

Reese hung up and laid the phone aside, then swiveled around to watch her. He could tell the instant she became aware of his gaze. She stood an inch taller. Became less soft. Tried to look tougher—and failed.

"Was that Jace?" She sounded as cool and unapproachable

as she tried to look, and never shifted her gaze one millimeter from the photograph in front of her.

"Yeah."

"He's not coming, is he?"

"No."

If he hadn't been studying her, he would have missed the nearly imperceptible shiver that rippled through her. "Then we may as well go. My bag is already packed."

If he took her to the jail, as he'd threatened, her presence in Canyon County would no longer be his and Jace's secret. She would be out of his house but not out of his life. He might be more comfortable—though he wouldn't bet on it—but she would be trading one difficult situation for another. She very well might be no safer there than she was here—maybe not even as safe. Everyone in the department and a good number of courthouse employees would know she was there, and who knew who they might tell?

No, transferring her to the jail wasn't the answer—not yet, at least. He would give his cousin a little more time, then reconsider, but he wasn't taking her anywhere today. "Jace said to tell you not to worry."

The faintest of smiles touched her mouth before disappearing. "Jace is an optimist."

"So are you."

She shook her head. "Maybe I used to be, but not anymore. These days I'm a realist."

And these days her reality wasn't too encouraging.

"You hungry? There's a casserole in the refrigerator—one of my aunt's Tex-Mex specialties." Reese went into the kitchen, and she followed, taking a plate from the cabinet to dish up a helping to put in the microwave.

"Smells wonderful," she said, breathing deeply. "How is Rozena?"

Pausing in the act of returning the casserole container to the refrigerator, Reese looked at her sharply. When they were together, she'd never met any of his family but his father and Jace. He couldn't remember ever mentioning his aunt by name, or believe Neely would remember after all these years. "You know Rozena?"

The suspicion in his voice stiffened her spine as she watched the food slowly rotate inside the oven. "We met the last time she visited Jace in Kansas City."

He didn't know Rozena *had* visited Jace in the city. And why in hell would Jace include Neely in a family visit unless… "You think he's going to marry you?"

Either the question itself or the hostility that made it so harsh startled her into looking at him. Her brown eyes were open wide and faintly amused, and her mouth wore the beginning of a smile that never quite formed. Instead she grew serious and thoughtful. "Does that worry you?"

"Jace deserves better."

"But we don't always get what we deserve, do we?"

And what did she think *he* deserved? Eternal damnation? "The family will never accept you."

"Why not? Because you'll tell them whatever is necessary to make them dislike me?"

"All that will be necessary is the truth."

The microwave stopped, and she removed her plate, carried it to the table, then returned for a Coke and silverware. As she settled in the chair she calmly said, "You can't tell them the truth, Reese, because you don't know it. All you know—all you can accept—is your narrow-minded version of what happened, but there's so much more to it than that."

"There's nothing more to it," he argued, moving to sit across from her. "Leon Miller tried to kill his wife. We arrested him and took him to trial. You manipulated the law to get the charges dropped, and he walked out of the courthouse and blew her away. Bottom line—if not for you, he wouldn't have gone free that day. If not for you, Judy wouldn't have died that day." He stared at her a long, cold moment before finally finishing. "The bottom line is *you* were responsible, Neely. *You* should have paid the price."

Neely held her fork so tightly that the beveled stainless edges cut into her palm, but she kept her hand from shaking and thought she succeeded fairly well at keeping the hurt and frustration out of her expression. In fact, even to herself, she sounded polite. Conversational. "It must be nice to be able to pass judgment on the rest of the world—to lay blame wherever you want, to condemn whoever you want and absolve whoever you choose. You decide which laws are worth enforcing and which to ignore in the name of right. You point fingers, lay blame, assign guilt, judge, condemn and sentence, all from your intolerant, mean little viewpoint, and all with the certainty that you have a God-given right to do so.

"Well, you don't, Reese. You're no wiser than anyone else. You overstep your authority, and you do incredible harm. You accuse me of manipulating the law. How could you possibly tell after you and others like you have twisted and subverted it beyond recognition? In your quest for justice as you define it, you trample all over people's civil rights, and then when your case gets thrown out, you look for someone else to blame. You don't have the guts to say, 'I shouldn't have conducted an illegal search, or beaten a confession out of the suspect, or failed to read him his rights. I screwed up.' Oh, no, you say, 'It's his lawyer's fault. It's the judge's fault. The D.A. wasn't prepared. It was that bleeding-heart jury.'"

She took a breath, forced her fingers to uncurl, and lay the fork on her plate. Folding her hands tightly in her lap, she met his gaze unflinchingly. "The bottom line, Reese, is that Leon Miller walked out of the courthouse a free man that day because *your* department screwed up. *Your* fellow deputies failed to read him his rights and coerced his confession. From the first time they hit him, it was guaranteed that those charges were going to be dropped. It didn't matter who his lawyer was or if he even had a lawyer. The judge had no choice but to dismiss the case. *Your* people set him free. *Your* people gave him another chance to kill his wife. Not me."

His face was a few shades paler than normal, which heightened the color staining his cheeks, and his eyes were a few shades darker. He wanted to argue with her—she knew that from too much experience arguing just such cases in the past—but he didn't seem able to get the words out. They would just be a waste of breath, just as all her words had been wasted.

He believed, as the rest of the Keegan County Sheriff's Department had, that, to some extent, the end justified the means. When Leon Miller had given his wife the worst beating yet, they'd shown him what it was like to be brutalized by someone bigger, stronger and angrier. They'd gotten a confession and some small satisfaction, and had left the D.A. with no case.

Thankfully, Reese hadn't been involved in that particular case, though he'd arrested Miller a number of times before. He hadn't approved of the beating, but he'd understood it, and he hadn't thought it a reason to let the man go. Well, hell, Neely had understood it, too. What woman, victim or not, hadn't fantasized at least once about some tough guy coming along and teaching a wife-beating bully a lesson he would never forget? And if it had merely been some tough guy, she probably would have cheered him on and volunteered to represent him if he was arrested.

But they'd been *deputies*. The so-called good guys.

And their crime had been worse than any Miller had committed until that day.

"It's an old argument that we may as well drop now," she said wearily. "I can't accept your point of view, and you won't consider mine."

"And what is your point of view, Neely? That fairness should always win out over justice? That Miller's civil rights were more important than Judy's life? That you can't be held responsible for what your client does once he walks out of the courtroom? Because that's all just so much bull. We don't *live* in the courtroom. If you make it possible for your client to walk out of the courtroom, free to commit other crimes, you share the responsibility for every one of those crimes."

Giving a shake of her head, she picked up the fork and took a bite of beans, shredded beef and cheese. Though she wasn't hungry and felt queasy, she forced herself to eat. She needed the strength if she was going to make it through one more day with Reese.

How had they ever hooked up together when they were such different people? Had the intense emotions they'd called love merely been stronger-than-usual lust? Had they wanted love so badly that they'd fooled themselves into believing they'd found it in each other? Surely at some point they'd realized that they could never make the relationship work. They must have known it was only a matter of time before their differences became so great that they couldn't be overcome.

But she didn't remember realizing any such thing. She'd loved Reese with all her heart. She'd believed they would be together forever. She'd thought differences of opinion were inconsequential in the face of such love. Maybe they would have been, if the love hadn't been one-sided. If he had been as committed to her as she'd been to him, they could have withstood anything.

But he hadn't been. At the first serious challenge they'd faced, he'd folded. Turned away from her. Betrayed her. Broken her heart.

"All right," she said flatly. "You've been damning me for nine years. I'll accept your blame, and I'll share it with Leon, with Judy and every one of the deputies involved in his confession, with the sheriff of Keegan County, the district attorney, and with you. There's plenty of guilt to go around, and I'll take my portion if you'll take yours."

Why shouldn't she? Despite her protests this morning that she'd done nothing wrong, she'd been living with her own guilt all those years. In the early months she'd tormented herself with it. What if she'd refused to represent Miller? What if she'd persuaded him to plead guilty in spite of the civil rights violations? What if she'd made it clear to the D.A. and the judge that she wouldn't raise any questions about the way the confession was obtained? That even though the state's entire case was tainted, she would stand quietly by and let her client go to prison because, after all, there was no question of his guilt?

It wouldn't have been fair, but it might have been justice. And it wouldn't have cost her much—just a lifetime of living with the knowledge that she'd betrayed her client and herself. Her ethics, her morals, her self-respect—the very essence of who she was—all would have been destroyed.

But Judy wouldn't have been killed, and Reese wouldn't have left her…though eventually *she* would have left *him* because her love would have been destroyed, too.

She ate as much of her lunch as she knew she could keep down, then pushed the plate away and lowered her face into her hands, rubbing her temples and the ache that seemed to have settled there permanently. She'd eased a bit of the tension when Reese spoke and the mere sound of his voice brought it racing back.

"Do you need some aspirin?"

She felt the tautness as her faint smile formed. "I need a new life—a normal life, where the people who say 'I wish you were dead' are generally talking out of anger or rebellion and aren't really intending to plant a pipe bomb in your car or redecorate your bedroom with bullet holes. But since a normal life doesn't seem likely at the moment, yes, aspirin would help."

He went to the cabinet next to the sink, then came back with an open bottle. He shook two tablets into her palm, then sat again. After she'd washed the pills down with pop, he quietly asked, "Did Forbes do that?"

For a moment she considered not answering, but those were quite possibly the only non-accusing, non-bitter, non-hostile words he'd spoken to her. Besides, she was hiding in his house. If Forbes found her, the next car bombed might be Reese's, the next house shot up, this one. It was only fair that he know.

Managing another tight smile, she nodded. "The verdict's not in on the bomb yet—whether it malfunctioned or their timing was simply off—but I wasn't in the car when it exploded. As for the shots in the night, I was lucky. The first one woke me up and I managed to crawl to safety. But don't worry. They say the third time's the charm. Then I'll be out of your life for good.''

His features darkened into a scowl. "I don't want—" Clenching his jaw on the denial, he dragged his fingers through his dark hair, then gave a shake of his head, as if he knew he was wasting his breath. "Look, we're stuck here until Jace makes other arrangements, and God only knows when that will be. If we don't start acting like reasonable adults, it's going to be the most miserable time of our lives. We can either stay in our respective corners, or we can negotiate a truce."

Staying in their corners hadn't worked very well so far, Neely admitted. She felt as if she'd gone five rounds with a much better opponent and couldn't possibly survive another five. Compromise was the only reasonable action, though it held risks of its own. If Reese quit attacking her, if he let her forget for one moment that he despised her, she could be foolish enough to fall for him all over again. He was more handsome than ever, surely—with others, at least—as charming as ever, and she'd always been so susceptible. She'd built such fantasies around them.

But he'd despised her so much more—and so much longer—than he'd ever loved her, and he wouldn't forget, or let her forget. He was offering to compromise on his behavior, not his beliefs. That damning look in his eyes, the one that shadowed every other emotion he was feeling, would probably never go away, no matter what.

"So what do we do?" she asked. "Agree that certain topics are off-limits?"

Reese shrugged.

"The Miller case?"

"Your noble profession."

Ignoring the sneer underlying his words, she smiled. "Your narrow-minded, damn-the-law-and-the-lawyers pigheadedness."

He opened his mouth to refute her statement, then almost smiled. It had been so long since he'd smiled at her that she stared and made silent, fervent wishes that he would let the smile form. He didn't. "At least we agree that we don't think much of each other professionally."

"You're wrong, Reese. I always thought you were the best thing that ever happened to the Keegan County Sheriff's Department...until you became just like the others."

"I was never just like them," he denied a little too quickly and too vehemently.

"Careful there. A person might think you find being compared to your former fellow deputies an insult, and that might suggest that you have a problem with the way they did their jobs. That maybe they weren't always so right. Maybe I wasn't always so wrong."

After studying her a moment he mildly said, "It seems to me that discussion encompasses all three topics we just agreed were off limits. So...how are your sisters?"

It was entirely too normal a question, one that left her feeling unbalanced, as if the gibe would come in a moment, when she wasn't prepared. She shrugged and cautiously replied, "My sisters are fine. Kylie is living in Dallas. Hallie is in Los Angeles, and Bailey lives in Memphis."

"Any of them married?"

"Hallie just divorced number three—no kids, fortunately. Kylie and Bailey are waiting for the right guy. They're learning from her example."

"And yours?"

"Hallie's got the relationship 'dos and don'ts' all to herself. I'm the 'don't' for everything else." *Don't try to make a difference. Don't make the mistake of thinking you can be important. Don't care too deeply or too passionately about anything. Don't mix relationship and career. Don't work where you might make men with guns angry with you.* And the biggie—*Don't piss off drug-dealing murderers.*

"And your mother?"

"She's also fine. She's living in Illinois with husband number two. She golfs, cooks, plays doting grandmother to his grandkids and routinely complains that none of us has provided her with grandchildren of her own." She heard the cynical note in her voice and was embarrassed by it. She'd long ago learned to not expect much from her mother. Doris Irene had done the best she could with the life she'd gotten. All she'd ever wanted to be was a wife, mother and grandmother, with a husband who would take care of all life's problems so she wouldn't have to bother her pretty little head with them. And that was what she'd gotten in the first ten years of her marriage.

Then the police had come in the middle of one winter night, kicking in doors, waving guns, shouting commands, and they'd taken Lee Madison away. To this day Neely remembered the cold, hard knot of terror in her stomach, her mother's tears and her sisters' screams. She'd stood there in her little flannel nightgown, the younger girls and Doris Irene huddled behind her sobbing, and her feet had felt like ice as she stared unflinchingly at the officers who dragged her father away.

"You never mentioned a father."

Her startled gaze jerked to Reese. Seeing curiosity in his expression, she forced herself to relax, to breathe deeply and hopefully get some color back into her face. Under the protection of the table, she rubbed her hands together, her fingers as icy as her heart that long-ago night. "You never asked."

"I figured he was a sore point. People who get along with their parents tend to bring them up from time to time. You never did."

"I got along with him beautifully. I loved him dearly. I adored him."

"Is he dead?"

The cold, hard knot was back, making it difficult to breathe. For years she couldn't think about her father without bursting into tears, or dissolving into a nerveless, trembling heap. *I'm not bitter,* he'd told her the last time she'd seen him. She had been bitter for him. That was when she'd learned to truly, intensely, unforgivingly hate.

Rising abruptly from the table, she carried her dishes to the sink and rinsed them. Her hands were unsteady—the silverware slipped through her fingers, and the plate clattered against the sink. When she dried her hands, she wrapped them tightly in the towel, knotting muscles and cotton as she flatly replied, "Yes, he's dead. He was murdered."

Reese didn't know what to say. It was strange, but even in his profession, he hadn't met the families of very many murder victims. Canyon County averaged about one homicide every couple years, and in Keegan County, he'd been too inexperienced to handle capital cases.

Though he'd seen Judy Miller gunned down not twenty feet in front of him. She was the first person he'd ever seen die, and he sincerely hoped she was the last.

"Your father was murdered, and you can still justify defending the bad guys?"

"My noble profession's off limits for discussion, remember?" she reminded him, her voice less than steady. Then she went ahead and answered. "It wasn't the bad guys who killed my father. It was the state."

"I don't under— He was *executed?*"

She turned from the sink, her arms folded across her middle. "Not formally. But he died in prison, killed after an assault by another inmate. And he was there for a crime he didn't commit."

Reese swallowed hard. "But...don't they all say that?"

The look she gave him was disappointed, as if she expected better from him, and scornful, as if she didn't. "Yes, most convicted felons say that. But my father's name was cleared by authorities. Unfortunately, it was too late for him."

So that was why she'd become a lawyer, why she defended people accused of crimes. She believed her father hadn't gotten a fair trial and was probably right. With a better lawyer, a better chance, he might still be alive today.

But if Leon Miller had had a less competent lawyer, Judy might still be alive.

Judy was one of the first people Reese had met in Thomasville. She'd been a waitress at the diner where he'd eaten most of his meals the first week—when Leon let her work— and they'd struck up a friendship. Her utter lack of knowledge of or interest in his injury-shortened baseball career had been a welcome change. With her he'd just been one more deputy in the long line that frequented the diner.

In the beginning he'd never guessed that anything was wrong. He'd seen an occasional bruise or two, but she'd always had a plausible explanation. Then one day he'd seen the distinct fingerprints that circled her arm, and soon after she'd been sporting a black eye. It had taken him weeks to coax the truth from her, months to convince her to file a police report.

Weeks before Leon's last arrest, Judy had confided in Reese that she was going to stop calling the cops. Nothing ever changed, she'd complained. He kept getting out of jail, kept coming back.

And she'd kept taking him back, he'd pointed out. She didn't throw him out. Didn't get a protective order against him. Didn't go for counseling, either jointly or alone. Didn't disappear someplace where he'd never find her. Didn't take his threats seriously enough.

The last time he'd beaten her, she'd taken him seriously. She'd wanted to run away. Reese had convinced her to go through with the trial. The sheriff's department would protect her, he'd promised. *He* would protect her.

And that was why he'd been so quick to put all the blame on Neely. Because Judy had believed him, had trusted him with her life, and he'd failed her.

Feeling queasy, he stood, neatly pushed the chair in and walked into the living room. He didn't stop until he was at the window, where he turned around and looked back at Neely, still standing by the sink, still holding herself because there was no one to do it for her. He was guilty, too, just as she'd said, but that didn't make her not guilty. It didn't make her role any more forgivable. There was plenty of blame to go around. It was just weightier for some than for others.

He turned back to the window and stood there a long time, staring and seeing nothing. When the floorboard in front of the kitchen door creaked, he didn't look. When the leather of his favorite chair made its familiar rubbing sound, he continued to gaze out.

"How is your father?"

The question was so normal, so expected when talking with someone he hadn't seen in years, that it was unexpected. Frowning, he turned to face her and found her watching him without expression. For all the life it showed, her face might have been a porcelain mask—beautifully detailed, delicate, perfect in its design and execution, but lacking life. Warmth. Hope.

"He...he's fine."

"Does he live around here?"

"In Buffalo Plains." Remembering that the truce negotiations had been his idea, he stiffly continued. "He has a garage over there with Jace's father, and he's thinking about giving marriage another try. I'm not sure, though, which is the bigger attraction—the pretty widow, or the fact that she owns a vintage Mercedes that he loves to tinker with."

"Tell him to marry for the car. It won't break his heart."

The muscles in Reese's jaw tightened. "Actually, my advice was to forget the widow and make an offer for the car instead. If she turns him down, he can find another one like it and be just as happy."

"Everything's interchangeable with you, isn't it?"

He didn't like the way she spoke—didn't like the bitter little smile that accompanied the words. He for damn sure didn't like the twinge of guilt they sent down his spine. "A car's a car," he said flatly.

"And a woman's a woman, and a crook's a crook, and any one can take any other's place."

If that were true, he would have replaced her nine years ago. As soon as he'd moved from Thomasville to Buffalo Plains, he would have found a job, a place to live and a woman to love, all in short order. Instead, it had been one hell of a long time before he'd even given thought to finding a woman to have sex with. He hadn't yet found the desire to look for one to love. "According to your reasoning, men are interchangeable, too. How many men have you used in my place over the years?''

''None.'' Apparently his cynicism showed on his face, because she smiled that bitter little smile again. It was a gesture he could easily learn to hate. ''I'm not saying I've been celibate all these years. I haven't. I'm just saying that you were a tough act to follow. I couldn't find many men out there who despised me as much as you did but wanted to sleep with me badly enough to sacrifice their self-respect.''

Reese opened his mouth to argue, then closed it again. He'd told her just that morning that his relationship with her had cost him his self-respect. He couldn't blame her now for throwing it back at him.

When he didn't say anything, she made a regretful sound. ''We got a little off track there, didn't we? You say your father's contemplating marriage again, and I'll say 'Oh, that's nice—how many does this make?' and you'll say…''

''This will be number four.'' This wasn't the conversation he wanted to have. He wanted to back up, to ask her how many men she hadn't been celibate with. Had they been relationships or affairs? Had she contemplated marriage with any of them, or had they merely been substitutes—making do with what was available?

''What happened to numbers one through three? And which one was your mother?''

''He and my mother were never married.'' His mother had wanted more from life than marriage to a man who couldn't keep a job and a trailer to call home in a dusty little town like Heartbreak. She'd been in and out of their lives for years, coming home during Del's ranching phase, leaving during his attempt at farming, moving in again while he worked in the oilfields and out again when he'd scraped together every penny he could to open the garage. Working with engines, it turned out, was where Del excelled, but even steady work and good money hadn't been enough to make Lena Harlowe settle down with a lowly grease monkey. Since she hadn't come around in twenty years or so, Reese assumed she'd found someone who made good money and had clean fingernails, too. He'd been glad to see her go.

"The first marriage was before I was born, and I don't know anything about it except that he's hated the name Karen ever since. Then came the on-again, off-again thing with my mother. The second marriage was doomed from the start. They'd been seeing each other awhile. She wanted to get married, and he didn't. They took a little trip one Memorial Day weekend—did a lot of partying. He woke up when the weekend was over with Lou Ann in his bed and a marriage certificate on the nightstand. The next April he woke up after another rowdy weekend to find that Lou Ann had filed for divorce and run off with someone else—which explains why, to this day, Tax Day is the high holy day of Del Barnett's nonreligious life."

"And number three?" Neely sounded vaguely amused, more like the woman who'd knocked him for a loop ten years ago by doing nothing more than walking into a courtroom, tripping over a loose board and dropping an armload of files at his feet. She hadn't been embarrassed, hadn't blamed the county or the faulty board, but had laughed instead, and that quick, he'd been a goner.

"She was a souvenir from a trip to Las Vegas. Her name was Georgie, she was only four years older than me, and she was an exotic dancer. She looked like a stripper, dressed like a stripper, stood out like a peacock in a flock of doves and generated gossip everywhere she went. She damn near wore him out before she got a calling to go help the less fortunate in South America." He smiled at the memory of Georgie with her magenta hair, multiple piercings, dramatic makeup and eyebrow-raising clothes. "She's the one he misses the most."

"And you miss your mother most."

His smile slowly faded into a frown. "Not at all. I miss Georgie, too. She kept things stirred up. I never really knew Lena—my mother. About the time we'd start to get acquainted, she'd take off for a few months or a few years. By the time she wandered back, we'd have to start all over again.

Then one day, when I was fifteen or so, she took off and never came back. By then I didn't care if I ever saw her again. That was somewhere in between Lou Ann and Georgie.''

"So your dad's been alone a long time.''

"Not alone. Just single. There's a difference.'' Turning his back on her, he stared out the window again, at grass in need of mowing, blackjacks and a thin blue sky. *He* was the one who'd been alone a lot. Thanks to Neely, he knew the difference intimately.

Thanks to her, he might never know anything different.

Chapter 4

There was another storm Tuesday evening that took out the power with the first lightning strike and left Neely and Reese in warm, muggy darkness. She was stretched out on the sofa, her skirt pulled up to expose her legs, with a magazine clutched in one hand to languidly fan herself, and he was comfortably slumped in the chair-and-a-half, with his bare feet propped on the ottoman.

Wishing for shorts and a T-shirt, a piña colada and a cooling breeze, she asked, "Does your electricity go off every time it storms?"

"Nah. Sometimes I lose the phone instead. Sometimes all it takes is one lightning strike and the power will be off for hours. On the other hand, last month a tornado passed between the house and the barn, and the lights didn't even so much as flicker."

"And you know it came that close because...?"

"I saw it."

"But the safe room doesn't have any windows."

"I wasn't in the safe room. I was in the barn."

She recalled her first sight of the barn out back, when she'd thought it was surely a hundred years old. "Is there any particular reason you took shelter in that old barn instead of your high-tech safe room?"

"I'd gone to check the horses. I thought I had time."

"You're lucky it didn't come crashing down on your head."

"Believe it or not, some people would have minded."

She gazed in his direction, but with no illumination, all she could see was shadows. Swallowing a soft sigh, she turned her head to look at other, less dangerous shadows.

She didn't doubt people around there would have been sorry if anything had happened to him. After all, the position of sheriff was an elected one, so enough people liked him to put him in office and keep him there. But, hell, people liking him had never been a problem. He'd been popular with the Royals' fans, and had been easily the most respected deputy in Keegan County. Heaven knows, *she'd* never had any trouble liking him. She'd thought he was the best thing that ever happened to her.

She'd proven herself a lousy judge of character.

Resolutely pushing away the ache in her chest, she aimed for a cheery, conversational voice and asked, "What brought you back to Oklahoma? As I recall, you had no intention of ever living here again." He'd had enough small-town living to last a lifetime, he'd insisted, and once he left Thomasville for a job with a bigger and better department, he was never living in a city with fewer than a hundred thousand people. And here he was, back home in a county with only a fraction of that population.

"I didn't. But I took some vacation time after…"

After Judy's death, which they'd agreed to not discuss.

"I stayed with my dad over in Buffalo Plains, spent some time with the family, saw some old friends. I found out things weren't quite as suffocating as I'd remembered. When the sheriff offered me a job, I decided to take it. It wasn't as if there was anything for me back in Thomasville, and getting out of Kansas certainly couldn't hurt my so-called career.''

A lump swelled to block Neely's throat, bringing with it a shudder of deep sorrow. There was nothing for him back in Thomasville…except her. Lying in a hospital bed the first four or five days, then struggling at home to manage alone and facing the anger and hostility of an entire community with no one on her side—and, in his eyes, that was nothing. The harassment, the vandalism, the threats against her life—nothing. The great love he'd claimed, the commitment, the forever-and-ever—nothing.

''What made you move to Kansas City?''

She barely restrained a choked laugh that could too easily dissolve into hysterical tears. ''You're kidding, right? I moved because I wanted to stay alive, and the odds were against that happening in Thomasville.''

''What are you talking about?''

''Oh, come on, Reese. Even if you weren't there, your buddies must have kept you informed. After all, they were doing it for you.''

''Doing what for me?''

Unable to sit still any longer, she surged to her feet and paced the length of the dark room as if she'd placed each piece of furniture herself and knew its location intimately. She went all the way to one hall door, then all the way to the other. When she returned, though, Reese was on his feet, blocking her way.

''Doing what for me?'' His voice was softer, lower, milder, and more demanding. She knew from experience that the angrier he got, the more reasonable he sounded. When people who didn't know him thought he was as harmless as a kitten, that was when he was most dangerous. And knowing that, she hesitated only a second before stepping around him.

He caught her arm just above the elbow and pulled her back. Her skin was clammy. His palm was warm and dry, his grip strong enough to hold her, but not strong enough to hurt. ''What were they doing, Neely?''

A flash of lightning showed the hard, unforgiving look on his face. She thought it probably matched her own look. "Harassing me," she replied in clipped, challenging tones. "Punishing me. Trying to make me leave town. Failing that, trying to kill me."

Abruptly the power came back on. Lights banished the darkness to the corners of the room and made them both blink in response. The television came on midshow, the air-conditioning unit kicked on, and the ceiling fan began turning lazily, picking up speed with each revolution. And she and Reese stood where they were, staring at each other as if one might persuade—or dissuade—the other with nothing more than the sheer force of their gazes.

He didn't believe her. She didn't expect him to, not without proof. Even with proof, he would find some way to shift the blame entirely to her. He was good at that.

But she was disappointed. Unreasonably, irrationally disappointed.

"You expect me to believe that Dave, Reggie and those guys tried to kill you because…they thought it was what I wanted?"

She gazed into his dark eyes—eyes that had once looked at her with such tenderness, that were now skeptical, cynical, distrusting—and she felt so lost, so hopeless. "Please…let me go. Just turn off the alarm and let me leave. You can tell Jace I escaped. You can blame me for everything. You've done it before."

His fingers tightened fractionally. "And where would you go?"

"Someplace safe. I know people who will help, people who wouldn't rather see me dead."

At that, something flickered across his face—dismay? offense? shame?—but it was gone long before she could identify it, and once it was gone, his features settled into stone-cold stubbornness. "Most people don't give a damn whether you're dead or alive. You have quite an opinion of yourself, don't you?"

Her eyes burned with tears she damn well wouldn't shed, and her throat was so tight that the words she forced through sounded raw. "No. I used to, but not anymore." He—and life and luck—had taken care of that. "Please let me go."

"We haven't finished discussing this alleged conspiracy plot against you in Thomasville."

Over the years she'd felt a great many things for Reese, but his smug words and his obnoxious smirk made her hate him for the first time ever. She wanted to slap that smirk right off his handsome face, but with her luck, any physical aggression would be rewarded with handcuffs. Instead she responded in kind. She gave him a smirk that made her feel dirty, and arrogantly replied, "Maybe you haven't, but I have. Now, let go of me before I decide to make your life a living hell." She wrenched free and made it as far as the hall before he got in his last dig.

"Too late, counselor. You did that years ago."

After another restless night—courtesy of Neely—Reese got up early, showered and dressed in his uniform, then headed for the kitchen to start the coffee. He didn't make it farther than the door into the living room, though, where he found her curled tightly in the chair-and-a-half, with the chair arm for a pillow and the quilt off her bed for cover. The position looked uncomfortable as hell, but, sound asleep, she didn't seem to notice.

Why give up a perfectly adequate bed for a backache-inducing chair? Granted, she'd said she was learning to love small, safe spaces, but this was stupid. This entire house was safe.

But theoretically no place should be safer than a designated safe house, and yet it was sheer luck that she hadn't been carried out of the Kansas City safe house in a body bag.

He watched her for a moment, then another, before finally giving himself a mental shake. He retreated into the hallway, then cut through the kitchen to the guest room, where he gathered her belongings. After removing the extra set of keys to his truck from the desk drawer and disconnecting the power cord from the computer, he carried it all, along with the phone from his nightstand, into the closet where he also kept his guns, then closed and locked the door. The lock was a two-inch dead bolt, and the only key was on his key ring. There was no way she was getting inside.

That done, he went back to the living room. He didn't like the idea of leaving her alone—didn't trust her to not do something stupid—but he had no choice. He'd missed two days of work already, and today he not only had a meeting with the county commissioners, but also a court appearance. Neither one could be put off.

The only question was whether he should wake her and tell her, or let her find out he was gone on her own. Wake her and put the fear of God in her, or trust her to realize that, like him, she had no choice. Wake her, with her face scrubbed clean of makeup and her hair falling every which way and looking delicate and vulnerable and making him feel so damn vulnerable, or save himself.

Taking a deep breath, he pivoted away from her. In the kitchen, he scrawled a quick note, telling her where he was going and when he would return, warning her that one of his men would be nearby at all times, hinting that she would be sorry if she didn't behave—though he had little doubt she couldn't be any sorrier than she already was. Sorry she'd ever met him. Sorry she'd taken his advice and gone to work for the prosecutor. Sorry she'd come here instead of taking her chances with the bad guys in the city.

He anchored the note on the table underneath her starry glasses, then left. Everything was locked up tight. The alarm was armed. She couldn't get out and no one else could get in without his knowing it. She couldn't have any contact with the outside world. She was more secure than she'd be in his jail.

He hoped.

It was a short drive to downtown Heartbreak, where he parked in front of Shay Rafferty's café. He'd had a relation-

ship with Shay for a while last year, and occasionally he'd
tried to imagine the two of them married, having a family,
planning a future. The images had always refused to form,
though—because he'd known from the start she would never
love him, he'd told himself.

Not because there was only one woman he'd ever wanted
to spend the rest of his life with.

Virtually every seat in the café was taken, and Reese figured
he knew every single soul by name and history. There were
some he liked, such as Ethan and Grace James, sharing breakfast with their little girl, Annie Grace, before they headed out
to open up the hardware store. There were some he didn't
like—Inez Taylor, her snotty sister-in-law and snottier daughter came immediately to mind as they turned three identical
scowls his way—and some he'd arrested, none of whom ever
bore him any ill will.

There were worse things than knowing everyone, he thought
as he settled into the back booth reserved for Shay's family
and friends. Not knowing anyone at all—that would be lonely.
Believing that people wanted you dead…

Scowling, he muttered a curse, then looked up as a coffee
cup appeared in front of him. Shay filled the cup, then slid in
across from him. "Howdy, Sheriff."

He removed the tan Stetson that was part of the uniform
and laid it on the seat beside him. "Ma'am."

"So…you've come out of seclusion, and except for a few
signs of fatigue, you look none the worse for wear. Who was
the lucky lady?"

"Lady?"

Tossing her head as if she still had the incredibly long mass
of blond hair that had made men weak, Shay batted her eye-
lashes and said in her breathiest, most seductive voice, "Oh,
by all means, darlin', go on. I don't mind stayin' here in this
great big ole house all by my little ole self one bit."

He continued to scowl at her, but his heart wasn't in it.
"You like to exaggerate, don't you?" Neely didn't go in for
breathy or blatantly seductive. She didn't need to.

"Maybe a bit. It's so much fun to watch you get all stern. Who is she?"

"Nobody."

"Oh, come on, Reese, I *heard* her voice. It wasn't *nobody*. Give it up, Sheriff, or I'll cook your breakfast myself." She grinned wickedly and affected a totally different accent. "I haf vays of makeeng you talk."

"Idle threats. I know you're not allowed in the kitchen, even if you do own the place. How's Easy?"

"Easy's beautiful. Is she from around here?"

"And your mom and dad?"

"They're fine. I'm fine. Everybody's fine. And you're no fun." Her blue eyes widened and she leaned closer. "Is she married?"

He gave her an annoyed look. "I'm not interested in married women. That's a good way to get yourself shot." To say nothing of losing any self-respect a man might have.

"Not even one married woman in particular?"

"Not even one."

Shay sat back and studied him a moment, then slid to her feet. "Give me your order so I can get it in, then make the coffee rounds."

He ordered, then stirred sugar and cream into his coffee and wondered about the way she'd looked at him—as if something he'd said surprised her. But he hadn't said anything of substance, except for the remark about married—

He mouthed a curse seconds before she sat again and folded her hands together. "Okay," she said cheerily. "Which one's the lie? Have you ever in your life had your heart broken by a married woman, or are you really not interested in any married women?"

He forced an unsteady smile. "You broke my heart when you picked Rafferty over me."

"Oh, darlin', I never touched your heart. It was already in pieces—broken by a woman married to someone else, or so you said. Wasn't true, was it?"

"I said she *belonged* to someone else. You made the leap

to marriage on your own.'' He tried not to squirm under her steady gaze, but wasn't successful. ''Look, it's a part of my life that I wish had never happened and would give anything to forget. I didn't want to discuss it with you or anyone else, so I lied.''

''So she wasn't married. And she didn't choose another man over you.''

In a sense, she did. She'd chosen to defend Leon Miller, knowing that he was guilty, knowing that Reese was opposed to it. She'd weighed her relationship with *him* against the rights of a wife-beating bastard to go free to do it again, and she'd chosen the bastard.

''Did you love her?''

''No.'' The flat lie didn't sit well on his conscience, but he ignored the twinge. ''We had an affair that never should have happened, and it ended badly. End of story.''

''You didn't love her, you were just using her for sex—but she broke your heart and you're still not over her.'' Shay squeezed his hand gently. ''Sounds to me like you're a long way from the end of this story.''

He forced a careless grin. ''Why are we even discussing it? It's got nothing to do with anything. It was a long time ago. It's over. Nothing's ever going to change. It was a mistake, and could never be anything but a mistake.''

''Hey, you don't have to convince me, darlin'. I'll believe you.'' She paused. ''I'm just not sure you believe yourself.''

''Change the subject or go take care of your customers.''

She glanced around the dining room, then turned back to him, apparently satisfied that her waitresses had everything well in hand. ''I'll change the subject. So...who was the woman at your house Monday night?''

''You know what you remind me of when you're like this, Shay? Pinky, Inez Taylor's little mutated rat dog. When Pinky grabs hold of something, she won't let go to save her life.''

''Yeah, and I heard the last thing she grabbed hold of was your ankle.''

''Tore holes in a pair of perfectly good uniform pants and

left teeth marks in my boot. Given a choice, I would've shot her right then and there, but Inez would have had my hide.''

''Given a choice, *I* would have shot Inez,'' Shay said sourly. There was no love lost between the Raffertys and the Taylors—between anyone in town and the Taylors. They were unpleasant people whose goal in life was to torment everyone around them, and they did it quite well, which meant Reese dealt with them more than he would have liked.

''So call me Pinky, and tell me about this mystery woman.''

One of the waitresses set his breakfast in front of him and flashed a smile before rushing off to deliver the other four plates she carried. He sprinkled everything with salt and pepper, cut the ham into bite-size pieces, then broke open the biscuit and ladled cream gravy over it before finally facing her. ''All right. I'm going to tell you this in confidence, and you have to swear to me you won't repeat it to anyone else.''

''Cross my heart and hope to die.'' She made the accompanying gesture, then waited expectantly.

''You remember my cousin Jace?''

''Six foot two of ooh-la-la?'' She pretended to fan herself. ''Oh, yes, I remember Jace.''

''You know he's a cop in Kansas City. He's got this case where this guy's trying to kill the assistant D.A. who sent him to prison. Jace put her—''

''The assistant D.A.'s a woman?''

He nodded. ''He put her in a safe house and the bad guys shot it up, so he brought her here.''

''To your house? Why didn't he lock her up in jail?''

''They found the safe house. Generally, only cops have that information. If he's got a dirty cop, she wouldn't be safe in jail. But here… She has no ties to Heartbreak. No one would think to look for her here. No one knows she's here except Jace and me—and now you.''

Shay's expression turned regretful. ''And Easy. And Olivia, Guthrie, Ethan and Grace.''

Once she'd finished blurting out names, Reese took a few minutes to eat and consider the news. Olivia and Guthrie Harris were the Raffertys' nearest neighbors, and Guthrie and Ethan James were half brothers. The six of them were best of friends and had few, if any, secrets. They were also decent, honorable people who knew when to keep quiet and what was better left unsaid.

"I'll tell them I forced the truth out of you this morning—that she was just an old girlfriend from college. You spent a few days together, which helped you remember why you dumped her all those years ago. No big deal."

"Works for me." After all, it wasn't so far from the truth. Unfortunately, in addition to remembering why their affair ended, he also kept remembering why it had started. Frequent reminders that the beginning wasn't important—that was what he needed, along with vivid reminders why the end *was* important. Those were easy enough. All he had to do was close his eyes, and he could easily summon an image of Neely in the courtroom, arguing Leon Miller's case, smugly, righteously insisting that the charges against him be dropped. That image was always followed by another—Judy Miller, sprawled grotesquely on the courthouse steps, blood turning her white blouse red, her eyes open, unseeing, yet somehow accusing.

His appetite gone, Reese pushed his plate away, then pulled his wallet from his pocket. Shay made a shooing gesture. "Your money's no good here, Sheriff."

"Hey, I'm not one of the deputies. I actually get paid a living wage."

"My apology for talking too much. Of course, if you'd get a steady girlfriend, we wouldn't all be so tempted to gossip about a woman at your place."

He slid out of the booth and picked up his Stetson. "If I ever get a steady girlfriend, *then* you'll have reason to gossip." With a sly wink and a lazy grin, he clamped his hat on his head and left the café. By the time he reached the Blazer, his grin had faded into a hard, flat line. He wanted neither a steady girlfriend nor a woman at his place. He'd been the subject of enough gossip in his lifetime, and the last thing he needed was more.

No, the very last thing he needed was Neely on his mind. In his house. And sure as hell not in his life.

In all her life Neely couldn't remember a time when she'd had the freedom to lounge around and do nothing but watch television all day. Throughout her father's arrest and trial, she'd run the house and taken care of the younger three girls while her mother went through what was politely described as a nervous spell. All through junior high she'd continued to shoulder responsibility for the family while Doris Irene worked, and in high school she'd spent every spare minute studying or working at one of three part-time jobs. She'd been obsessed with getting through college and law school, with gaining the education and the expertise to help people like her father, and since her mother couldn't help her, she'd helped herself. She'd won scholarships, baby-sat, clerked in a store, flipped burgers, cleaned houses—had done everything, it seemed, but get enough sleep and food.

Now she had an entire day to do nothing. She didn't have to get dressed or shower or brush her teeth if she didn't want to. She could eat soup straight out of the can or cook a full meal, could sleep all day, veg out with the TV, read or snoop through the house from top to bottom.

Of course she did shower, dress and brush her teeth—but the clothes she put on were the same shorts and T-shirt she'd slept in, and the toothbrush she used came from Reese's medicine cabinet. That was because hers was gone—her toothbrush, toothpaste, clothing, shoes, purse, everything. He'd taken every damn thing except the clothes she was wearing and her reading glasses—left behind, no doubt, so she could read his smug little note.

She'd searched the house and found the locked closet in his bedroom and the locked truck in the garage and assumed her stuff was one place or the other. He was smart to lock it away, because if she could have found one clean outfit, one pair of shoes and the money and credit cards stashed in her purse, she would have been long gone, and he never would have seen her again.

Which would make him very happy.

And her, too. That was what she wanted. Really, it was.

She sat at the kitchen table, a can of pop in front of her, watching the second hand on the wall clock sweep around. His note had said he would be back "this evening." In her book, evening started at six. Did that mean she had only one more hour to go nuts with boredom before he came home and gave her a target for her frustration? Or did evening to him mean eight, nine, ten o'clock?

She smiled thinly. If it did, she would kill him.

She heard the sound of the garage door opening first, then saw the lights flicker on the alarm keypad next to the back door. If she had a pair of shoes, she could dash out one door while he was coming in another. She would head north because there were no windows on that end of the house and by the time he realized she was gone, she would be... Where? In his pasture? Racing down the driveway into his town? Pleading with one of his neighbors to help her escape? Oh, yeah, like *that* would work.

He was whistling tunelessly when he came into the kitchen. When she turned her iciest glare on him, he stopped short, ended the song and simply looked at her.

He looked better in the green and khaki uniform than any man had a right to. In spite of a day's wear, the creases were sharp, the fabric hardly wrinkled. The shirt fitted snugly across his broad shoulders and tapered just as snugly to his narrow waist, and the pants—

She was better off not noticing how snugly *they* fitted.

After laying his hat upside down on the table, he unhooked the radio attached to his belt and set it aside, also. *Keep going,* she silently urged. *Take off the gun belt and give me just one lousy chance at the pistol...*

He started to pull apart the Velcro fastener that secured the heavy black belt, then gave her a narrow look and thought

better of it. Instead he went to the sink to wash his hands.
"Jeez, Neely, you didn't even bother to get dressed?"

Her fingers curled around the pop can as she tested its
weight. It was half full—enough to make a mess, enough to
let him know he'd been hit—and while he reacted to that, she
would have time to grab a knife, a frying pan, a chair. But
she didn't throw the can, though she did crumple it a bit.
"Where are my shoes? My purse? My suitcase? My *clothes?*"

"Oh. Guess I should have left something out for you."

"Get my stuff."

"I will in a—"

The can crumpled a little more as she slowly stood. "Get
my stuff now."

He looked from her to the can, then picked up the radio and
the cowboy hat and disappeared down the hall. A moment later
he returned with her suitcase in one hand, her purse in the
other. She thought of all the rude things she would like to say,
but settled instead for snatching her property from him and
stalking into the guest room.

The first thing she did was change into a lavender jumper.
It was sleeveless, as soft as a well-worn T-shirt and reached
to her ankles with a slit to one knee. Immediately she felt
better.

Her next step was to locate a pair of sandals...or loaf-
ers...or tennis shoes. She had dresses, shorts, jeans, shirts and
lingerie, but no shoes. Even her fuzzy little house slippers
were gone.

"Bastard," she muttered as she reached inside her purse for
her wallet. If he was going to insist on locking up her pos-
sessions every time he left—and she would bet he was—she
would be prepared next time. Her toothbrush would be in the
guest bath and her cash and credit cards would be easily ac-
cessible under the—

Dumping the contents of her bag onto the bed, she sorted
through everything, though it was obvious her wallet wasn't
there. It was easily the largest item she carried in her purse,

to say nothing of the fact that it was cherry-red. "Damn him! Damn, damn—"

"Looking for something?"

She dropped her empty bag on the bed, then slowly turned to face Reese, standing in the doorway, hands in his pockets. How did he manage to look so damn honest and open when he'd *stolen* from her? "I want it back."

He pretended neither innocence nor ignorance. He simply shook his head.

"You can't do this! You can't just take my stuff!"

"Oh, come on, Neely. It's not as if I'm going to go out and run up your credit cards, spend your cash or sell your ID. I'm just...holding it. You'll get it all back."

There were things in the wallet besides the credit cards, cash and ID, she wanted to point out—sentimental things such as photographs of her family, a note or two, a single dried flower. The photos were replaceable—her sisters each had copies— but the notes and the flower weren't. If he recognized them— and how could he not?—Reese would be more likely to destroy them than preserve them.

If he gave them back to her at that very moment, she would happily consider destroying them herself.

Her cheeks were flushed with anger and more—the prospect of humiliation?—as she fought the urge to childishly stamp her foot. "I want my wallet back."

He leaned against the door frame and folded his arms over his chest. "What's in it that you don't want me to see?"

The temperature of her blush climbed a few degrees higher. "N-nothing. It's...it's the principle. It's mine, and you have no right to take it."

"If I hadn't taken it, and your clothes and your shoes, you wouldn't have been waiting to greet me so warmly when I got home, would you?"

She saw no reason to admit that she'd spent at least half of her long, boring day fantasizing about escaping—how she would do it, where she would go, what name she would give herself. Would she be a redhead or a mysterious brunette? A demure Southerner or a no-nonsense Yankee? Would she hide in plain sight or choose someplace impossibly remote?

And the big question: could she possibly survive?

She didn't know, but she'd rather take her chances out there alone than here with Reese.

"I foolishly agreed to stay here a few days," she said stiffly, hearing her voice quaver and hating it. "I *didn't* agree to become your prisoner, and I *didn't* agree to give up my right to privacy. There's not much left in my life that's all mine, and I'll be damned if I'll give up even one small part of it to you just because you get an ego boost from playing the big, arrogant, controlling cop."

After a long silent moment, he left the room. Undecided whether to follow, Neely remained where she was, rubbing one bare foot uneasily over the other. When he returned before she could make up her mind, he was tight-lipped and scowling. With his dark, unforgiving gaze fixed on her, he offered her her wallet, then left the instant she took it.

Clasping it tightly, she closed the door, then slid to the floor. She knew without looking that the important things—the things that could help her get away—were gone, and she didn't care. She would have thought him an incompetent cop if he'd given them back, and while Reese Barnett was many things, incompetent was *not* among them.

But the rest of it… She slid her fingers behind the wedding photo of Hallie with husband number two and pulled out two smaller items. One was a snapshot of Reese, twenty-two years old, handsome, just drafted by the Royals with a quite impressive contract. The other was a card insert, and both had been delivered years ago with a dozen coral roses. On the back of the picture he'd written, "The second best day of my life."

On the card he'd added, "May 17. *The* best day of my life."

The day they'd met. The day he now cursed.

Laying the notes aside she unzipped the outside wallet pocket, which was too small for coins and too inconvenient for anything else, and carefully removed one of those dozen roses. It was pressed almost flat, its color and fragrance long since faded. Her first impulse was to crumple it to dust. After all, it was dead, just like the love it was supposed to represent.

But even though her fingers curved around the bud, she didn't crush it. She couldn't. As she'd told Reese, there wasn't much left in her life. He was gone, her father was dead, her family scattered all over. Her career was done for, and no matter what happened, her quiet existence in Kansas City was finished. But she still had the rose—physical evidence that, at one time, she had made a difference in someone's life. He had loved her—maybe not well, clearly not for long, but for a while. For a while, she'd mattered. She'd been happy.

And it had been the best time of her life.

Chapter 5

"I want to go somewhere."

The petulant voice made Reese blink a couple of times before he turned from the computer. It was nine-fifteen on Thursday night, and Neely hadn't spoken one word to him since calling him a big, arrogant, controlling cop Tuesday evening. She hadn't come out of her room again that night, and she'd come out only for dinner the next night.

But both Wednesday and Thursday mornings he'd found her asleep in his leather chair.

"You can't go—"

She rolled her eyes, reminding him of Guthrie and Olivia's twin girls when they needed a nap. "It's nighttime. It's dark. Your truck has tinted windows. It's in the garage so no one would see us get in or out. Just for a drive in the country. I need to smell fresh air. I need to see something besides this house." Abruptly her gaze narrowed. "If you don't take me someplace, I'm going to walk out the door. You'll have to choose between calling the dispatcher first, which means I'll have a head start, or going after me first, which means the dispatcher will think you're an idiot—again.''

"I have a third choice,'' he said mildly. He reached in the desk drawer, then let a pair of handcuffs dangle from his fingers. "I could make sure you can't go anywhere.''

She gave the steel cuffs a flippant look. "Been there, done that.''

Then heat flooded her face and spread through his body, making his skin clammy and his hand unsteady, making his voice rough and husky as hell when he softly added, "And enjoyed it a lot.''

Looking away, she shifted uncomfortably. She cleared her throat a couple of times, but couldn't seem to find the words she wanted. What could she say? They *had* been there, done that, and they had most definitely enjoyed it. Of course, they'd been ten years younger and a hundred years more innocent. They'd been adventurous, foolish, deeply in love and incredibly in lust.

He'd never felt that way before or since. Had never wanted a woman the way he'd wanted her. Had never been so weak or felt so powerful. Had never felt so…complete.

The handcuffs swayed, glinting in the light. The steel should have felt cold, but if he closed his fingers around it, it would sizzle. And if he fastened the cuffs around her wrists, *he* would sizzle, and before he let her go, so would she.

He returned them to the drawer, then took an unsteady breath. Turning back to the computer, he signed off the Internet, then stood and gestured toward the hall. "Let's go.''

For a moment she was too surprised to react; then she popped to her feet. "I need shoes.''

Though he tried to simply glance at her feet, it wasn't that easy. His look started at her shoulders and slid slowly downward, but it wasn't entirely his fault. Her outfit left little to the imagination. The sleeveless top hugged the gentle swell of her breasts and her flat middle before ending a scant inch above her waist. With its ribbons and lace and soft white fabric, it was innocent and virginal for a woman he knew all too well—all too gratefully—was neither.

Below a thin strip of pale skin, her skirt, the color of a well-washed chambray shirt, fell in a full sweep, hiding lush hips, lean thighs, shapely calves, before finally reaching her feet. Delicate, narrow, perfectly arched, with nails painted pale, pearly pink. He'd rubbed those feet after a long day, had warmed them through a Kansas winter, had tickled them a time or two and made her squirm.

Remembering where she'd been sitting when she'd squirmed, he grew warm and stiff—play on words intended—again.

"If we're just going for a drive, you don't need shoes," he said dismissively, roughly.

She didn't protest, though the go-to-hell look she gave him suggested she wanted to. Instead she turned in a swirl of chambray blue and stalked toward the garage door. After a stop in the bedroom, he joined her.

"You expecting trouble?" she asked, giving the pistol he'd clipped onto his belt and the shotgun he carried a suspicious look.

"You haven't given me anything but trouble. I'm just trying to be prepared." As soon as they were both belted inside the truck, he backed out of the garage, closed the door and reactivated the alarm, then made certain the truck doors were locked. "If Jace knew I was doing this, he'd snatch you out of here in a heartbeat."

"I won't tell if you don't." Then she glanced at him in the dim glow from the dash lights. "Oh, I forgot. Getting rid of me is your number one priority."

Reese ignored the discomfort her flat statement sent down his spine. "Oh, yeah, like you haven't spent your time trying to figure out how in hell to get away from me."

She didn't deny it but smiled coolly instead. "Maybe I'll go to Seattle or Vancouver. Or maybe Alaska. I read about this family who lives on an island off the coast of Alaska, and they get mail and supplies only two or three times a year. The rest of the time they're totally isolated. They raise their live-stock and tend their crops and fish, and the rest of the world leaves them alone. I'd like that.''

"No, you wouldn't. No restaurants? No movie theaters or shopping malls? No poor unfortunates to help?"

"No one to hurt," she murmured before turning to stare out the side window.

He looked at her a moment, disconcerted by her answer, then shifted the focus of the conversation. "Running away to Seattle, Vancouver or especially Alaska is a dumb idea. What are you going to do? You can't practice law without a license, and as soon as you get a license, you go in a dozen databases, complete with new address. Forbes wouldn't even have to leave Kansas City to track you down."

"I'm not going to practice law."

"Yeah, right." Neely giving up the law was about as likely as him giving up law enforcement. It just wasn't going to happen. "Jace will make this case, Forbes will go to prison, and you'll go back to the pursuit of liberty and justice for all. No, sorry, I forgot who I was talking to. You'll go back to the pursuit of liberty and fairness for the guilty."

The look she gave him would have made a lesser man quake. "Can you honestly tell me you've never made a mistake? You've never arrested someone based on an eyewitness identification that you knew was shaky? You've never had to choose which suspect to believe and had this niggling doubt that you chose the wrong one? You've never turned over a case to the D.A. that was based on nothing more than weak circumstantial evidence?"

"I've never made the kind of mistakes you did."

"Never," she repeated doubtfully. "Every arrest was a good one? Every conviction arising from your arrests was a just one?"

"Yes," he said stiffly. To the best of his knowledge.

"That's what the district attorney who prosecuted my father said. And you know what he said when he heard my father had been exonerated? 'Well, gee…you win some, you lose some.'" Her voice trembled, and the tension radiating from her made the air inside the truck damn near vibrate. "My father was lying in the prison morgue after spending seven years behind bars for a crime he didn't commit, and that *bastard*—" Breaking off, she pressed her hand to her mouth, then took a long ragged breath. "I envy you, Reese. I'm not infallible. I've made mistakes…but not anymore. I'm not playing with people's lives anymore. Right now I can't even be responsible for myself. I'm not competent to be responsible for anyone else."

Reese drove silently for a while, through dark side streets, past brightly lit houses where normal people were living out their normal lives, and he thought about her father's circumstances. He'd never bought into the argument that it was better for a hundred guilty men to go free than for one innocent man to be wrongly punished. One innocent man's freedom to rid society of a hundred violent criminals, even temporarily, was a fair trade in his book.

Unless you were that innocent man, or the family who loved him dearly. He couldn't begin to imagine the fear the little girl Neely had been must have felt at seeing her father taken away, the anger when people said things about him that weren't true, the emptiness his absence had left in their lives. When Reese was a kid, his father had *been* his life. It would have destroyed him to lose him that way or any other way. He'd worshiped his dad and would have hated anyone who'd taken him away.

They were in the country now, on the west side of Heartbreak, traveling along a dirt road that went everywhere in general and nowhere in particular. If a person had the time and knew the turns, he could eventually reach the highway that would take him to Stillwater, Oklahoma City, or Tulsa, and see a fair part of Canyon County while he was at it. He could go to Buffalo Lake or Buffalo Plains, could wind up at Grandpa Barnett's hunting cabin back in the middle of nowhere or find himself back in the heart of Heartbreak.

Neely shut off the air conditioner, then rolled the window

down and leaned against the door so the breeze ruffled her hair. After a moment, he rolled his own window down. The night was a bit warm, but everything smelled fresh and clean. The recent rains kept the road dust to a minimum, and the endless chorus of tree frogs filled the silence.

After a mile or two, Reese broke the quiet himself. "What was your father convicted of?"

She planted her feet on the dash board and tucked her skirt in snugly before glancing at him. "Murder. But he never could have hurt anyone. He was the sweetest, gentlest man I've ever known."

"So how did he wind up in jail?"

"He was a bookkeeper for a small tool and die company in Wichita. He'd asked for a raise, but one of his bosses said no. They exchanged words, and he went home. A short time later he got a call from the other partner, saying that the first one wanted to speak to him in his office. Daddy went back, the man said he knew nothing about any such call, and he fired my father for harassing him. The man's body was discovered by his secretary the next morning. She told the police he'd argued with Daddy. The partner claimed Daddy had been fired before he left work the day before, and he denied ever calling him. Witnesses came out of the woodwork to say that my father and his boss had argued frequently—people my dad didn't even know—and my father's fingerprints were on the murder weapon."

"And the real killer was the partner."

She nodded. "Six months after my dad was convicted, the partner sold out, took the money and the dead man's wife and disappeared. Presumably he's still out there somewhere, living the good life."

Her voice was dark and angry. He'd heard that bitterness before, when they'd argued the merits of the law, of justice versus fairness, and had mistaken it for simple passion. But it was so much more.

"Hypothetically, let's say you know beyond a doubt that this man is guilty of the crime your father died for. But he's been arrested for a different crime—one that you know beyond a doubt he *didn't* commit. Justice would be letting him go to prison anyway. But under your definition, that's not fair. What do you do?''

''I'd do my best to help the D.A. convict him and bury him under the prison.''

''And fairness be damned.''

''To hell.'' Catching the smug look on his face, Neely went on before he could point out how inconsistent she was being. ''In the first place, I would never represent the guy. I'd kill him myself before I'd lift a finger to help him. Second, my father didn't get a fair trial, so why should he? And third, a highly personal hypothesis like that isn't fair. What a person would do in a situation with someone he has strong feelings about is obviously different from what he would do in the same situation with ten million other people. Take you and me. If asked how you feel about convicted felons who try to kill the D.A.s who send them to prison, I feel fairly confident you would be against it. But when you were told that a convicted felon was trying to kill *me* in retaliation for my prosecuting him, your response was, 'Good. I wish him luck.'''

She stretched her right arm out the window and closed her eyes as the warm, fragrant air brushed her skin in an unending caress. Wishing for the easy, soothing sensation to never end, she made her point and finished her little speech. ''Under the circumstances, no one would think it odd that you'd wish I was dead, but they would know it was a special case. They would never think you believed every assistant D.A. deserved to die for sending felons to prison. As I would never believe that justice gained by illegal means *is* justice.''

With an uncomfortable silence—a guilty silence, she thought—filling the truck, Reese slowed to make a turn, then proceeded at a snail's pace. Gravel crunched under the tires and off to the left she heard the quiet, rhythmic lap of water against shore. From somewhere on the right came the low hoot of an owl, along with the steady calls of bobwhites and whip-poorwills.

Neely smiled faintly. She wasn't a nature girl. She'd never gone hiking or camping, wouldn't make it fifty feet into the woods without getting lost, and didn't know how to get along without indoor plumbing. But the sounds in the otherwise still night made her understand how a woman could develop an appreciation for a sleeping bag, a starry sky, a dying campfire—and, of course, a special someone to make it worthwhile.

Reese brought the truck to a stop, then shut off the engine. The water was on three sides now, and the birdsongs were more distant, though she heard the flap of impressive wings overhead. They were sitting at the end of the line on a narrow peninsula stretching out into a lake. There was no beach, no boat ramp, just a few concrete picnic tables and benches scattered around in grass that, with a few cows, could pass as pasture.

Of course, so could Reese's yard.

After opening the door, she slid to the ground. The grass was prickly and the soles of her feet were tender, but she carefully made her way toward the nearest table. She was almost there when a sharp pain pierced her foot. Gasping, she shifted her weight to her other foot, where the pain was duplicated several times over. "Ow, ow, oww—"

Unexpectedly Reese swung her into his arms. She felt curiously light-headed—swept off her feet—and strangely uncomfortable. She wanted to go limp and enjoy the experience, and wanted to struggle down and run, not walk, all the way back to Kansas City. She settled for holding herself very still, for barely breathing or thinking and certainly not feeling, and when he set her down on the tabletop, she gave a great, silent sigh of relief. Not disappointment. Not regret. Neither pleasure nor hunger for more.

"Stick your foot up here."

The sane, rational, intelligent part of her insisted she refuse and remove her own stickers. The reckless, irrational, once-a-sucker-for-this-man part of her obediently presented first one foot, then the other, to him.

"Guess I should have given you a pair of shoes after all,"

he said gruffly as he plucked a half dozen stickers from the bottoms of her feet. "Between stickers and copperheads—"

"Copperheads," she repeated. "There are copperheads out here? In the grass?"

"And curled up places that still hold the heat of the day, like the dirt road, rocks, stone."

She jumped to her feet in a whirl of fabric and gave the tabletop a thorough look, then subjected both benches to the same. He watched her, waited until she gathered her skirt close and sat again, then dryly said, "I wouldn't have set you there without looking first."

"Oh, right. You expect me to believe you'd pass up a chance for me to die from natural causes and to save yourself from having to do me in?"

"Damn it, Neely, stop it!"

His sharp response startled her into silence. She'd just been teasing…sort of. She wasn't sure she *really* believed he wanted her dead. She just couldn't convince herself that he would feel even a moment's regret if it happened.

After a moment of silence, she made another effort at conversation. "What is this place?"

"Buffalo Lake." He answered grudgingly, like a recalcitrant child not yet ready to give up his pouting. After a moment, though, he sat at the opposite end of the table, feet braced on the bench. "It's where the kids go on Saturday nights to party, which means my deputies spend a fair amount of their time out here, too."

"Is this where you came when you were a kid?"

"Yeah. Sometimes."

"With your girlfriend?"

He merely shrugged.

"Can you swim here?"

"Sure—if you watch out for the water moccasins."

"Oklahoma's just full of dangerous creatures, isn't it?" And she was sitting four feet from one of the most dangerous. A bite from a water moccasin or copperhead could leave her dead, but Reese could make her wish she was dead. She knew that from painful experience.

She rubbed the ache in her right shoulder, feeling the thickened scar tissue through the fabric of her top. As gunshot wounds went, it had been fairly minor. She'd required surgery to remove the bullet and then some physical therapy, but she'd regained full use of her shoulder and arm. But at times the healed wound hurt worse than it had nine years ago. There was no reason for it, the doctor had said. It was all in her head.

Maybe he was right. Maybe it was merely a reminder to her to keep herself safe.

And sitting here in the moonlight with Reese, with the water lapping and a soft breeze blowing, she needed all the reminders she could get.

"Where do kids go in Wichita?"

His question pulled her from her thoughts and coaxed a faint smile. "I don't know. I never went anywhere."

"Why not?"

"No boyfriend. No time. No opportunity."

"You didn't have a single date in high school?"

Turning to face him, she sat crosslegged, her skirt tucked over and around her legs. "Five nights a week I went straight from school to a job at the neighborhood burger place. I got off at eleven, home by eleven-thirty, studied and did homework. On Saturdays and Sundays I worked twelve-hour shifts as an aide at a nursing home. I didn't have much time for dating." She hadn't had her first date, first kiss, first sex, until college, but she hadn't minded. She hadn't met the man who could compete with her drive to succeed.

Not until she'd moved to Thomasville and practically fallen at the feet of the handsomest, sexiest, most charming man she'd ever met.

"You, on the other hand, probably spent far more tim‑ ing than working, studying and doing homework she said lightly.

"Life was easier then." He wa‑

turned slightly away from her, and what little she could see
of his expression was as distant as he sounded. "All I had to
worry about was not getting anyone pregnant and keeping my
arm in good shape. I was going to graduate and get a college
scholarship regardless of my grades. By the end of my soph-
omore year at Oklahoma State, a pro career was pretty much
guaranteed as long as I stayed healthy. When I went to the
Royals, I thought I had it made. I was getting paid big bucks
to play a game I would have played for free. I had a great
condo, a great car, more women than I knew what to do with.
People asked for my autograph wherever I went. Kids were
starstruck around me. Baseball fans around the world knew
my name. And then it ended."

After she'd met him, Neely had gone to the library and
looked up all the old newspaper stories. He'd been considered
something of a phenomenon—so good, so controlled, so
young. Sportswriters had routinely compared him to the greats
in baseball history, had made predictions about how far he
could go. And then one day he'd thrown a pitch, just as he
had ten thousand times before, and something went wrong.
He'd suffered a torn rotator cuff—not a particularly serious
injury as a rule, but the kiss of death to his pitching career.
He'd had the corrective surgery, done the rehabilitation and
tried to come back, but Reese before the injury and Reese after
were as different as night and day. As different as a hot-shot
pro pitcher and a weekends-only, beer-belly-league softball
lobber.

"You'd lived a charmed life," she said. "Then you had to
come live in the real world with the rest of us."

He gave her a long, heavy look. "I liked the charmed life

charmed he found the adulation from sports fans and
          re satisfying than the complete love and
                    lawyer? Had being a sports hero
              her hero? Did he prefer the
                        have been a part of it?

So he wished he'd never met her. That was no surprise. Plenty of other people had made the same wish.

But none of them had claimed to love her.

Deliberately she turned away from him, looking back the way they'd come. The moon showed open grassy areas and glinted in fractured ripples on the water's surface, but even its silvery light couldn't penetrate the woods. The only light capable of that was headlights, she thought as she watched twin lights move far too quickly for a handheld lantern. She watched them move for a moment before suddenly realizing what that meant. "Someone's coming."

Reese looked over his shoulder as the vehicle broke free of the woods and started the long, straight shot toward them. Sliding to his feet, he swung her into his arms, carried her to the passenger side of the truck and set her down, then unsnapped the strap that secured his pistol in the holster. "Stay here."

The truck was parked at an angle and offered her some cover. She watched the second vehicle, a battered pickup, pull into the grass some fifty feet away and a dozen or more kids pile out. "Hey," one of them called in their direction as he lowered the tailgate. "We're gonna have a party. Ya want to join us?"

"Is that you, Robbie Langley?" Reese asked from the other side of the truck.

"Yeah. Who are— Oh. Reese."

"That's Sheriff Barnett to you. Does your daddy know you're out here?"

There was a moment's silence, then, "No."

"Does he know you're hauling all those kids around in his truck?"

Another silence, then another grudging response. "No."

"Does he have any idea that you've raided his liquor supply?"

"Aw, hell, Reese—Sheriff. How'd you know...?"

Because he'd probably done the same thing when he was young, Neely thought, suppressing a smile. He'd come out here with his friends and girlfriends—had probably gotten drunk more than a few times, had probably gotten lucky every time.

A young girl came to stand beside the boy. Her blond hair gleamed like platinum in the moonlight. So did her skimpy little white top and shorts that exposed a tremendous amount of skin. "What are *you* doing out here, Reese? And who's that with you?"

"I'll ask the questions here, Tiffany," Reese replied.

"Why is she hiding back there? Is she married? Is she naked? Are you trying to recapture your lost youth by coming out here and pretending you're kids again?"

He ignored her sarcastic questions. "Robbie, how many ice chests you have there?"

"Two."

"Bring 'em over here."

"Aw, Reese…"

"Come on. Some of you kids help."

Neely sank down onto the running board as, with much grumbling, Robbie and three other boys carried the two ice chests over and loaded them into the back of Reese's truck.

"That's my dad's ice chest," one of them said sullenly. "He's gonna want to know what happened to it."

"He can have it back. All he has to do is come by the office. Your dad, too, Robbie." As the boys headed back to their group, Reese called, "You guys be careful—and enjoy your party."

"Oh, yeah, like *that's* gonna happen," someone muttered.

As Neely cautiously stood up again, Reese reached through the truck's open window, flipped a switch, then opened the door. The interior light didn't come on. "Come on, Neely. Let's get out of here."

She climbed inside and fastened her seat belt, then softly sang, "'Every party needs a pooper. That's why we invited you.'"

As thanks for her serenade, he scowled at her. "Duck until we're past them."

Obediently Neely bent forward, her arms on her knees, her chin on her arms. Through the open window, she heard a whistle or two, along with a few disgruntled words. Once he gave the all-clear, she sat up again and combed her fingers through her hair. "Let me guess…Robbie is the Reese Barnett of this class, and Tiffany is his cheerleader, homecoming queen, senior-class-vice-president girlfriend. She comes from money and considers a public servant exactly that—a person there to serve her. Her primary goal in life is to marry someone rich and powerful so she can be pampered and powerful and can turn out spoiled children just like her."

"Sounds about right."

"What happened to your Tiffany?"

"Her name was Jana. She went to the University of Oklahoma and dated the star quarterback of their national championship football team. He got drafted, she got pregnant, they got married. She followed him from team to team, popped out two more kids, plus he had a couple more with various girlfriends. He developed a drug habit, eventually got kicked off the team and divorced her to marry a girl half his age. Jana got half of everything he owned, which by that time was basically nothing and, last I heard, was selling real estate somewhere down in Texas."

"I'm sorry."

She sounded as if she meant it, Reese thought. She was sincerely sorry that the life of someone she didn't even know—someone who wouldn't have given her the time of day back in high school—hadn't turned out the way it was supposed to. He didn't bother telling her to not waste her time. Jana felt sorry enough for herself, and she hadn't even learned anything from the experience. She was actively searching for another man with a lot of money and power and a weakness for her. But this time she intended to get her share of the fortune from the beginning. He wouldn't have the chance to leave her with nothing.

"She got pretty much what she deserved," he said with a shrug.

"That's a bit cold. But then, I forgot who I was talking to. Mr. Never-Made-A-Mistake-In-His-Entire-Life Barnett. Never arrested an innocent man, never condemned an innocent woman. Never judged anyone unfairly or loved anyone unwisely or— Oops. Looks like you did make one mistake."

His fingers tightened fractionally around the steering wheel. "Knock it off, Neely. I'm not in the mood."

"Did you tell people that about me, too? That I got what I deserved? That I'd deserved your walking out on me because I was a criminal defense lawyer who'd defended—surprise, surprise—a criminal? That I'd deserved to get shot by your deputy friend because I'd gotten his grossly mishandled case thrown out?"

Reese brought the truck to a halt in the middle of the dirt road, sending up a spray of gravel and dust. "You didn't 'get shot' by one of the deputies," he argued hotly. "Your client murdered a woman in cold blood in front of a half dozen cops, and you had the misfortune to get caught in the cross fire."

She stared at him a long time before smiling thinly. "Misfortune. Right."

Frustration made his neck itch and his face hot. Impatiently he switched the air conditioner on high, then rolled up both windows. "You're implying it was something other than bad luck. What's your story?"

"I don't have a story."

"Come on, Neely—"

"From the beginning you've chosen to believe what's comfortable for you—what makes you feel innocent and blameless. Fine. It's gotten you through nine years. Maybe it'll get you through the next ninety."

"Are you saying one of the officers deliberately shot you?"

"I'm not saying anything. I was merely asking a question. Did you tell people that, like Jana, I got what I deserved?"

He ignored her. "Because I don't believe it. Not for a minute." The Keegan County Sheriff's Department might not have been the best law enforcement agency around, but the deputies had been good cops. A little gung-ho sometimes, but in police work, dedication was a good thing. And they *had* been dedicated. They'd done a difficult job with long hours, lots of headaches, its own share of danger and too damn little pay. Maybe they had screwed up Leon Miller's arrest, but it was because they'd been overzealous and frustrated by the system's inability to deal with him properly. But for one of them to deliberately shoot Neely... He couldn't believe it.

He wouldn't.

She planted both feet on the dashboard and tapped them in rhythm to music only she could hear. She didn't look at him. Didn't argue with him. Didn't seem to even notice that he'd implied she was lying. He thought about demanding an explanation from her, about shaking, intimidating or scaring the words from her, but he was better off not touching her.

Finally he eased the accelerator down. They returned to town, and to his house, in silence. Once they were safely inside the house with the alarm activated, he went to his bedroom, closed the door and went straight to the phone.

Jace sounded otherwise occupied, but Reese didn't offer to call back later. He didn't bother with useless chatter or to even ask when his cousin intended to move Neely elsewhere. He just got straight to the point. "Back in Thomasville, the day Leon Miller killed his wife, Neely got shot, too. What do you know about that?"

"Not as much as the two of you do. You were there. I wasn't."

"Did they ever figure out who shot her?"

"There wasn't any question about that," Jace replied scornfully. "It was that Dave guy, and his only regret was that he'd aimed too high."

Reese sank onto the bed and raised his free hand to rub his temples. Dave Dugan had been one of the deputies involved in obtaining Miller's tainted confession. He'd also been the most outspoken against Neely, particularly after she'd refused to go out with him when she'd first moved to town. He'd taught Reese a lot about police work—both what to do and, he admitted grudgingly, what not to do—and he'd been…not a close friend, but a friend. Or so Reese had thought.

"Didn't you know that?" Jace asked. "You were there."

"Hell, when a bunch of people start shooting guns from all directions, I tend to keep my head down," Reese replied sarcastically. That wasn't true, though. He'd been talking to Judy when Leon shot her. The force of the blast had knocked her against him, and he'd lowered her to the ground, then held her until the ambulance came. He hadn't realized Neely had been shot until the gunfire ended and Leon lay dead.

"Didn't you hear anything about it afterward?"

"I only stuck around a few days, and I didn't see or talk to anyone. I didn't hear… Why wasn't he charged?"

He didn't need Jace's laughter to know that was a ridiculous question. "It was just Neely, the bleeding-heart lawyer who beat them damn near every time she faced them in court, who helped guilty men to go free, whose own boyfriend walked away from her and left her bleeding on the ground. No one cared—not the sheriff, not the D.A., not you."

"I didn't know—"

"Come on, Reese. You knew she'd been shot. If you thought about it at all, you knew she wasn't standing in the right place to get caught in the cross fire. You knew they had it in for her in the department because she was showing them up for the incompetent, corrupt bastards they were."

But he hadn't thought about it at all, Reese acknowledged, because then he would have had to face what a bastard *he* was for walking away from her. After the ambulance had arrived, he'd stood there with Judy's blood on his uniform and watched the paramedics work, knowing it was futile, before he'd finally looked at Neely. The pharmacist from the drugstore across the street had been kneeling beside her, putting pressure on her wound, but she'd been watching Reese. She'd been in pain, frightened, heartsick, in shock. She'd needed him more at that moment than anyone had ever been needed, and he'd looked at her, then at Judy, and he'd walked away. He hadn't known how badly Neely was hurt—hadn't even known for sure she would survive—but he'd walked away from her.

Every man involved in the incident was a bastard, and he was the worst of all. His behavior had been unforgivable.

"Reese? You there?"

"Yeah."

"You okay?"

He sighed wearily. "I didn't know... I didn't *want* to know. It was easier to believe that I was right, that I was justified in everything I did because she was so wrong in everything she did. It was...more comfortable."

"You've gotta be able to live with what you've done, bubba. If not knowing is what works for you..."

"You've never said what you thought," Reese remarked curiously.

"I think a lot of things. You have to be specific."

"About Neely and Judy and me."

"I try not to stir up trouble."

"Meaning?"

"I think the way you left her was wrong. I think the way you treated her was wrong. I think she deserved a hell of a lot better than anyone gave her. And no matter what, bubba, the ends don't justify the means. Not in law enforcement. Your department blew their case against Leon Miller. If anyone besides him is responsible for Judy's death, it's the Keegan County Sheriff's Department. Not Neely."

"Gee, don't hold back."

"Don't ask the questions unless you're prepared to hear the answers." In the background a soft feminine voice murmured something, then Jace said, "Anything else you want to know had better take sixty seconds or less 'cause that's all the time I can spare."

There were plenty of things he wanted to know, but Jace wasn't the person he should be asking. "Have fun," he said sourly.

"I do. You should try it sometime...if you remember how. See ya, bubba."

Reese hung up, then lay back on the bed and stared at the ceiling. He remembered how to have fun. He just didn't remember how to have the sort of fun that didn't require some sort of emotional commitment. He'd been really good at it in college and in the years he'd played baseball. It had been so easy then. But Neely had been right. That wasn't the real world. And though he'd said he preferred that life, he'd lied. He'd loved playing pro ball, had thrived on the celebrity, had gotten damn near giddy over the money and lived for the adulation, the attention and awe. But it hadn't been real life. It hadn't been conducive to keeping a manageable ego, to maintaining steady relationships or keeping life in perspective. It hadn't been normal.

Truth was, he enjoyed being a small-time Oklahoma sheriff. He could honestly say he'd made a difference in his job—had contributed something to society. He'd saved some lives, had brought some new ones into the world and helped direct a few onto different, safer paths. There were people who would be worse off if he wasn't doing this job, while his quitting baseball hadn't made a bit of difference to anyone but him.

And what a difference it had made. It had sent him looking for a new job—had helped him wind up in Thomasville where he'd met Neely.

Slowly he sat up and stretched. It was nearly eleven o'clock, a half hour past his usual bedtime. It would be perfectly all right if he shut off the lights, stripped down and crawled back into bed. After all, six o'clock came mighty early in the morning. But he didn't switch off the overhead light, turn on the ceiling fan, undress or turn back the covers. Instead he left the room, listened for a moment, then headed into the dimly lit living room.

He hadn't taken the time before they'd left for their drive to shut down the computer, much less remove the power supply. Neely was sitting at his desk, crosslegged in the old oak chair, and her gaze was riveted on the card game on the computer screen. At least he knew she hadn't tried to sign on to the Net and possibly send out a general broadcast letting family and friends know she was all right, since he had only the one phone line and he'd been using it.

She glanced at him, then clicked on one card that sent all the other cards flying to the four suits at the top of the screen, then started a new game.

"I never could get the hang of that game," he remarked as he stood a safe distance behind her.

"The goal isn't to get the cards up here." She clicked at the top where she'd placed two of the four aces. "It's to build your sets down here at the bottom. If you do that right, the rest happens automatically."

He watched, but she moved cards too quickly for him to keep up and finished another game in little more than a minute. He turned the nearest chair so it faced her and sank down into its deep made-for-slumping seat. He watched her face as she completed another four or five games, her eyes glazed, her expression intent. Finally he spoke. "I never told anyone you got what you deserved."

She glanced at him briefly before returning her attention to the game.

"Jace knew the truth, of course. Dad knew part of it, and he passed that on to Aunt Rozena and Uncle James. None of my friends around here knew anything except Shay, and the story I told her was…misleading." In his opinion. A lie in Shay's.

"Afraid to let anyone know how fallible the great Reese Barnett could be?" The cynicism in her voice was sharp enough to cut. "Or were you ashamed of the truth?"

"I wasn't ashamed of you."

"Sure, you were, but that's a different story. I meant ashamed of yourself and the way you dumped me. Because if you weren't ashamed, you should have been." She finished the game and closed it, then gracefully unfolded to her feet. "Thank you for the drive. Good night."

Chapter 6

On Saturday morning Neely started a load of laundry as soon as she got up, then ate a bowl of cereal while gazing at a note that said Reese had gone to the grocery store. She wished *she* could go to the grocery store. She was so tired of being inside that she would even gladly mow the grass for him if he'd just give her the chance. But she'd asked yesterday, and he'd refused.

She washed the few dirty dishes on the counter and put them away, then swept up the faintest dusting of dirt from the floor. She wiped an already-clean counter, stove and table, then did a little unnecessary cleaning in the living room and both bathrooms. Because they were both relatively neat people, and because she wasn't a good enough housekeeper to care about dusting door frames or washing windows, she was finished in no time and was just about to pop with the need for something to do.

She was standing at the French doors that opened from the kitchen onto the deck when she heard the garage door open. The red light on the alarm keypad next to her blinked off and the green light came on. She looked from it to the hall connecting to the garage door, then back to the green light and made her decision. A twist of the lock, a turn of the knob, and she was out the door.

The heat was intense, wrapping itself around her, sucking the very energy from her pores. It was great sunbathing weather for someone like young Tiffany, who'd already toasted herself to a lovely bronze. A radio tuned to a great rock station, an icy can of diet pop, a skimpy bikini and maybe an occasional mist from a garden hose... For someone who'd never done it, it seemed an absolutely perfect way to spend a hot summer day.

Sliding a chaise longue into the sun, she stretched out, unbuttoned her skirt until it was almost indecent, undid a few buttons on her blouse, then tilted her face to the sky and closed her eyes. The sun warmed her air-conditioned skin, seeped into her bones, started the tanning process that so many doctors warned against and so many people coveted anyway. For the first time in her life, she understood why. She felt warm, lazy, relaxed, languid—and faintly, barely aroused.

She was listening to the rustle of the breeze in the trees and the nearby drone of a bee, and thinking how easy it would be to fall asleep there when she heard Reese call her name. So he'd brought the groceries in and begun looking for her. When she'd moved from Thomasville to Kansas City, she'd had dreams about him coming looking for her. She'd known that, as a cop, he could find her whenever he wanted, but she'd tried to make it easy for him. She'd had her home number listed in the phone book, had filed a change of address with the Thomasville post office, had made certain Jace knew how to reach her at any time.

But he'd never come. Never had a change of heart. Never forgiven her. Never missed her.

She'd missed him so much she'd thought she would die.

His next shout was louder and edged with frustration. Opening her eyes, she saw him standing in the kitchen, a few feet back from the window over the sink. She waved to catch his

attention, then wiggled her fingers with an innocent Hi-here-
I-am smile.

A moment later the French door slammed behind him.
"How the hell did you get out here?"

She shielded her eyes to look up at him. "Is your alarm
supposed to be set so that when you shut it off at one door,
it goes off at all of them?"

"I don't know. I guarantee, it won't be any longer." He
scowled fiercely. "It's hot as hell out here. What are you doing?"

"Sunbathing."

"You're wearing way too many clothes for that."

"That thought occurred to me. Would you mind if I took
some of them off?" She hadn't thought any such thing, but
she had to admit, in heat like this, the more skin she could
expose, the more comfortable she would be. Besides, it wasn't
as if her bra and panties were any more revealing than—or
even *as* revealing as—a lot of swimsuits.

He swallowed hard, started to speak, then swallowed again.
"You do that, I'll have to arrest you for indecent exposure."
His voice was rough and hoarse, as if he needed immediate
cooling.

Neely slowly stretched her arms over her head. "You never
minded me being indecent before, and if you stayed inside
away from the windows, no one would see anyway."

He blew his breath out in a heavy rush, then took a step
back into the shade provided by the roof overhang. "Come
on. Inside."

She considered refusing. Unbuttoning the last few buttons
on her skirt and letting it fall open. Undoing the buttons on
her top and slipping it off, too. Stretching out. Daring Reese
to make her obey.

But he didn't back down from dares, and if he touched
her...

Slowly she sat up, swung her feet to the floor, rose from
the chair. Her front was all toasty warm, her back hot and
damp. Pretending she didn't mind giving in again, she passed

him with a phony smile and went inside. She shivered the instant her bare feet made contact with the cold tile, felt goose bumps rise and her nipples harden as she walked underneath a ceiling vent.

He returned to putting away the groceries as she moved laundry to the dryer, then started another load in the washer. When she went back to the kitchen, he was standing in front of the refrigerator, the freezer door open and a half gallon of ice cream pressed to his forehead. "Get a little warm out there?" she asked, deliberately making her voice sultry and low.

He flinched, put up the ice cream and closed the door, then scowled at her. "You don't take it very seriously, do you—this threat against you?"

Sliding into a chair, she propped her feet on another seat, and her skirt immediately fell to either side, drawing his gaze. As if it were of no consequence, she buttoned it practically to her knees, then combed her fingers through her hair. "When I was nine years old, I saw my father dragged away in handcuffs by police officers who burst into our house in the middle of the night, and I watched my mother fall apart, leaving the care of my three younger sisters to me. When I was sixteen, I made the arrangements for his funeral while my mother fell apart again, and after he was buried, I listened while the authorities admitted that there'd been a terrible mistake, that my father had been as innocent as he'd claimed. Ten years later I got shot by a corrupt deputy, which was painful, and at the same time got dumped by the man who'd said he loved me dearly, which was worse. I have been harassed, threatened and intimidated. My car's been bombed and I've been shot at fifty times or so." She shrugged. "It's serious. I understand that. It's just not particularly unusual."

For a long moment he looked at her. There were too many emotions on his face to identify every one, but she recognized guilt. Frustration. Anger. Just the barest hint of sympathy. Then abruptly he turned, gathered empty grocery sacks and

wadded them into a tight ball. He'd just tossed them in the
wastebasket in the pantry when the doorbell rang.

Neely didn't wait for his command to disappear—just his
nod that it was clear to cross in front of the open doorway.
The bell rang a second time as she closed the bedroom door,
locked it, then leaned against it. She couldn't hear the conversation but could tell the visitor was a woman. Maybe his
friend's wife Shay, the only one outside the Barnett family
that he'd ever acknowledged Neely's existence to, or Ginger,
too young to be his kid sister...and most likely not the least
bit interested in filling that role, anyway. Or maybe it was
Isabella, with much more than horses on her mind, or any of
a countless number of women. God knows, he'd had no shortage of them.

After a moment she unlocked the door and eased it open a
crack. Now she could hear better. More importantly, she could
see. Reese was standing in the doorway that led to the living
room, leaning one shoulder against the jamb, and a blonde
with amazing looks was unpacking a box on the dining table,
storing some items in the freezer, taking others to the pantry.

"You know, your mom's a great cook, but she doesn't have
to keep me fed."

"I've tried to tell her that, but she figures it's her civic duty.
Besides—" she flashed a blinding smile "—if it wasn't common knowledge that Mom and Rozena stocked your larder,
every single woman in the county would be knocking at your
door. You wouldn't want that, would you? Especially now."
She took a look around. "Where is she? Do I get to meet
her?"

Neely blinked. He'd just accused her of not taking Forbes's
threat seriously, when he'd gone off and confided the secret
of her visit to some drop-dead gorgeous beauty queen? That
said a lot for how seriously *he* took the threat...or how completely he trusted this woman.

"I don't think that would be a good idea, Shay," Reese
was saying as Neely, acting totally on impulse, pulled the door
open wide and walked out of the bedroom and into the kitchen.

His mouth tightened into a thin, flat line and his eyes turned bitterly cold. She might live to regret this, she thought as he folded his arms over his chest, but regrets were nothing new. She'd had plenty, and she'd survived.

"Why not, Sheriff?" she asked coolly. "Are you afraid I won't be on my best behavior?"

The blonde looked from him to her, then offered her hand. "I'm Shay Rafferty. And you're…an assistant D.A.?"

"Used to be. Before that I was a bottom-feeding, scum-sucking criminal defense lawyer. The past few years I've just done the easy stuff—the sort people generally don't try to kill you for."

Neely accepted Shay's hand and was surprised to find a few calluses and short, unpolished nails. She would have figured the beauty queen to be allergic to hard work and addicted to fake nails. "I'm Neely Madison."

Her name clearly meant nothing to Shay. He may have told the woman about her, but apparently not her name. Guess she hadn't been that important.

"Under the circumstances, I wouldn't normally come here," Shay explained, "but my mother delivers a box of food to Reese every other Saturday, and nothing would have kept her away except my volunteering to bring it. Believe me, the last thing you want on a hot Saturday morning is Mary Stephens giving you the third degree." She gave Neely an up-and-down look with piercing brown eyes, then grinned. "Of course, being a former assistant D.A., you just might be able to hold your own against her. You must have been something in court. You look so sweet and innocent. I bet a lot of people underestimate you."

"Some make that mistake." Reese had a time or two, but he'd learned. Dave Dugan and his cohorts in the sheriff's department had never learned, and they'd finally succeeded in getting rid of her. But she'd gotten out alive, so they couldn't claim complete victory.

"This must be interesting—spending twenty-four hours a day with a total stranger," Shay remarked.

"There are worse things. Like spending twenty-four hours a day with someone I once knew intimately."

"Or being dead," Reese added snidely.

Shay looked from one to the other, obviously wondering at the source of the tension between them, then extended her hand again. "I wish you luck, Neely. You're in good hands with Reese. He'll take good care of you."

"I'm sure he will," Neely replied in a voice that suggested otherwise.

Reese walked to the door with Shay and exchanged a few quiet words while Neely watched from the kitchen. When he returned a moment later, she was leaning back against the counter, arms folded, one ankle crossed over the other. "The wife of a friend—is that what you told me?"

"I said Shay and her husband Easy are friends of mine. What about it?"

"Did she become his wife before your affair with her or after?"

A crimson tinge crept into his cheeks. "My relationship with Shay is none of your business."

"Does *he* know you had an affair with her?"

"They hadn't seen each other in eight years," he said defensively. "He had no claim on her."

Eight years, and they'd gotten back together, were married and were, she suspected, very happy. Neely and Reese had been apart nine years. Did that mean there was a chance for them, or was there some magic cutoff point there? Eight years and eight months, ten, even eleven, you were fine, no problem, everything could be fixed. But nine years, you were flat out of luck.

And which of them would ever be foolish enough to want to get back together? They'd had one sweet, wonderful year, followed by nine years of misery—well, misery for her. Affairs with beauty-queen blondes for Reese. Why would she want the source of such heartache in her life again? Why would he give up women like Shay for a woman he'd hated far more than he'd ever loved?

Feeling unsettled—heart-sore—she lost her taste for the conversation, swallowed up in a sudden, irrationally teary need to be alone. Before Reese could say anything else, she pushed away from the counter. "I'm going to take a nap."

"But what about—"

She closed the bedroom door, cutting off the rest of his words, stripped off her skirt so it wouldn't tangle around her legs, then curled up on the bed. She was a survivor, her father had often told her. She could endure anything, according to Jace. Two of the three most important men in her life couldn't be wrong. She had survived Reese once. She swore, she would do it again.

Please, God, for the last time.

Driven by the urge to get out of the house, Reese changed into a pair of ragged cutoffs and sneakers and headed to the barn out back. Until this house, he'd made it a practice to live in apartments where the yardwork fell to someone else. Now, with a three-acre yard, he owned a riding mower, which he'd bought last month, and a push mower his father had given him when he'd first moved in. That was the one he chose this hot summer morning. More than just the feeling that he was accomplishing something, he needed exercise, too.

Since Neely had been planning to sleep, he started in the front yard, mowing on the diagonal from one corner to the other. It was mindless work, and fairly rewarding, since he could monitor his progress with every row. As sweat dripped from his brow and trickled down his spine, he felt the tension that knotted his muscles easing, felt his jaw and neck relax for the first time in days. He hadn't even been aware of just how tense he'd been until much of it was gone. For the first time in a week, he was able to notice utterly mundane details, like how badly the grass had needed cutting. That the rains had dislodged much of the gravel in the driveway. How bare and unfinished the front of the house looked without something planted up close, and the short-term absence of the mounds and tunnels that meant there were gophers and moles about.

For the first time in nearly a week, for a time he felt like a perfectly normal man doing perfectly normal chores.

A cooling breeze out of the west brought clouds that turned the sky dark. They might bring rain or might not—might be accompanied by thunder and a little heat lightning, or might break up and disappear under the sun's blazing glare. June in Oklahoma was a good time for anything to happen.

Weather-wise, *any* month was a good time for anything. He'd seen snow in April, 80-degree temperatures in December, flooding and drought in the same place in the same month. He'd gone to a Christmas parade in shorts and T-shirt and shivered under a quilt at the Fourth of July fireworks a few years back. Hell, in one day he'd watched it change from high eighties and sunshine to low thirties and snow in less than six hours.

It was a good thing he liked change.

Then he thought of Neely and his grin faded. Some change, at least. There were a few things he'd wanted to stay the same forever.

He'd finished the front yard and the side across the driveway before he finally gave up and traded the antique for the shiny new lawn tractor. It made short work of the back yard and the other side, and required his attention so he couldn't spare more than a glance when he passed the guest room windows.

The weather still hadn't decided what to do by the time he returned the tractor to the barn. When the sun shone, it was brilliant and hot, the air seemed unusually clear, and everything was still. Then the wind picked up, blowing the clouds in again, sending huge shadows creeping across the land. The temperature dropped a degree or two, the humidity went up a percent or two, and the air turned heavy. He figured they would have a storm before the day was over, maybe even a tornado. With heat like this, who knew?

The house was still when he went inside, with only the air

conditioner breaking the silence. He went to the master bath, took a quick shower and shaved, then put on a pair of jeans as the phone rang.

"Hey, Reese, it's Brady. You busy?"

Brady Marshall was the undersheriff for Canyon County. He took over when Reese was off, and the two of them traded off weekends so the deputies couldn't complain. He was a good officer, had a mind that worked like a master criminal's, and kept pretty much to himself. As far as Reese knew, he had no family in the area and, although he had the respect of virtually everyone who knew him, no friends, either. He was a loner, and the best undersheriff Reese could ask for. "What's up, Brady?"

"We've got an injury accident out on the highway about halfway between Heartbreak and Buffalo Plains, involving one of our vehicles. I'm headed that way and thought you might want to come, too."

"Who is it?"

"Tommy Lee, and the injuries are minor. Apparently his girlfriend was driving the patrol unit and she lost control."

Reese swore hotly. "I'll meet you there. And don't let Tommy Lee leave the scene before I get there." He hung up and swore again as he finished dressing, this time a string of virtually every obscenity he knew.

But, some small desperate part of him thought, at least he had someplace to go and something to do besides hang out here with Neely.

On his way out, he detoured past her bedroom. Her door was ajar a few inches, and it swung wide when he laid his palm against it. She was lying on her side in bed, her back to him, her knees drawn up. Her skirt lay discarded at the foot of the bed, and though she still wore her top, under the best of circumstances, it barely reached her waist.

He knew he should retreat, out of respect for her privacy as well as for his own safety, but his brain couldn't give the command and his body, he was fairly sure, wouldn't obey.

Her skin was pale, creamy, and looked soft and warm. It

molded over delicate bones and incredible curves, disappearing under the scrap of peach satin masquerading as underwear before stretching over long muscles in her thighs and calves. She looked amazing. Designed to torment.

Exhaling heavily, Reese let his head fall forward until his forehead bumped the door frame. He needed a date. It had been too long, and he was only human. Maybe on the way back into town, he could stop by Callie's place to see if Isabella was interested in a *real* riding lesson. Maybe she could help him control these reactions to Neely.

He didn't wake her, though that had been his original plan. Even half asleep, she would see…would know… Instead he left the room as quietly as he'd come, went to the kitchen and followed what was becoming a routine—left her a note, slid under her glasses on the table.

He was slightly more than halfway to Buffalo Plains when he saw the flashing lights of several sheriff's vehicles, a highway patrol car, an ambulance and a tow truck ahead on the shoulder. He parked at the end of the line, then got out and swore again when he saw Tommy Lee's patrol car on its roof in some farmer's cornfield.

The clouds that had only threatened rain over at his place had delivered here. The air was unbearably muggy, steam rose from the pavement, and the normally empty ditch he had to cross was overflowing with runoff.

Tommy Lee Curtis sat in the shade of a scrub oak, holding a square of gauze pads to his temple. His uniform was torn and dirty, his grin was dim-witted, and the glazing of his eyes had nothing to do with the accident, Reese would bet, and everything with what he'd had for lunch. "He-ey! Reese." He tried to stand, but Brady pushed him down again. "I thought this was your weekend off."

"Give me your badge and commission, Tommy Lee."

It took the kid a moment to process the information and another several moments to get it off. "Well, sure, but…yours is a whole lot cooler."

Reese slid the badge into his pocket, then held out his hand once more. "And your weapon."

"Sheriff, I can't be working without a weapon," Tommy Lee said in all seriousness.

"You can't be carrying this weapon when you've been fired."

He grinned again. "True. But I'm not— You're *firing* me? For *what?* I didn't do nothin'! I wasn't even driving!"

"You didn't do nothin'?" Reese repeated. "Drunk on duty. Dereliction of duty. Misuse of a county vehicle. And that's just off the top of my head."

"I'm not drunk," Tommy Lee said with great astonishment. "And I *wasn't driving!* You can't fire me 'cause she's a bad driver!"

"Tommy Lee, every deputy in the state of Oklahoma serves at the pleasure of the sheriff. Your sheriff is damned displeased, and you're fired. No hearing, no appeal." Reese bent forward and removed the pistol from its holster, then shifted his attention to Brady again. "Tell the doctors over at the hospital that I want him tested for drugs and alcohol. And then I want him charged with everything you can come up with. Where's the girl?"

Brady gestured a few yards away where another deputy and the trooper waited with a sniffling redhead. "Selena Hampton. Is your mama ever gonna be mad at you." Trudie Hampton owned one of only two insurance agencies in Heartbreak. She'd been a housewife until her worthless ex-husband ran off and left her with five kids to feed. She hadn't even known how to type when she got her first job, and now she owned the whole shootin' match. She had no patience for imprudence and recklessness, especially from clients or family.

Selena burst into tears. "It wasn't my fault! It was raining, and the road was slick, and it—it just happened!"

"Near as we can tell," the trooper said, "she was doing about seventy coming into the curve. But that wasn't her fault, either."

"What were you doing driving one of my department

cars?'' Reese asked, rubbing the ache that was settling at the back of his neck.

"Tommy Lee came over for lunch,'' she replied, ''and time got away from us, and he was going to be late getting back, but he wasn't in any condition to drive, so I did.''

"Why didn't you just call in and tell the dispatcher he wasn't in any condition to drive?''

"I didn't think about it,'' she said with a pout. ''Besides, you probably would have fired him. You're always picking on him.''

Reese looked at the two officers who were shaking their heads. "And I was actually looking for a reason to get out of the house. Gee, what was I thinking?''

"Can I go home now?'' Selena asked, getting unsteadily to her feet. ''I don't feel so hot.''

"You're going to the hospital to get checked out,'' Reese said harshly. ''Then you're going to jail until your mother sees fit to get you out.'' If she were his daughter, that would probably be a week—or three. Of course, if she were his daughter, she never would have been foolish enough to get behind the wheel. Whatever faults he and Neely had, neither of them were stupid, and their children wouldn't be, either.

"You can't arrest me!'' she cried, slapping one hand against his chest. ''I was just trying to help Tommy Lee 'cause you're out to get him! You can't take me to jail!''

The trooper pulled her back and fastened his handcuffs around her wrists. "I'll charge her with unauthorized use of a county vehicle and reckless driving. That'll give her something to think about for a while.''

A fine she couldn't afford and possibly a year in jail, to say nothing of the fact that what the county couldn't collect from her insurance for the damage to the patrol car, they'd take from her... Reese grimly shook his head. That was enough for *anyone* to think about for a while.

Selena was wailing too hard to walk so one of his deputies had to help the trooper get her across the ditch to the shoulder of the road. Ten feet away, Tommy Lee was alternating claims of innocence with every obscenity Reese had run through that morning. Reese's head was already aching from the voices when one more joined in from the cornfield.

"Your boy done knocked down my fence and damaged my corn crop, Reese," Bill Taylor said in his thin, ninety-some-year-old voice. "And now they're plannin' to cut down more fence so's they can git that car outta here. Who's gonna put the barbed wire back like it was? Who's gonna clean up the mess left behind? Who's gonna reimburse me for my loss? Don't be shy, son. What do you have to say for yourself?"

Reese raised his gaze to the sky, turned dark and leaden. Of course it was going to rain again. How could it not, when he was standing out there without a slicker? When thirty-five thousand dollars of his department's assets was lying battered and pretty much totaled in a cornfield? When Bill Taylor was five feet behind him and feeling particularly cantankerous? When he did his best to avoid Bill, cantankerous or not?

He had only one thing to say for himself as the sky opened up with a ground-pounding torrent.

"I want to go home."

He didn't get his wish for another two hours. That was how long it took to wait out the rain, retrieve the patrol car and persuade Bill that it was safe to leave the fence down until Monday morning. It wasn't as if anyone would come in and steal the rest of his unripe crop, and, even up and intact, the fence wouldn't stop anyone determined to get into the field. Climbing over or through barbed-wire fences was a skill they all learned before they started school.

Finally, though, everyone was gone except him and Brady. They were both soaked and muddy. "Firing Tommy Lee will leave you shorthanded tomorrow," Reese remarked.

"We'll get by. If I need extra help, I'll call the sheriff," Brady replied with a rare grin.

"Guess we'd better get the word out that we're looking for a replacement. Don't suppose you've got a kid brother that's the spittin' image of you and is looking for work, do you?"

The distance that came into Brady's expression was familiar—and puzzling. "No, 'fraid not. I'd better get changed and get back into the office."

"Call me if you need anything." Reese climbed into his truck, watched Brady drive away, then made a U-turn and headed back toward Heartbreak. If he hadn't had a more pressing concern on his mind, he would have spent a few miles wondering about the undersheriff and the mysteries in his life. But that would have to wait awhile.

Back there when he'd been talking to Selena, he'd thought no daughter of his would pull such a stunt, and he'd made the automatic assumption that any children of his would also be Neely's. For one short year, that had been a perfectly reasonable expectation. For the nine long years since, it had been out of the question. Utterly impossible. So why had he thought it today?

Because he'd intruded on her privacy and seen her half-naked just before leaving the house? Because it had been a compelling reminder that he hadn't had sex in a very long time? Because a man could go only so long before he started getting tempted by the most inappropriate women at some damned inappropriate times?

Or, maybe, because there'd been a time when marrying Neely and raising a family with her had been the one thing he'd wanted most in his life.

About a mile outside Heartbreak was the turnoff to Callie's house. He debated making the turn and following the dirt-and-gravel road two-and-a-half miles back through the woods. He always carried a change of clothes in the truck, and Callie wouldn't think twice about giving him the use of her shower. Hell, he might even convince Isabella to wash his back for him, along with anything else that caught her attention.

Despite the temptation, he didn't slow down. Using one woman to forget another was cold, and wasn't fair to either of them. Maybe he and Neely didn't deserve better, but Isabella did.

Once he got home, he left his shoes and socks in the garage, then went into the kitchen. Neely, standing at the counter, looked his way, then burst into laughter. "Where did you find mud to roll in?"

"In Bill Taylor's cornfield."

"You wrestling the pigs for the corn?"

"These have not been the finest few hours of my week. Don't laugh again, or I might have to scrape some of this mud off and let you get an idea how it feels."

"You wouldn't."

Though he'd cleaned off the worst of it at the accident scene, he easily filled one hand. "Where would you like it? In your hair? On your face? How about inside your shirt? Or dripping over your peach satin—"

As he broke off, her eyes widened and her mouth opened in a silent gasp. "How did you know—"

"I've gotta take a shower."

Careful not to touch him, she moved to block his way. "Uh-uh. How did you know?"

The heat in his face was so intense that he wondered if he might have gotten sunburned this morning. He was naturally dark enough that it didn't often happen, but he'd spent more time outside today than normal.

Of course, he knew the difference between the burn of too much sun and plain old embarrassment.

"I, uh, went to your room to…to tell you that I had to go out, and you…you were asleep, so I, uh, uh…"

Neely folded her arms across her chest. "You stood there and…ogled me?"

"That sounds a lot worse than it was. Let's say I admired you. Thought how incredible you looked. Remembered how incredible…" He didn't finish. He could tell by the smoky look that softened her brown eyes that he didn't need to. *She* remembered how incredible they used to be.

For a long time she looked at him, her lips barely parted in the slightest of smiles, and for that same long time, he had an insane urge to kiss her. To forget that he was muddy, that he despised more about her than he'd ever admired, that her great passion in life was letting bad guys go free. To pull her close and kiss her until they both forgot everything except need. Hunger. Lust. Heat. Torment. Pain. Pleasure. Satisfaction.

She broke the spell, though, with one whispered question. "Do you have any idea how much I loved you?"

Bitterness welled inside him, sending the more tender feelings on their way. "Yes," he said flatly. "Not enough."

Hurt crept into her eyes and chased the smile from her lips. "You're wrong, Reese. I would have died for you."

"Instead Judy died."

She raised her hand to her right shoulder, rubbing as if it ached. He brushed her hand away and lifted the fabric, but she stepped away too quickly.

"You want to see the scars?" Her voice was taut, reckless. "Want to see if they're as gruesome as I deserved?"

"No." There was no way he could look without touching, no way he could touch without wanting. Besides, he didn't need to see the physical proof from when he'd let her down. "I'm going to take a shower now."

"Oh, come on, Reese. Everyone in Thomasville got such a kick out of seeing me with my arm in a sling. You can be the first one to see the actual scars." She began unbuttoning her blouse with trembling hands. "Dave Dugan wanted to see them, but I wouldn't let him. I told him if he ever broke into my house again, I'd kill him. He laughed and said I didn't have the guts, but he never broke in again, so who knows? Maybe he did believe me."

As she reached the last button, Reese pivoted on his heel and started for the hall. Her broken voice stopped him at the doorway.

"Please...don't walk away from me again."

He couldn't think, couldn't breathe, couldn't go back to her, couldn't leave. It was one of those situations where every possible action was wrong, where he had to determine which was least wrong, and he didn't have a clue.

From behind him came a soft, choked sob, and he realized abruptly, as if it were somehow important, that he'd never seen

Neely cry. He knew she did—he'd seen the proof of it from time to time—but he'd never witnessed it.

But she was crying now. When he turned, she was standing in the middle of the kitchen, head bowed, shoulders slumped, blouse unbuttoned and hanging open. Her arms hung limply at her sides, her hands open, and she was sobbing helplessly.

He reached her in two strides, pulled the edges of her blouse tightly together, then wrapped his arms around her and pulled her close. Closing his eyes, he stroked her hair, patted her back and thought how curious it felt to have her in his arms again— familiar, awkward, wrong.

And eternally right.

Clutching handfuls of his shirt, she cried until the fabric was damp, until her eyes were puffy and her sobs turned to hiccups. For a long time after she fell silent, she didn't move and neither did he. Well, not voluntarily. It wasn't his fault that holding her felt so damn good, or that he'd been celibate too long, or that every pore in his body remembered the exquisite pleasure of her body. It wasn't his fault that she'd cried—not entirely—or that he'd had no choice but to comfort her, or that he found such comfort too erotic for his weak will to resist. He'd never been able to resist her, even under the best of circumstances. How could he be expected to now, when she was vulnerable and he was aroused? When she needed somebody and he needed her?

When she became aware of his erection pressing against her belly, tension flitted through her. He felt it, and knew instinctively it was sexual in nature. He could kiss her. Slide his hands inside her blouse, his tongue inside her mouth, other parts in other places. He could open his jeans, lift her skirt, remove those tiny peach satin panties, and he could take her right there—standing up, on the table, on the floor. Neither of them was a stranger to places less common.

Her fingers tightened on his shirt, pulling the fabric taut, but she didn't raise her head, didn't look at his face. "Do you…" Her whisper faded, and she cleared her throat before trying again. "Do you want to make…"

A shiver rippled through her—maybe arousal, maybe hurt—and she discarded the phrase she'd been about to finish and chose a shorter one. A blunter, bolder, cruder one. Most often it was obscene, but in her delicate voice it became sexy, hot, erotic as hell. It sounded damn near proper, and in that moment his need for it—his need for her—was damn near killing him.

Finally she did look up at him. Her red-rimmed eyes were glittery and hard, her smile brittle, her demeanor wounded. "It's pretty obvious you want to—" she shifted against him, making him choke back a groan "—do it to someone. Do you think you can use me without hating one or both of us afterward?"

His hand was unsteady when he touched her cheek, her jaw, then slid along the silky length of her throat to the pulse at its base. She was so soft where he was hard, so warm where he suddenly felt cold. "I already hate one or both of us," he murmured. "It wouldn't be anything new."

Bitterness stole into her eyes. "So is that a yes or no? You want to set your self-respect aside long enough to take the edge off, or are you planning to make that shower a cold one?"

He wanted her—sweet hell, he wanted her! But not enough to sacrifice his self-respect or to endure that bitter little smile of hers. Not enough to deal with the fallout of having her. No matter how they approached it, she would be hurt. He knew that as surely as he knew he would feel worthless, selfish, a first-class bastard, when it was over. He deserved better than to feel that way.

So did she.

"I…" He touched her face again, brushing away a smudge of dirt. "I think we could both use a cold shower."

Her expression was impossible to read. Disappointed? Relieved? He didn't have a clue. "Are you being noble?" she asked flatly as she took several steps back, then pulled the edges of her shirt together so tightly that the fabric flattened her breasts into soft, malleable mounds…with hard, dusky pink crests that would get harder still if he touched them...kissed them...dragged his tongue slowly, roughly across them. "Or are you simply repulsed?"

It took a moment for her last word to register, for his gaze to move from her breasts to her face. "Oh, yeah, I really look repulsed, don't I?" he asked scornfully. His jeans were stretched taut, his skin was clammy and his hands and voice were less than steady.

"Then why...?"

"Is this what you do, Neely? Offer yourself to any man who gets hard around you? You used to have more self-respect than that."

"I used to have you."

And when he'd left, he'd taken some of that self-respect with him. One more thing to feel guilty for—not that he needed anything else.

"It would be wrong," he said with a heavy sigh. "There's too much between us." *Yeah, like too much distance,* his libido taunted inside his head, *and too many clothes.*

Too much history, his conscience countered. *Too much anger, disappointment, love, hate.*

For a time she stood very still, looking like a lost little girl. Then she nodded once in agreement and walked away. He let her get as far as the hallway before he spoke.

"Neely."

She looked back.

"Are you okay?"

Again she stood very still. With her bare feet, her long skirt half unbuttoned, her blouse held together by only her fingers, her mussed hair and the dirt still smudged across her cheek, she looked wanton. Wicked. The best time he might ever know. Then a smile eased across her face—not a bitter smile, or a hurt one, or one with even a hint of anger. This was a womanly smile—slow, lazy, confident. The kind that could bring a man to his knees and make him grateful to be there.

"Sure," she replied. "I'm a survivor. I can endure anything."

Chapter 7

When Neely found herself Monday afternoon, arguing with people on a TV talk show that had been taped weeks earlier, she knew she had to do something or go nuts...which might not be a bad thing, as long as she got to take Reese with her. He was responsible for at least half the mental duress she'd been under, so it was only fair that he suffer half the insanity.

He still refused to give back her credit cards and money, and had every pair of shoes she'd brought with her locked up in his closet. He also refused to give her the code for the alarm, even though she'd sworn she would never set foot off the front or back porch. He wouldn't leave the power cord for the computer, even after she'd solemnly promised to do nothing more than play Free Cell, and she hadn't seen an intact telephone for eight days now.

She appreciated that he was trying to keep her safe. She just hoped he appreciated that when she did go nuts, she couldn't be held accountable for her actions.

She was curled up in the chair-and-a-half with a diet pop and a bowl of buttered popcorn, muttering insults to the snotty teenagers on television when a car coming down the driveway caught her attention. The bowl slid from her lap and balanced precariously on the leather cushion before she found the presence of mind to grab it and jump to her feet. Should she go to the bedroom and lock the door? Barricade herself inside the safe room? Curl up in a dark corner and pray for Reese to come home right that very instant?

Or maybe first see who the visitor was?

She hurried into the hallway, then peeked around the corner of Reese's bedroom door. The sidewalk from the driveway to the porch went right past his window. If whoever it was walked past there, she would see, and if he looked particularly dangerous, she could be secure inside the safe room before he could kick in the front door. And if he *didn't* come past there, she could assume he was up to no good, trying to sneak in the back, and she'd lock herself up.

But it was no *he* who walked past the window, and she was only dangerous to susceptible men and jealous women. Of course, Neely fell into the latter category.

Shay Rafferty was peering in the windows when Neely returned to the living room. She waved and beckoned Neely closer. "I thought you might be getting a little stir crazy, so I brought some lunch. You want to come out or let me in?"

Neely shrugged helplessly. "I don't know the code to the alarm."

"Oh, I forgot about that. Are the windows wired, too?"

She nodded.

"Well..." With her hands on her hips, Shay tapped one foot rapidly. "What happens when you open the door? Is there some kind of horn or siren here?"

"No. It just calls in to the dispatcher at the sheriff's department, and he sends someone out to check."

Shay's smile was broad and smug. "The sheriff's department is over twenty miles from here, and it's lunchtime. Unless there's a deputy in town that I missed—and trust me, in Heartbreak, it's hard to miss *anything*—by the time anyone got here, we could be finished with lunch and just getting started on gossip. What do you say?''

Okay, so she was beautiful. Had a body to die for. Wore a white denim skirt that hugged her curves and was a good six inches shorter than the shortest of Neely's shorts. And her blouse…Neely had handkerchiefs that were bigger.

But she liked the way Shay thought.

''Meet me at the door.''

Neely took a deep breath before turning the lock, then placing her hand on the knob. With her luck, Reese would answer the dispatcher's call, and she wouldn't have to worry about Forbes anymore because he'd kill her himself. Then she turned the knob and it was too late to worry, so why not enjoy the company?

''Do you mind if we eat outside? I've been stuck inside for so long that sometimes I crave just one breath of fresh air.''

''Grab some drinks and lead the way,'' Shay agreed. ''I have no idea what I've brought to eat. I told the cook to wrap up two meals and surprise us.''

Neely took two cans of pop from the refrigerator, then opened the back door. ''You have a cook?'' she asked enviously. Not that she couldn't afford household help. It just seemed pointless when she was always alone.

''I own a café in town, and it has a cook. Anyone in town will tell you that I'm not allowed in the kitchen because I'm a disaster at any sort of food preparation. But I'm pretty good at taking orders and chatting up the customers.'' Shay hooked a small table with her foot and pulled it between two patio chairs, then gracefully sat. ''What about you? What are you pretty good at?''

''Making Reese angry. I excel at that.''

''Every woman should be able to get under at least one man's skin. What else?''

Neely peeled back the foil from her plate, uncovering a chicken sandwich, still warm from the grill, her favorite kind of dill pickle spears, a dish of creamy cole slaw and a bag of

chips. "That's really about it," she replied with an awkward shrug.

"Of course that's not it. You were good enough at sending bad guys to jail to make one of them want to kill you for it."

"He hasn't tried anything in a week."

"O-oh, a whole week. You getting bored?"

"Trust me, being locked up alone all day with no telephone, no computer, no one to talk to, and no shoes—" she wiggled her toes "—and then spending all evening with a man who can hardly bear the sight of me is *not* how I would choose to spend my time."

Shay frowned at her. "How could he already 'hardly bear the sight' of you? You just met a week ago...didn't you?"

Neely filled her mouth with food to buy time for the crimson heat that warmed her face to fade. When she finally had no choice but to swallow, she gestured with the sandwich. "This just might be the best grilled-chicken sandwich I've ever had. If the rest of the café's food is this good, I'm surprised they can spare you at lunchtime."

"I'm the boss. They don't have a choice. How long have you and Reese known each other?"

"I'm not sure we ever did know each other."

"Quit hedging. How long?"

Neely took another bite before finally replying. "Ten years."

"So you're the one," Shay said softly.

"Who? The naive, self-absorbed, bleeding-heart witch who wanted to win, whatever the cost, who would say anything, do anything and destroy anyone who got in her way?"

"The one who broke his heart."

Neely's laughter sounded phony and tearful in her own ears. "No, ma'am. You must be thinking of some other manipulative, shameless, bleeding heart witch." The only heart she'd ever broken was her own, by loving him too much.

"My gosh, this must be hard for both of you."

For one more than the other, she thought scornfully. "We're

both agreed that I don't want to be here and Reese doesn't want me here. I'd leave in a heartbeat if…''

"If what?"

Neely slowly raised her gaze to Shay's face. "If someone would help me. I need shoes. A small loan. A way to get away from this house."

Shay's curiosity instantly gave way to apprehension. "Oh, Neely, I can't help you with that."

"A pair of sneakers, five hundred bucks and a ride to Tulsa. I'd pay the money back just as soon as I could get my bank to transfer it. I have cash, Shay—plenty of it—but he's locked it up where I can't get to it. Please…I've got friends and family all over the country. They'll help me if I can just get away from here."

"Look, Neely, I'd love to help you, but…Reese would kill you and me both."

"He'd have to find me first."

"He would, trust me. Besides, I know you're bored and lonely here, but…you're *safe*. If you go off by yourself, God only knows what could happen."

Neely tamped down the disappointment rising inside. It had been a long shot—she'd known that the instant she'd opened her mouth. Reese was Shay's friend, her former lover. Neely was nothing. She forced a smile as if it were no big deal. "Oh, well…I figured it couldn't hurt to ask. How about a smaller, less deadly favor? Could you call my sister and let her know I'm all right?"

The apprehension remained in Shay's blue eyes. "I always wanted a sister. Does yours live in Kansas City?"

"No. One's in California, one's in Texas, and Bailey, the one I'd like to get a message to, is in Tennessee." Hallie had her own problems, and Kylie…there was just something about turning to her youngest sister for help that felt wrong. Bailey, though, was the second eldest and had helped raise the other two. She was responsible, capable, and, as a newly licensed private investigator, she was somewhat trained for the task.

Given the chance, she would find some way to get in touch with Neely and then help her escape.

"Three sisters. You're lucky."

There had been times when Neely wasn't so sure of that, such as when she'd tried to feed a family of five on a budget inadequate for two, or when she could never spend time with her friends after school because she was cooking, cleaning and doing laundry, or when she desperately needed time to study but Kylie needed cuddling or Hallie couldn't learn her times tables or Bailey needed patching up after another fight defending their father's name.

Most of the time, though, she'd appreciated her sisters more than she could say. They got together whenever they could—not often enough, since they all had lives in other places. When she'd gotten shot nine years ago, one phone call would have brought all three of them to Thomasville and they would have stood up for her to every narrow-minded citizen and corrupt cop in the county. Once she'd realized Reese was never going to forgive her and her heart had finished breaking for good, if she'd told them, they would have come, armed with chocolate and tissues, and they would have cried with her, told her what a fool he was, convinced her she deserved better, mourned his leaving, celebrated it, and just generally made everything better.

But she hadn't made that phone call. She hadn't told them it was over with Reese until she'd recovered to the point that she didn't need their support. They'd been angry, and had demanded to know why, and she hadn't had much of an answer to give them beyond the fact that she was the oldest. *She* took care of them, not the other way around. She'd always been strong for them and hadn't known how to let them be strong for her.

Well, she needed them now, even if it was for nothing more than a loan and a way out of Oklahoma. She wouldn't stay with any of them, wouldn't endanger their lives, but she would use them to get away. To save her sanity. To protect her heart.

"I am lucky," she agreed with Shay. "If you could just

call Bailey and let her know that everything's all right and that I'm safe here in Heartbreak…''

''And what would she do?''

''She'd thank you, and pass it on to Kylie and Hallie.'' And, being the curious sort, she would wonder why Neely had sent such a message when she'd been closemouthed about her problems in the past. She would take a few days off and do some snooping around—would find out about Forbes's threats and the attempts to make good on them. She already knew about Neely's friendship with Jace, and that Reese was from Heartbreak, and she would head west to the rescue.

''What's her name?'' Shay asked reluctantly.

''Bailey Madison. She lives in Memphis. She's listed in the phone book.'' Neely drew a tentative breath. ''You'll call her?''

''I—I'll think about it.''

Neely would bet that translated to Shay couldn't think of any reason why such a phone call would be out of line, but some part of her strongly suspected it was. She made a none-too-subtle effort to convince her. ''Normally, I wouldn't ask you to do this. Reese has his reasons for not letting me near a phone. He's protecting me—I understand that. But they're my *sisters*. Since our father died and our mother remarried, we're all we've got. He doesn't understand how worried they are.''

Conveniently she didn't mention that fifteen years had passed between their father's death and Doris Irene's second marriage, or the fact that the four daughters spoke to and saw their mother regularly. If they sounded like abandoned little orphan girls… Oh, well.

''I'll think about it,'' Shay repeated.

At least it wasn't a flat refusal. Neely couldn't ask for more than that.

Shay glanced at her watch. ''It's been about twenty minutes. Someone should be showing up to check on you about…'' She smiled at the sound of a powerful engine that nearly drowned out the crunch of tires on gravel. ''Would you think

I'm a coward if I slipped around the house, got in my car and hustled away while you dealt with Reese?''

"That's what I would do, given the choice," Neely said dryly. But she didn't have many choices these days. All she could do was go along and hope for the best. "Would you think *I'm* a coward if I go inside where I can be berated and threatened in private?"

"Go ahead. I'd like to talk to him a minute."

Neely hesitated only an instant. Hearing a car door slam, followed by her name in an angry roar that was approaching the rear corner of the house, she jumped to her feet and hurried inside. She waited at the door long enough to catch a glimpse at Reese, whose expression was as dark and ominous as anything she'd ever seen, then she disappeared into her bedroom. No doubt, he would come looking for her, and no doubt, he would find her, but she didn't have to make it easy for him by waiting meekly on the deck.

She didn't have to make it easy for him at all, she thought as she locked the door.

Reese wasn't surprised to find Shay sitting on his deck, beautiful, tanned, wearing an outfit flashy enough to catch any man's eye. It said a lot about the strength of her relationship with Easy that he didn't mind her dressing that way.

Of course, if *he* had a steady woman in his life, he wouldn't mind her dressing that way, either—but he'd sure as hell hate her going out in town like that. Fortunately, Neely had never been comfortable in anything overly revealing unless they were home alone, so he'd never had to worry—

The scowl that lately seemed to have become a permanent fixture on his face deepened, drawing his brows together. Neely was *not* a woman in his life, and she could wear whatever kind of clothing she damn well pleased. It didn't matter to him.

He took the steps two at a time, then stopped just out of arm's reach of Shay, planted his hands on his hips and glared at her. "Where is she?"

She pulled a pair of dark glasses from somewhere and put them on before looking up and smiling brightly. "Nice to see you, too, Reese."

He took a controlling breath. "Hello, Shay. It's good to see you. Where is she?"

She patted the empty chair. "Sit down. We need to talk."

"No, darlin', you need to tell me where in holy hell Neely is so I can put her in handcuffs and take her back to the Canyon County jail where there's a nice, luxurious cell waiting with her name on it."

"You can't take her to jail."

"I'm the sheriff. I can do whatever I damn well please." He removed his hat and ran his fingers through his hair. "Do you know where I was when the dispatcher called? On my way to pick up a prisoner in Stillwater. *Five miles* from the city limits, but there wasn't anyone to take this call, so I had to turn around and come all the way back, and after I take her to jail, I'll have to go back to Stillwater."

She didn't say a word, but merely patted the chair again. After a long moment he grudgingly sat.

"Which was worse?" she asked. "The worry that she'd done something stupid, like run away? Or the fear that the people trying to kill her had found her?"

"Neither," he lied. He'd driven faster than was safe over narrow, two-lane roads, telling himself mile after mile that she was probably just getting some sun on the back deck or had gone to the pasture to see the horses. That the biggest danger to her safety was Neely herself—though he ran a close second. Eddie Forbes just had to wait in line with everyone else who held a grudge against her.

But he hadn't convinced himself, not for a second. Even now, his heart was still beating too fast and the tension that had knotted his muscles the instant the dispatcher called hadn't yet begun to ease. It wouldn't, he thought, until he saw Neely and knew for a fact that she was all right.

"Liar," Shay said mildly. "Why didn't you tell me?"

"Tell you what?"

"That you were in love with her."

"I'm not—I wasn't—" He sank back and pressed one hand against his middle where the tension was making him regret that greasy burger for lunch. "She told you about that," he murmured, then commanded, "Take off your glasses and look at me."

When she obeyed, he knew Neely hadn't told her everything. Shay wouldn't be able to look at him so clear-eyed if she knew how he'd turned his back on Neely after she'd been shot. No matter what had happened, no matter how many people had died or who they were, he should have gone to her. Should have held her, reassured her, helped her. Should have prayed for her to be all right.

He shouldn't have had a single thought to spare for anyone but her until he'd known she was going to be all right, and even long after.

"You were in love with her, and it didn't work out," Shay said softly.

Didn't work out. It sounded so harmless. She could have died, and there'd been days when he'd believed death was preferable to living without her. It hadn't been harmless at all. "No, it didn't work out," he agreed, grimacing with the words.

"Poor Neely."

Reese gave her an aggravated look. "Why poor Neely? You hardly even know her. Why not poor Reese?"

"Because you obviously did something unforgivable."

He couldn't deny it, and he couldn't admit the truth—couldn't face it in the bright afternoon sunlight—and so he ignored it and got to his feet. "You'd better get back to work, and I've got business to take care of inside."

"Reese..." Rising, Shay laid her hand on his arm. "Consider how difficult this is for her. She spends most of her time alone with nothing to do but watch television. The only person she sees is you, and you're carrying a load of guilt for the way you once treated her, but instead of trying to make it up to her, you're taking it out on her. She's scared, bored, hurting, suffering from cabin fever... This is really hard for her.'' She hesitated, then lowered her voice. ''Ordinarily, I wouldn't tell you this, but...I like Neely, and I don't want to see her do something foolish. She...she asked me to let her sister Bailey know she's safe and in Heartbreak. I—I suppose it could be as innocent as it seems, except...just before that, she'd asked me to take her to Tulsa and loan her the money to get away from here.''

He wasn't surprised, Reese told himself. Neely had made it clear that she'd rather be anyplace than with him. He'd been expecting some stunt like this. Wasn't that why he'd restricted her access to the telephone and the computer? Because he couldn't trust her?

No, he wasn't surprised at all. Just...a little disappointed.

He hugged Shay, noticing in some distant part of his mind that it felt different from holding Neely. Shay was an incredible woman, but for all his body noticed, she might as well be his sister. Ignoring the disturbing difference, he said, ''If you'd ever gotten over Easy Rafferty, I would have happily married you.''

Her arms tightened briefly around him. ''No, you wouldn't have. Not happily, because you'd never gotten over Neely. You know, second chances don't come around every day. Take some advice from someone who finally got it right. Don't blow this one.''

She pulled away and started for the steps, and Reese watched her go. He didn't bother arguing with her that he didn't *want* a second chance with Neely. Except maybe in bed. Lust was the biggest part of what he was feeling lately, and there were a million easier ways of satisfying that than Neely Madison.

Once Shay had turned the corner, he gathered the remains of their lunch and went inside. For a moment he stood at the kitchen sink, staring out at the barn and the horses grazing idly in the pasture. From the living room came the sounds of conflict—shouting, screaming and the audience's boos. Trash

TV, his dispatchers called it. They loved it. He bet it drove Neely right up the wall.

Other than that, the house was silent.

Wishing he could just reset the alarm and leave again, Reese walked to the guest room door and knocked once. "Neely?" When he got the expected response—none—he tried the knob and found it locked. He felt along the top of the door frame for the handy key that fitted the lock and opened it with a click, but he didn't open the door. Instead he leaned against the wall. "I won't come in without an invitation, but…we've got to talk. This can't continue."

For a long time there was no answer. He knew she was in there. He could practically *feel* her sitting or lying on the bed, upset, defiant, embarrassed and helpless. And she hated feeling helpless.

"Listen, I've got to get back to work. I've got to pick up a prisoner from the Payne County jail. When I get home, we'll renegotiate the terms of your…visit."

The bed creaked, then he swore he heard the whisper of bare feet on the wood floor. An instant later the door opened a few inches, giving him a view of one narrow strip of her face. "You aren't going to yell at me and threaten to throw me in jail?"

Was that all she expected of him? Anger and threats? "No."

Her look turned accusing. "Did you yell at Shay?"

"Honey, if I'd yelled at Shay, you would've heard her yelling back. She doesn't take orders kindly." And why should she? She was intelligent, capable, efficient, and deserved to be treated as such.

And so did Neely.

"I—I'll be back around the usual time. We'll talk then, okay?"

Though she nodded, her expression lacked any hope at all. That nagged at Reese as he headed back for the kitchen. Before he got there, he turned back. "Do you want anything? Books? Magazines? Any particular food or pop?"

For one distrusting moment after another, she simply looked at him, then finally answered. "Books. With happy endings. Chocolate kisses. And that chocolate sauce you put on ice cream that turns hard."

Books with happy endings and ice cream sauce that turned hard. He was going to have fun asking for help in finding those at the store. But he didn't comment on that. He simply nodded and left.

He'd made the drive to Stillwater so many times that he didn't need to think about it. After high school, he'd gone to Oklahoma State, located in Stillwater, on a baseball scholarship. A free ride to a college degree just because he could throw a baseball fast and hard, while Jace, who'd actually cared about getting a degree, had gotten academic scholarships and still had to work part-time every semester. It wasn't fair, but life wasn't fair. He'd accepted that a long time ago.

It seemed Neely had finally accepted it, too.

Unfortunately, it had been too late for them.

Unless you believed in second chances.

Unless you blew it the second time, too.

Or unless you did something the first time that was unforgivable.

He *wasn't* looking for forgiveness, he reminded himself. He just wanted to keep her alive until it was safe for her to return to Kansas City, and then he wanted to go back to life as usual. Quiet. Peaceful.

Lonely.

Scowling again, he stopped at the store once he reached Stillwater and found a salesclerk old enough to be his mother to help him choose the books. With a wink and a grin, she led him to the end rack in the book section. "Happy endings guaranteed, Sheriff," she said, indicating the books with a flourish. "That's so special, that you're not embarrassed to buy romance novels for your sweetheart. Maybe you two will find a happy ending all your own."

"She's not—we're not—" Giving up, he scanned the shelves. Determined not to endure the clerk's beaming smile

any longer than necessary, he didn't bother to choose carefully. He grabbed six or eight books whose covers caught his eye, tossed them into the cart, then turned to the next item on his short make-Neely-happy list.

The clerk helped him find both the chocolate kisses and the ice-cream sauce, then even accompanied him to the checkout. "He's shopping for his lady friend," she told the checker as she helped unload the cart. "Isn't that sweet?"

He'd never been so relieved to get out of a store in his life.

From there he picked up his prisoner, returned to Buffalo Plains and turned the man over to the jailer, then interviewed a couple of prospective deputies. The state of Oklahoma gave sheriffs tremendous latitude in the hiring and firing of staff, but he tried very hard to not take advantage of it. He'd never hired anyone who wasn't competent, and had never fired anyone who didn't deserve it.

By four o'clock, he was happy to walk out the door and was almost eager to get home and give Neely her stuff. Because it proved he had at least a speck of consideration? Because it might make her feel more kindly toward him? Because he wanted her to stop trying to run away?

He was about to open the door to his truck when a strong hand clamped onto his shoulder and pulled him around. Startled, he dropped his right hand to his holstered weapon, then gave his father an admonishing look. "That's a good way to get yourself shot."

"I called your name a half dozen times, but you were preoccupied. You're heading home early."

Reese glanced at his watch. "It's quitting time."

"For everyone else in the department, maybe. You hardly ever get out of here on time." Del turned to lean back against the truck. "I heard you had to fire Tommy Lee Curtis."

"Did they tow the patrol car into your yard?" At his father's nod, Reese said, "Then you saw why. Is it going to be fixable?"

"I don't know yet. Your uncle James was looking at it when I left. We'll let you know probably tomorrow." Del's gaze narrowed. "When did you develop a hankering for chocolate?"

Reese glanced at the nearly transparent plastic bag he held in his left hand. With the afternoon high predicted to be in the low nineties, the kisses would have melted into gooey globs if he'd left them in the truck so he'd taken them to his office. The books had stayed in the truck. Wrapped inside two plastic bags. Stuck under the passenger seat.

With the heat in his face approaching the temperature of the pavement beneath his feet, he tried not to stammer. "I—I like chocolate."

"Son, you lived half your life with me. While you did eat chocolate cake or pudding or ice cream on occasion, I don't believe I've ever seen you eat a piece of chocolate candy in my life." Suddenly Del grinned. "You seeing somebody with a sweet tooth?"

A sweet tooth, a sweet body, an incredibly sweet face…and a not-so-sweet disposition, for which he was at least partly responsible.

Rather than make some effort at the truth, Reese let his father's misinterpretation stand. "I won't be seeing her if I don't get home pretty quick."

Laughing, Del moved back, then opened the truck door. "By all means, don't let me stand in the way of true love…or just getting lucky for the night. But you know, you might want to keep in mind that before long, I'm gonna be too old to enjoy any grandkids I might have."

"Right, Dad," Reese agreed dryly as he settled behind the wheel. "You've got more energy and strength than most men half your age."

"Good luck with your young lady. I'll look forward to hearing the results later."

Reese made it to Heartbreak in good time. He didn't abuse his authority as sheriff in any way but one—he did like to get to places quickly without having to worry about a speeding ticket. But the same was true of virtually everyone with a driver's license. He just happened to be in a position to make it happen.

When he got home, he found Neely sitting in the kitchen. A magazine was open on the table in front of her, but she was ignoring it and staring off into space instead. She looked forlorn. Defeated.

He set the bags on top of the magazine, then removed his hat. She stared at the bags, looked blankly up at him, then opened the first one, studying each book, stacking them neatly together. The second bag held the chocolate—three bottles of the ice cream topping and three large bags of kisses. She looked at him again, one brow raised, and he shrugged as he removed his gun belt.

"These are plain, with almonds and white chocolate." The cellophane bags crinkled as he touched each one. "And the ice cream stuff is chocolate, fudge and chocolate with some kind of crunchy stuff in it." His face warm, he shrugged again awkwardly. "You didn't say what kind you wanted, so I got all of them."

She stood and surprised the embarrassment right out of him by rising onto her toes to brush her mouth across his. For an instant he was too stunned to move. He caught his breath, which teased him with the faint scent of her, and a shudder rocketed through him, making his skin tingle and his muscles tighten.

That tiny, little-nothing kiss was all she meant to give. He knew that. He also knew he wanted more. Snaking his arm around her waist, he held her tightly when she tried to back away, pulled her body hard against his and claimed her mouth as if he had a right. She tasted sweet and hot, full of secrets, of mysteries and incredible pleasure. When she opened her mouth to his tongue, he grew hard where her hips cradled his. When she clung as if she needed him, he wondered crazily, seriously, if they could make it to the bedroom, if he could hold out long enough to get inside her.

And when he tasted the salt from her silent tears, his lust died an instant death.

He ended the kiss, pulled her arms from around his neck, hushed her protests and simply held her. He *didn't* have a right to kiss her, hold her, have her. After everything he'd done, and everything he hadn't done, he didn't deserve to even want her.

But God help him, he did.

"Are you okay?" His voice was thick, hoarse.

Without lifting her head from his shoulder, she nodded.

"So all it takes to make you happy is three pounds of chocolate candy and a little ice-cream topping?"

At that, she did raise her head and smile faintly as she dried her cheeks. "It's not the chocolate."

He knew that. It was the fact that finally he'd thought to ask what she wanted. That he'd bought all the choices rather than disappoint her with the wrong one. That at last he'd shown her some consideration.

The chocolate was wonderful, Neely thought with a sniffle, but that wasn't the reason for her tears. It was the fact that he'd kissed her, just like old times. Gotten turned on by her, just like old times. Even would have made love to her like old times.

And he still would have hated her when they were done.

She wasn't sure how much longer she could bear his hatred.

Moving out of his embrace might have been the hardest thing she'd ever done. Even if he did despise her, she felt safe there, and always had. She'd known from the first time he'd held her that nothing bad could happen to her in his arms. The problems in her past seemed less important there. Her world felt more secure. Even getting shot would have hurt less if he'd held her.

But those were *her* feelings. His were vastly different. He felt lust, tempered by derision.

"I—I— Thank you for the books and…and the chocolate." She nervously brushed her hair back, laced her fingers together, then shoved her hands into the pockets of her jumper. "I'll behave better. I promise."

His mouth tightened into a thin line, and the emotion that

had softened his dark eyes disappeared. "It wasn't a bribe, Neely."

"I know. I didn't mean…" Behind her the timer beeped, and she spun on her heel, grateful for the excuse to turn away. She opened the oven door and unnecessarily checked the ham and the rice casserole on the rack above it. "It's awfully convenient, having your freezer filled with wonderful food that needs nothing more than a little time in the oven."

"You like to cook," he said flatly.

Her smile was unsteady. "I'm surprised you remember."

"I remember everything."

So did she. She remembered how much she'd loved him. How even the most mundane chores had been special when shared with him. How sometimes she'd awakened in the middle of the night, cold or startled or unsettled by a dream, and he'd automatically pulled her close and wrapped himself around her. How she'd soaked in the tub some mornings and watched him shave at the bathroom sink and thought those few quiet minutes were her favorite part of the day.

And what did he remember? That she'd refused to take his advice on which cases to accept and which to refuse. That she'd caused him no end of teasing, sometimes friendly, usually not, from the other deputies. That he'd liked having sex with her. And that he could walk away from her without even a moment's regret.

Still smiling shakily, she turned from the stove. "Do you remember that we're supposed to renegotiate the terms of my imprisonment?"

"Your visit."

"My incarceration. I'm locked up. I can't go anywhere. I can't use the phone. I can't have visitors. I'm your prisoner." She would have changed those last words, given the chance, because they reminded her of the night last week when he'd held up the handcuffs. *Been there, done that,* she'd quipped. *And enjoyed it a lot,* he'd replied in that lazy, husky voice that always made her hot. He could damn near talk her to climax with that smooth-as-honey, turned-on Oklahoma-cowboy voice. Put that voice, her and those handcuffs in the same room, and…

Some parts of her body turned hot and dry. Some were hot and damp enough to steam. "Let's not quibble over words. What are you willing to offer?"

"You can call Bailey and let her know you're all right, but I get to listen."

So Shay had told him what she wanted, and he had figured out why. Neely couldn't even blame the other woman. She never should have asked for her help. "All right."

"I'll give you the code to the alarm system. You can go out back, but you have to promise to keep the alarm on when you're inside and to stay alert when you're outside. If anyone—*anyone*—comes to the house while you're out there, you hustle your butt into the safe room and lock yourself inside, and you stay there until I get home."

She nodded. "Shoes?"

"No. And don't ask Shay to loan you a pair. Her feet are smaller than yours."

"Her everything is smaller than mine—except her breasts," she replied dryly. "She's a breathtaking woman." Then, after a beat, "Were you in love with her?"

For a long time he simply looked at her. Then he picked up his hat and gun belt, paused in the doorway long enough to say, "No," then disappeared down the hall.

She followed, watching from the door as he unlocked the closet, set his hat on the shelf beside several others and pushed his gun belt out of sight on the tallest shelf. "That sounded like a guilty no."

Still standing in the closet, he removed his uniform shirt, pulled off his T-shirt and unbuckled his belt. "There was nothing guilty about it. We were friends."

"Who slept together."

After a glance at her, he nudged the door shut. She sat primly on the side of the bed—what had once been *her* side of the bed—and waited. There were lots of family pictures in the living room, but the only photograph in the bedroom was on the nightstand nearest her—a simple five-by-seven snapshot of Reese in his Royals uniform. It had been taken an hour before the game that had ended his career, and he looked so handsome. So invincible. She had the same photo on the desk in her office at home. She had dreamed about it, talked to it, cried over it, thrown it a few times and mostly used it, face-down, as a paperweight. She had asked for the picture when they'd started dating, and he'd had a copy made, put it in a beautiful sterling filigree frame and given it to her, and then they'd made love for the first time.

So long ago.

With a heavy sigh, she returned to the subject, raising her voice loud enough to be heard through the door. "So you were friends with Shay. You dated her. You slept with her. Presumably one or both of you hoped something more would develop. But you didn't love her."

He came out of the closet, wearing jeans and nothing else. Her mouth went dry at the sight of so much warm tanned skin, such nicely defined muscles, such temptation. She swallowed hard and redirected her gaze.

He dropped his badge and brass nameplate on the dresser, then pulled on the white shirt he carried. He buttoned it, rolled the sleeves up his forearms and left the tails hanging out before facing her. "Would it matter to you if I did?"

If the man who'd sworn he would always love *her* had made the same vow to Shay? "Yes. It would."

"Why? Why would you care?"

"I always cared. From the first time we met. We were in the courthouse and I tripped and you—"

"I remember the day we met, Neely. You were wearing a dress the color of cotton candy and shoes that looked like ballet slippers, and your hair was long and shiny and…" His tone lightened, as if he were smiling but his mouth wasn't cooperating. "And when you knelt to pick up your files, I could see down your dress. You weren't wearing a bra. Shay's breasts might be bigger than yours…but yours are perfect."

The simple compliment brought her far more pleasure than

it merited. It warmed her already-heated blood and made her nipples tighten and pucker. Hoping her voice would be steady, she forced a carelessly amused smile. "So that's why you asked me out. If I'd known that was the way to get dates, I would have tried it on every attractive man in the city."

He leaned against the dresser, hands beside his hips, ankles crossed. He looked wicked. Sexy. More addictive than all the chocolate in the world. "Were you looking for dates?"

"No."

"Then what were you looking for?"

"Absolution. Oblivion. Freedom from the pain and the guilt."

"And did you ever find it?"

"No. Judy's dead. She can't forgive me. You never will, and I can't forgive myself. I just have to live with it. It's not easy…" She stood, moved to the door, then looked back. "But I'm learning."

Chapter 8

Dinner that evening was baked ham, a brown-rice-and-broccoli casserole and green beans from Mary Stephens's garden, followed by Reese's favorite dessert—plain white cake with plain vanilla frosting. He was loading the dishwasher while Neely cut the cake. When he finished, he asked, "You want to take dessert outside? If the bugs aren't bad, it should be nice."

She was surprised but quick to agree. Handing him a plate with cake and a fork, she picked up her own dessert—vanilla ice cream with chocolate sauce and sprinkled with chocolate kisses—and headed for the French door.

There was a nice breeze blowing, enough to keep the mosquitoes and gnats at bay. They settled in chairs that still held the day's heat and ate the sweets in silence. For the first time, though, it was almost companionable.

"Did you ever think, when you were a kid, that you'd wind up like this?" Her voice was soft, tantalizing. It slid along his skin and eased the tension in his muscles as surely as any massage could have—and, with the right words, it could just as easily bring it back stronger than ever. Words such as *I want you, Reese.*

Take me to bed.

Make love to me.

He had to clear his throat to speak. "Like this? You mean, a backwater sheriff in a redneck town?"

"*No.* Working as a sheriff, living back in your hometown, raising horses, living in a lovely house all your own, surrounded by trees, pasture and friends."

He set his plate on the side table, then stretched out on the chaise longue, his gaze fixed on the stars. "I thought maybe I'd win a World Series, or be a cop or a cowboy. I thought I'd live in L.A. or Houston or Detroit, or maybe Texas, Montana or the Dakotas. I knew I'd have a house, some land and horses…but I never counted on being alone."

"You could change that. There are a lot of women around."

He didn't want a lot of women. Even when he'd had them, when he was playing ball, he hadn't wanted them.

Because he wanted Neely.

Aware that she was watching him—and grateful she couldn't see much in the dim light—he shrugged. "I don't want a woman just for the sake of having someone." He wanted someone who mattered, who made his life better by being a part of it. Someone who was so important that she was irreplaceable. Someone so special that only she could be the mother of his children. Someone who wouldn't leave him.

Nine years ago he'd believed Neely met all those qualifications, and she hadn't left him. *He'd* abandoned *her.* Had they both suffered all this time because he'd been so terribly wrong in judging her? Or so terribly right?

"What about you?" he asked, pushing the unanswered questions out of his mind. "When you were little, what did you think you'd be?"

"A princess," she answered without hesitation. "Daddy said I could grow up to be anything I wanted, so I wanted to be a princess and live in a castle and marry Prince Charming. Then he was sent to prison, and for a long time all I wanted to be was someone else. Life was so hard without him. I needed his help, his support, his love. Then he was killed, and all I wanted was to survive. I loved him so much, Reese."

"Why didn't you ever tell me about him before?"

This time it was her turn to shrug. "It hurt. And you never asked. I thought you weren't interested."

"It would have helped explain so much…"

"Just accepting me the way I was would have helped, too. There's no denying that my father's life and death helped shape my opinions and beliefs, but regardless of how they were formed, they *are* my opinions and beliefs. I believe the concept of 'justice for all' is a joke in this country. I believe everyone truly does have the right to a *fair* trial without regard for their ability to pay. If my father had had some hot-shot attorney, he never would have gone to prison and he would probably be alive today. Instead he had an overworked, underpaid, inexperienced public defender who really didn't much care whether he won or lost. He got paid the same either way. He went home to *his* wife and children either way." When she stopped for a breath, she apparently noticed that Reese was grinning, because she petulantly said, "Don't laugh at me."

"I'm not laughing. I was just thinking that everyone should feel that sort of passion about something." He'd had it in varying degrees for the law, for baseball, but most especially for her—

"I was always that passionate about you."

His grin faded into regret. "I'm sorry."

She rose gracefully from the chair and walked to the deck railing, turning to face him in the full moonlight. It gleamed on her hair and gave her long, pale dress an otherworldly glow—made her look like an angel. "That I loved you? I'm not sorry. Never. But I am sorry that I lost you."

For a time she stood there, face tilted to the sky, eyes closed, the faintest of smiles curving her mouth. Then, with a great breath, she pushed away from the rail. "I think I'm going to read myself to sleep,'' she said, touching his shoulder lightly as she passed. ''Good night.''

He didn't repeat her ''good night'' until the door closed behind her. He stayed where he was a moment, then went to stand where she had stood. Though he knew it wasn't possible, he would have sworn he could still smell the delicate fragrance of her cologne in the air. But that was just wishful thinking. The breeze was blowing too steadily. The only ones out here smelling her cologne were the horses in the southeast pasture.

He turned to face the barn, his hands gripping the too-new-to-weather railing. How different would their lives have been if he'd accepted her the way she was—made good on his promises to love her and stay with her forever? He would have taken her away from Thomasville after the shooting, would have packed her away someplace safe where no one could ever hurt her again. He would have suffocated her with worry. Would have married her. Protected and pampered her. Made love to her. Made babies with her. Eventually he would have dealt with the fear of losing her. He would have been happy. He would have done his best to see that she was happy. And Eddie Forbes never would have known that she existed.

But the life he'd lived wasn't so bad, was it? Going to work, spending time with his family, caring for the horses, occasional relationships—nothing special. But not too bad, either. Just a little lonely. A little sad. A little less than he'd expected. A lot less than he'd hoped for.

Deciding he'd better find something else to occupy his thoughts before he talked himself into a bad mood, he went inside. He watched television, checked his e-mail and was grateful to hear the distant ring of the cell phone in the bedroom. It was Jace, calling from what sounded like a crowded bar. ''How's it going, bubba?''

Reese wondered how his cousin would react if he told the truth—*I've been having erotic fantasies about your witness, and this afternoon I kissed her the way we used to kiss, the way that always ended in sex, and I can hardly think for want-*

ing her. And how are you? He settled on a simpler version. "We're okay. How about you?"

"We've had better weeks. Remember I told you about the witness we mislaid? Somebody broke into her office over the weekend. Trashed it really good. As far as her secretary can tell, nothing's missing, but she says there wasn't anything of a personal nature there, anyway."

"What do you think they were looking for?"

"Clues to where she's gone. But she's too smart to leave anything like that lying around."

"You're sure about that?"

"Absolutely. So…what's going on with the Canyon County Sheriff's Department?"

Reese stretched out across the bed and opened the night-stand drawer while recounting Tommy Lee's adventures. Removing three frames from the drawer, he arranged them in a neat line on the floor beside the bed. Neely alone, with his father and Jace, and with him. She was so beautiful and looked so damn innocent, and Del was looking at her as if she was the daughter he'd always wanted.

His father had never looked at any other woman that way, Reese realized. Whenever Del had met the women in Reese's life, he'd always been polite, usually friendly, sometimes downright welcoming. But Neely was the only one he'd fallen so hard and fast for. Marriage had crossed Reese's mind only in a vague, sometime-in-the-distant-future sort of way until the meeting caught here on film, when Del had proudly commented, "That girl's going to give me smart, beautiful grandchildren."

"You there, bubba?"

Reese blinked. "Yeah. I was just thinking…"

"About a pretty woman, I hope."

"Actually, about Dad." It was sort of true. "Did I tell you he's thinking about getting married again?"

"You're kidding. I hope this one's like Georgie. She certainly inspired a few fantasies in this young boy."

"This one's a widow with a Mercedes, and that's all I know."

"Usually Uncle Del talks more than that. Of course, you've got a good reason or two to be distracted."

"I'm not—" Realizing he was stroking his fingertip over Neely's image in the photo where she was alone, he scowled, jerked his hand away and rolled onto his back.

Jace laughed. "I'll ask Mom about the widow. I'm sure she knows a lot more than you do."

"I'm sure she does. If she ever wants to get paid for her ability to ferret out information, send her down to my office. I'd put her on the payroll in a heartbeat."

"I'll tell her that. Take care of everything."

"I will." Catching himself by surprise, Reese blurted, "Hey, Jace... How important is that to you? That I take care of everything?"

"I don't think I understand the question, bubba."

With a grimace, Reese closed his eyes and rubbed them with his free hand. He couldn't just come right out and ask what Jace's relationship was with Neely, whether there was anything more than friendship between them. It was highly doubtful that anyone was monitoring *his* calls, but Jace couldn't be so sure. Since Neely's case was his case, he could be under the scrutiny of both the good guys and the bad. "I—I was just wondering about...your interest...in..."

Jace laughed. "Hey, if I can get off for the Fourth, I'm coming down and bringing my girlfriend with me. She's a city girl, and is convinced that towns like Heartbreak don't really exist anymore. You can figure out what you want to ask me and ask it then."

As he said goodbye, Reese was embarrassed to admit how relieved he felt. Not that a different answer would have made him want Neely any less. Knowing that she was involved with his cousin wouldn't stop him from taking anything she chose to offer. He wasn't proud of it, but there it was.

Now all he had to worry about was finding a way to stop wanting her long enough to fall asleep.

* * *

Sleep had come easier than Reese had expected. He showered the next morning and dressed for work, then walked into the living room to find Neely in her usual place, curled up in his chair. Usually he covered her, if she wasn't already covered, and left her there. That morning, because he wanted to, he scooped her into his arms, started toward the guest room, then made a U-turn and took her to his room. He laid her on his side of the bed, where the sheets still held a little of his warmth, tucked the covers around her, lowered and closed the blinds, then left the room and the house.

His first stop was the Heartbreak Café, where they were getting a slow start on a gray morning. Shay's husband Easy was among the few customers, sitting in the back booth with Guthrie Harris and Ethan James. Guthrie's girls, Emma and Elly, were spinning on stools at the counter.

Though Ethan held two-month-old Annie Grace, there was no sign of her mother. Reese was a bit disappointed. If the powers that be had offered him a kid sister, Grace would have been his choice. She was sweet, shy and innocent as hell—or, at least, she had been until she'd gotten mixed up with Ethan. Reese had thought the most disreputable son with the most dishonorable family name in the county was *not* a good choice, but Ethan had turned himself inside out for her and their baby. Reese wasn't a hundred percent sure he trusted the transformation, but Grace was, and that was all that mattered.

"Hey, Mr. Sheriff Reese!" Elly Harris jumped off the stool and landed in front of him with a flourish. "Shoot any outlaws lately?"

"No, ma'am," he replied, lifting her into his arms, then taking a seat on her vacated stool. "You know, that blood all over the place gets messy, so I try not to shoot 'em unless I have to."

Beside him Emma giggled. "You don't shoot 'em 'cause there aren't any outlaws around here."

"Hmm. You think that's why I haven't seen any lately?"

She nodded wide-eyed before going back to her breakfast.

The two girls were identical twins—so identical physically that Reese doubted even their parents could tell them apart. But everyone in town knew Elly was the tomboy, tough and sturdy and able to stand up to anyone on her own, while Emma was delicate, sensitive and—Elly's favorite word—prissy. Elly had a style all her own—today she was wearing red cowboy boots, purple jeans, a lime-green shirt and a cowboy hat cinched under her chin—while Emma was the perfect little girly girl. She wore a dress this morning, like something Neely would wear, with pink sandals, a pink bracelet and a straw hat, very much like Neely's, circled with a broad pink ribbon that tied in a bow in back.

She made him ache dead center in his chest.

He forced his attention from her to their dishes. "What are you having for breakfast? Pie and ice cream? I can tell your mom's not here."

"She's home with Taylor 'cause he's got the sniffles," Emma said of her baby brother. "But it's a good breakfast. Ice cream's made from milk, you know, and growing bones need milk."

"And pie's made from flour and eggs, and that's almost like bread," Elly added. "And it's apple, and that's fruit, and you're s'posed to have fruit, you know."

"Good argument. But I don't believe your mom will buy it for a second." He stood, set Elly on the stool, then continued to the booth.

Easy made room for him on the bench, then called, "Hey, waitress, we need some service out here!"

"I'll 'waitress' you upside the head, Ezekiel Rafferty," Shay said as she came through the swinging door from the kitchen. "Hey, Reese, how's the sheriffin' business?"

The glint in her eyes made it clear her question was more than a casual inquiry. "If you're asking if I've locked up anyone lately, the answer is no. Hell—" he glanced at the two girls a short distance away "—heck, I haven't even yelled at anyone lately but Tommy Lee, and he deserved it."

She poured coffee all around, then planted one hand on her

hip and subjected him to intense scrutiny. "You know, you look a bit tired. You probably need some time off."

"No, I don't."

"I think you do. When's the last time you took a vacation?"

"I don't know. A while back."

"When?" Guthrie asked. "I don't remember you going anywhere since you came back here."

"You don't have any room to talk. You didn't even take a honeymoon when you married Olivia."

"Yeah, but that's because I had a herd of cattle to take care of. All you have is five horses, and any one of your neighbors would be more than happy to look in on them."

Reese knew that was true. He also knew the sort of vacation Shay was recommending didn't necessarily involve *going* anywhere. But it did involve spending a lot of time with Neely, and that idea was mighty tempting. "We're short-handed at work," he said with more than a little regret. "I can't go anywhere until we replace Tommy Lee."

"Sure you can," Shay disagreed. She bent close and lowered her voice to little more than a tantalizing murmur. "You're the sheriff. You can do whatever you damn well please."

Except take time off work right now. Or take Neely someplace where she would be truly safe and anonymous. Or get her off of his mind. Or out of his system.

Hell, for someone who could do anything, he couldn't really do much at all.

A crack of thunder jarred Neely awake. She felt better rested than she had in months, but thought if she rolled over and closed her eyes, she could probably sleep another hour or two, just until the sun came up. Intending to do just that, she rolled over, snuggled under the covers and breathed deeply...of Reese.

The instant her eyes opened, her gaze fell on the window seat that looked out onto the front porch, and next she saw the safe room door. She was in his room, she realized. In his *bed.* How on earth… There were only two ways she could have gotten there—under her own power, or in Reese's arms. Since she couldn't imagine the first, it must have been the second. But why would he put her in his bed when her own room was just as close? A not-too-subtle hint that he wanted her there? Or had he realized why she wound up asleep in his chair practically every morning? Because it *was* his. She felt safe there, and the dreams left her alone there.

But safe as his chair was, his bed was that and a lot more comfortable. She stretched, then curled into a ball on her side…and caught sight of the alarm clock. It was nearly two o'clock! She'd slept half the day away—and it had felt so good.

She slid out of bed, straightened the covers, then peeked out the blinds. Last night's nice breeze was a full-blown wind this afternoon, and the sky was dark with pewter-colored clouds. The golden outline at the distant edge of the cloud bank hinted at the brilliant sun that shone somewhere, but the light here was harsh, eerie, with a faint greenish tinge.

But by the time she'd showered and dressed, the sky was clear, the clouds were puffy and white, and the day looked hot enough to broil. Neely made a sandwich from leftover ham, took pop and some chocolate and stretched out on the sofa with one of her books. She was finishing both the chocolates and the book when Reese came home. The memory of waking up in his bed that morning made her suddenly shy. She couldn't quite meet his gaze when she said hi.

He removed his gun belt, then sat and dangled it over one bent knee. "It is hot out there."

"It looks it." She thumbed the book's pages, then asked, "Have a good day?"

He shrugged. "On the car my deputy wrecked, it'll take about twice as much to fix it as it's worth. On the brighter side, I hired a new deputy. He's got experience, and he didn't whine about the salary." He gave her a sidelong look. "My deputies are seriously underpaid."

"They shouldn't be."

He blinked and looked at her again, making her squirm. "I don't hate cops, Reese. I just hate corrupt ones. And so do you. If you didn't, you would have kept in touch with your fellow officers in Thomasville when you left, at least for a while."

"How do you know I didn't?"

"Because Dave Dugan was quite proud of the fact that he'd shot me. He would have bragged about it to you. He would have expected your gratitude."

"He wouldn't have gotten it."

She believed him—believed that as much as he'd blamed her for Judy's death, he would have been appalled by Dugan's decision to shoot her for it.

"Why didn't you demand that the D.A. bring charges against him?"

She smiled ruefully. "I was fortunate to get out of there alive. I wasn't going to push my luck."

"What else did they do?"

Laying the book aside, she sat up and tucked her skirt around her legs. Part of her wanted to lie—to brush off the harassment, the vandalism and the threats. She wanted to say it was no big deal, nothing to be curious about. Truthfully, she didn't want to give him anything else to feel guilty about.

But when she opened her mouth, no denial came. "The day I went home from the hospital, all the windows in my house had been smashed. They slashed my tires. They spray-painted obscenities across the front of the house. I got threatening phone calls, changed my number and continued to get them. I was run off the road twice. I lost every single client I had. Some left voluntarily. Others were warned of the consequences of associating with me. And my office was burned to the ground. That's when I left."

With each sentence, Reese's expression had grown grimmer. His look was harsh, and so was his voice when he asked, "What happened when you reported the incidents to the sheriff?"

"I'd call 9-1-1, and the dispatcher said she would send a

car around. Sometimes a deputy would show up three or four hours later. He would smirk and spout something about kids these days. The other times no one ever showed up.''

''You shouldn't have let them get away with it. Once you'd moved out of their jurisdiction, you should have gone to the FBI or the state attorney general or the Kansas Bureau of Investigation. You should have stopped them.''

''I'd been shot by a cop because *he'd* mishandled a case and gotten it thrown out of court. My practice was destroyed. You had left me without a word. A woman was dead because of me. Every time I left the house, I was afraid I would be killed. Every day I didn't go out, I was afraid they were winning, afraid they were controlling my life.'' She remembered the helplessness and the overwhelming fear with a shudder that made her voice quake. ''I didn't have the strength, physically or emotionally, to fight them any longer. I stuck it out for a month, and then I got out before they succeeded at killing me.''

As if too restless to sit still any longer, he popped up from the chair and paced to the window to stare out. ''Do you really think they would have killed you?'' There was no skepticism in his voice, no condescending just-a-little-woman-over-reacting tone. He was dead serious. He wanted to know.

Neely hesitantly approached him, then veered off to one side before reaching him. She took a position next to the window, facing him with his stony expression, his granite-hard jaw, his flint-tough eyes. She folded her arms across her chest to contain the shivers, and to stop herself from reaching for him, and she schooled her voice into a quiet, unemotional tenor. ''Late one night I got a call from Doreen Hughes.'' Doreen had been a secretary at the local middle school and was married to Reggie Hughes, chief investigator for the Keegan County Sheriff's Department. Neely and Reese had done much of their socializing with Doreen and Reggie, Dave and his girlfriend du jour and other deputies. None of them had accepted her, though. They'd tolerated her for Reese's sake, and she'd put up with them for the same reason.

"She was distraught, crying. She pleaded with me to meet her at the office at eleven o'clock that night. She said Reggie had hit her, threatened her, and she was afraid he was going to kill her. She wanted my help. I agreed—stupidly. By then I was pretty paranoid. I expected something bad to happen every time I left the house. I got to the office early, turned on the lights and waited. A few minutes before eleven, Doreen called. She said she was running late and she begged me to wait. I said I would…but I panicked. I left by the back door, left the lights on and my car in the parking lot, and I went across the street to the library and hid in the shadows. Doreen never showed up, but about 11:15, an orange pickup full of men wearing ski masks arrived."

She saw Reese flinch. The only orange pickup in all of Thomasville, probably in all of Keegan County, had belonged to a young man by the name of Dub—another of the sheriff's badge-wearing finest.

"Some of them had gas cans. Some had two-by-fours and hammers. They nailed both doors shut while the others spread the gasoline around. When they were done, they lit the gasoline, stood back, broke out the beer and had a party while they watched the building burn." Believing that *she* was trapped inside. Men who had sworn to uphold the law, to serve and protect the citizens where they lived, had celebrated in the mistaken belief that they were roasting one of those citizens alive.

"I crawled around to the back side of the library, and then I ran all the way home and called Jace. He drove out from the city, and we got the hell out."

Finished, she waited for Reese to say something, but he continued to stare out the window. His face was pale, his eyes dark, his skin stretched taut across his cheekbones. His breathing was shallow and rigidly controlled, but he couldn't control the twitch of a muscle working in his jaw.

"That was the long answer," she said softly. "The short answer is yes. I believe they would have killed me."

Abruptly he spun around and strode away—into the kitchen,

out the French door and across the deck. Feeling…bereft, Neely remained where she was for a long time, then just as suddenly, she went after him.

By the time she reached the steps, he was approaching the barn. She ignored the blazing heat that brought an instant sheen of perspiration to her skin, and the rocks, twigs and acorns that pricked her bare feet, and the smell of horses, made more pungent by the sun. Catching up with him at the door, she grabbed his arm with enough suppressed emotion to swing him around. "Stop walking away from me!" she shouted, so angry she wanted to scream, stamp her feet, throw things.

"How am I supposed to look at you?" he shouted back.

Hurt sliced through her. She released his wrist and took a step back. "I—I'm sorry. I didn't realize you found me so…"

"I should have been there! I should have put a stop to it, protected you, taken you away! I should have…" Making a frustrated, anguished sound, he turned away and paced to the end of the barn. When he finally spoke again, his voice was low with defeat, but Neely didn't move closer. She could hear.

"That last time, Judy had had enough. She was going to leave town—go someplace where Leon couldn't find her and start a new life. I persuaded her to stay. I convinced her to go through with the trial by promising that we would protect her. That *I* would protect her. That this time Leon would go to prison and he wouldn't be able to hurt her again. I promised her, and she believed me."

And instead Leon had walked out a free man and killed her. And for Reese, as everyone else, it had been easier to blame Neely than himself.

"I let her down, and it cost her life. I let you down, and it damn near cost your life."

She smiled tearfully, even though he couldn't see it. "But you never promised to protect me."

"I should have been there. Jace hardly even knew you, but he was there when you needed him. I should have been…"

If Reese hadn't stuck Jace's business card, with his home number scrawled across the back, on her refrigerator, Neely figured she would have been dead long before she'd found anyone close enough to help. She'd rousted Jace out of bed, explained to him who she was—after all, they'd met only twice before—and begged for his help, and, because of Reese, he'd given it. He'd saved her life.

She made her way carefully across the dirt floor, stopping behind Reese. She hesitated, her hand inches from touching him, then took a breath and slid her arms around his middle. He remained stiff and unyielding, but she held him, anyway. "It's not your fault. None of this would have happened if I hadn't objected to Leon's confession or his treatment at the hands of the deputies..."

"The confession was inadmissible," he said harshly, "and the beating was a violation of his civil rights."

"But his rights to a fair trial weren't more important than his wife's right to live."

Turning, he gave her an intensely serious look. "Don't start blaming yourself, Neely. Don't change your beliefs to make me feel better. If Dugan and the others hadn't beaten the confession out of him, chances are very good that Leon would have gone to jail and Judy would be alive today."

Neely knew he was right. Leon Miller hadn't been a very likable man. He wouldn't have engendered trust or sympathy in the jurors, wouldn't have found any leeway with the judge. *She* hadn't liked him at all and she hadn't wanted him released. She just hadn't been able to watch him get convicted on the basis of a tainted confession and do nothing about it.

And so she had done something, and a violent man had gone free and an innocent woman had died.

She sank down on a nearby bale of hay. Oh, God, Reese had been right in all those arguments. Fairness had nothing to do with justice. In the bigger scheme of things, what did it matter if Leon Miller's rights were violated? He had been guilty. Period. No doubt about it. He should have gone to prison for a very long time. He should have been locked away like the uncontrollable animal he was. *That* would have been justice.

She covered her face with both hands, rubbing away the weariness there, then sighed. "I'm like a surgeon who meticulously repairs a minor cut without caring that the patient's got a severed artery. Sure, he'll bleed to death in a minute, but hey, look how neatly sutured that cut is. What did it matter that Judy and Leon both died that day? At least his civil rights weren't violated. To me, that was all that mattered."

Reese sat beside her, his leg brushing hers. "That wasn't all that mattered to you," he disagreed. It had been too important, in his opinion, but she'd cared about her cases—about her clients and their victims. She'd cared about justice, fairness and doing the right thing. She just hadn't realized that there wasn't always a right thing, that sometimes the choice was between the least wrong things, or that fairness for her client usually didn't translate into justice for their victims.

And he was no better—was worse, in fact. Her failing had been one of ideology. His had been a character flaw—the inability to accept responsibility and blame for what he'd done. The lack of courage to ignore the easy way out and instead take the honorable route. She'd been naive. He'd been a coward.

"I didn't know what was going on, Neely, I swear. If I had, I would have gone back." He believed it—truly believed the threat against the woman he'd still loved would have overcome the guilt, the anger and everything else. He never would have allowed the harassment and the threats to continue.

She didn't say anything. Not, *I know*, or *I believe you*. Not, *Yeah, right, easy to say now*. She didn't point out that he didn't know because he'd left her in so dishonorable a way, or that he'd known what kind of men he'd worked with and should have known what they were capable of.

Honest to God, he hadn't. He'd known that they considered more than a few laws open to interpretation, that they were likely to let their buddies or the county's influential leaders slide by on minor offenses, that occasionally they misused their authority to give someone's ex a hard time. He'd known they weren't sticklers for following the letter of the law, and that a few prisoners showed up for booking with bruises or a black eye they hadn't sported earlier. But he'd never believed, not for an instant, that one of them would deliberately shoot Neely in front of two dozen witnesses. The thought had never even crossed his mind that they would try to kill her, and in such a cold-blooded fashion.

For whatever it was worth, if they'd succeeded, and come bragging to him, he would have killed every last one of them with his bare hands. And then the State of Kansas could have locked him away forever, because he would have had nothing left to live for.

Neely swayed to one side, bumping his shoulder. "Remember when you were a kid, playing games, and you messed up your turn really badly, sometimes the other kids would let you call 'do-over.'" She smiled regretfully. "I'd like a do-over on that part of my life. There are so many things I'd like to change…except you. The only thing I'd do differently with you is not give you a reason to leave me."

"You didn't give me a reason. You didn't do anything in the Miller case that you hadn't done before."

"I never got anyone killed before."

Reese looked at her. She was one of the most capable career women he'd known, and yet somehow, except for that sad, regretful expression on her face, she looked as if she belonged beside him on a hay bale in his barn—to say nothing of in his house, in his chair, in his bed. She looked like the best thing to ever happen to him, and the biggest mistake he'd ever made, tied up in one. He wasn't sure he could survive another mistake with her.

"You've never gotten anyone killed," he said quietly. "There's plenty of blame to go around for that, and very little of it is yours."

She smiled tightly, unconvinced, then they sat in silence for a time, until finally he stood. "Want to meet my horses?"

"Sure."

He pulled her to her feet, then outside into the hot sun. Most of the pasture was fenced with barbed wire, but the sides surrounding the yard were board, old, warped, unpainted and worn to the same silvery gray as the barn. He rested his arms on the top rail, then pointed out each of the horses in turn. "That one over by the water is Lucky. The one pretending we're not here is Rio, and those two—" he gestured to two nearly identical geldings "—are Walker and Morgan…or Morgan and Walker. And that paint back there by himself is Rowdy."

She mimicked his position, then rested her chin on her arms. "Which one do you ride?"

"All of them from time to time, but mostly Rio."

"And which one did you let 'Ride me, cowboy' use?"

"Rowdy. His name is deceiving." He whistled, and the paint ambled over, in no hurry at all to answer the summons. Rowdy was the gentlest, most even-tempered and laziest of the bunch. He would never throw a rider, no matter how inept, because it would take too much energy.

But the paint surprised him. When Neely reached out to pet him, the gelding bared his teeth, tossed his head, then snapped at her.

"Hey, stop that." Reese folded his hand around hers and pulled it back, then apologetically said, "He's usually not testy with women." Or men, kids, pesky dogs or even horseflies.

"I suppose he warmed right up to 'Hey, cowboy—' What *is* her name?"

He told her, and she snorted. "Isabella. Figures. The idiot warmed right up to her, didn't he?"

"Well…yeah. But she talked sweet to him."

"He wasn't the only male she sweet-talked around here, was he?" she murmured sourly.

"No, he wasn't. And how many men have *you* sweet-talked in the past nine years? How many have you given that innocent, wicked, womanly waif look?"

She responded by looking at him in exactly that way. "We're talking about you, not me."

"Actually, we're talking about Isabella."

"Who has a thing for you."

Reese called Lucky over, then moved to stand behind Neely, trapping her between him and the fence. Holding her hand, he stroked her fingers over the horse's nose, then his neck, then slowly eased his own hand back. Though he didn't need to stick close—no way Lucky was going to give up a good scratching in favor of a bite—he did, anyway, just because it felt so damn good. "You've never even met her. You heard *one* short message, and you think you know what she wants?"

"'Hey, cowboy, this soreness will be gone in a day or two. When can you saddle me up for another go-round?'" she drawled in a passable imitation of Isabella's sultry, sexy voice. "You honestly think she was talking about ol' Rowdy there?"

"You think?" He pretended to consider it. "Maybe I should see if she's free for dinner tonight."

"Go right ahead. And maybe I won't hot-wire your sheriff's truck and take it for a spin." She smiled that incredibly innocent smile. "I always did want to go a hundred and twenty miles an hour with lights flashing and siren blaring."

"You don't know how to hot-wire an engine."

"Look at the people I've dealt with in the past ten years. Car thieves, burglars, check kiters, prostitutes, murderers...I might have picked up all sorts of questionable skills."

He wondered what she'd learned from the prostitutes and what it would take to persuade her to show him. He bent close to her ear and smelled the almond fragrance of her hair, the honeysuckle on her skin, the faint whiff of fabric softener from her dress, and a fainter, more tantalizing scent. Exotic, elusive, erotic. Neely herself.

"I don't believe you," he murmured between deep breaths. "If you could hot-wire my truck, you would have been gone a week ago."

"Maybe I've just been waiting to catch you off guard," she replied, then added, "I imagine *she* has all sorts of unspeakable skills."

"Hmm." Reese closed his eyes and breathed deeply of all

her scents, then choked the air out in a cough when she slapped his arm. "What was that for?"

"Nothing," she replied with a sweet smile.

"Assaulting a police officer is a serious offense. I'd hate to have to slap the handcuffs on you and haul you in."

"Liar."

She was right—he was lying. He'd like nothing better than to haul her into the house, handcuff her to his bed and keep her there until this damnable need for her had been satisfied. When she turned to face him, he knew she wanted it, too, by the smoky haze that turned her eyes a softer brown, by the way her breathing had grown shallow and the way her lips parted, inviting his kiss. He didn't bother to look beyond those signals—didn't acknowledge the doubt in her eyes or the nervous flutter of her pulse. He refused to even see her hesitance, her reluctance, her uncertainty.

He just kissed her. Took her mouth. Tasted her. Teased her. Tormented himself. He backed her against the fence and held her there with his body, stroked her tongue with his, fed her desire with his. He was thinking about heat, lust, rolls in the hay, getting down and dirty, when a wet tongue slurped across his ear. For an instant he didn't know what to think, then regrettably the instant passed as the tongue made another swipe.

Jerking away from Neely, sputtering curses, he staggered back a few steps, then dragged his shirtsleeve across his ear and neck. "Damnation! What in the hell do you think you're doing?"

Neely looked bewildered, but beside her, Reese swore, Lucky looked as if he was grinning. Reese scrubbed harder at his ear as he glared at the animal. "It's a damned good thing you're already gelded, you worthless piece of horsemeat, because if you weren't, you would be by this time tomorrow."

Lucky really did grin, then rubbed against Neely, who was trying her best not to laugh. He scowled at her, then more fiercely at the horse.

"Looks like you've got some competition for the girl's affection."

Reese whirled around, automatically stepping in front of Neely, blocking her from view. He recognized his father's voice, of course. He was just surprised that Del had managed to sneak up on them without him hearing a thing. "Dad."

"Son." Del leaned to one side to see past him, but Reese didn't cooperate.

"Actually..." Neely slid out from behind him and smiled. "I think *I've* got some competition for Reese's affection. Micky was kissing *him*, not me. Hello, Mr. Barnett."

Del clasped her hand in both of his, then pulled her into his arms. "Neely Madison! I didn't know... He didn't tell me... I can't tell you how glad I am to see you. You know, I'd always hoped you two would patch things up. You were the best thing ever happened to that boy, in my opinion." He held her at arm's length for a quick look. "You were always a beautiful girl, but, darlin', you've grown into one hell of a beautiful woman—pardon my language. How about leaving the boy here and you and me running away together?"

Del Barnett could sweet talk with the best of 'em, Reese thought, but there was no exaggeration there. She *had* been the best thing in his life, and she was one hell of a beautiful woman.

"So...you're here to stay." Del said it as fact. That was what he wanted, and so he wasn't open to other possibilities. "We'll have to introduce you around. We can have a cookout this weekend—"

"Not so quick, Dad," Reese interrupted, then changed the subject. "What brings you all the way over from Buffalo Plains?"

Del's smile dimmed and he became serious. "I wanted you to know before you heard it from someone else. Remember I told you I was thinking about getting married again? We set a date—the end of July. I brought her over so you two could start getting acquainted."

Reese looked past him to the silver Mercedes barely visibl in the driveway. "Where is she?"

"Waiting on the front porch. Come on." He tucked Neely' hand in the crook of his arm and set off across the yard "She's gonna love you, Neely. A son, a daughter-in-law maybe grandbabies real soon. I keep telling Reese, if he wait much longer, I'm gonna be too old to be a grandfather. If I' known how stubborn he was going to be, he never would hav been an only child."

"I take after you, Dad," Reese mumbled. "Except I don' marry every beautiful woman I meet."

"I heard that, son."

"I intended for you to," Reese lied as he followed them uj the steps to the deck.

At the back door, Del came to a sudden stop. "Now, sor you behave yourself. Be polite and respectful—"

"Dad, I've been through this before. And it may surpris you, but I pretty much behave all the time." Though h sounded aggravated, he wasn't. He didn't mind his father' nagging, especially when it made Neely smile.

They filed through the house to the front door. Del wen out, disappeared to the side for a moment, then reappeared "Reese, Neely, say hello to the latest—and last—woman it my life." He held out his hand and, after a pause, the futur Mrs. Barnett laid her hand in his and stepped into view.

Reese's gaze caught on the enormous ruby ring on her hand A widow with a Mercedes implied money. That ring suggeste a lot of it. He was hoping his father knew what he was getting in to—hoped the widow knew what *she* was getting in to— when she spoke.

"Hello, Reese. You…you look good. We're a few year late, but…your father and I are finally getting married. We'r going to officially be a family now. Isn't that wonderful?"

He stared at her as if he'd never seen her before, and wishee he hadn't. He looked her over from the top of her perfectl styled blond hair down to her feet in three-inch heels that matched her suit, and his jaw tightened. ''You guys be a family,'' he said derisively. ''But it'll be a cold day in hell before there will be a place for you in *my* life.''

Chapter 9

Neely stood at the living-room window, leaning one shoulder against the frame, and stared out though her eyes were gritty and her vision was blurry. It was nearly 2:00 a.m. and she was tired, but too restless by far to sleep.

It had been an interesting evening. A heavy-duty conversation with Reese. An incredible kiss. The surprise visit from his father with his soon-to-be mother.

His mother.

After making his pronouncement, Reese had stormed out of the house. Del had followed, leaving Neely and Lena Harlowe Winchester embarrassedly exchanging chitchat while listening to Reese and Del's shouting match on the deck. After a time, Del had come back in, muttering about hard heads, stubborn mules and tanning hides. He'd grabbed Lena's arm and stomped out. As the front door slammed, so had the back door. Reese had gone straight to his room, changed clothes and was gone before she could think of anything to say.

She'd eaten dinner alone, tried to watch television, tried to read. Finally she'd gotten ready for bed, shut off the lights, turned on the stereo and sat down to wait. Then paced. Then stood. She was thinking about curling up in the leather chair when headlights creeping up the driveway caught her attention. Her first response was relief that Reese was home. A few minutes later, he came inside the house and she went to the hallway to meet him.

It took a long time for the heavy garage door to close again, and a longer time for Reese to stumble inside. Muttering to himself, he turned on the hall light, then made several efforts to reset the alarm before succeeding. When he saw her, he grinned. ''Neely. What are you doing up?''

If the overwhelming odor of alcohol wasn't enough to tell her he was drunk, his unsteady gait, glazed eyes and carefully enunciated words were. He'd never been much of a drinker, but she'd seen him intoxicated a few times and remembered that the tipsier he got, the more precise his speech became.

''I was waiting to see if you made it home in one piece. Since you did, I believe I'll go to bed.''

He stepped forward, blocking her way. ''How about picking up where we were when Lucky interrupted us?''

She thought of the kiss—sweet and hot and leading up to oh, so much more—and shook her head. ''I don't think so. It's late and I'm tired.''

He caught her arm and pulled her close. ''Oh, come on, Neely,'' he coaxed. ''You can sleep all day tomorrow. Come and play with me.'' His hands slid down to her bottom, lifting her against his arousal, and his mouth brushed her ear. ''Come and let me play with you.''

She wished she could say the shiver that rocketed through her was born of distaste that their first time together after nine years should be a drunken tumble that would mean nothing more to him than easy gratification—provided he remembered it at all in the morning—but while she might be that noble, her long-deprived-of-any-satisfaction body wasn't.

''Reese, let go.'' She tried to wriggle loose but succeeded in only bringing herself into even more intimate contact with him. It would be so easy—remove her shorts, open his jeans, indulge in the sweetest pleasure she'd ever known. She wanted it, wanted him, even if he didn't remember in the morning. Even if he was only using her. Even if sexy Isabella would do as well—even better.

Even if she would have trouble facing herself in the morning.

"Don't be difficult, darlin'. You know you want it, and the devil knows, I can't hide that I do, too." He moved suggestively against her, then started backing her toward his bedroom. She tried to hold her ground, but he was bigger, stronger and more determined, and her feet, in thick socks that belonged to him, glided over the wood floor like skates on ice.

There were legitimate reasons why she shouldn't do this, Neely reminded herself when the mattress bumped her knees. Reasons why they would both be filled with regret. But when he released her with one hand to remove his T-shirt, when he unfastened his jeans and, with some effort, kicked them off, then tumbled her down onto the bed and stripped her shirt over her head, when he was naked and she was halfway there… Who cared a damn about reasons?

Pinning her wrists at her sides, he slid down her body, one hard-muscled thigh between hers, and took her nipple in his mouth. She gasped, feeling the erotic tug through her entire body. She should have more pride, more dignity, some part of her demanded. She should be fighting, screaming—should refuse to submit to a meaningless drunken grope. But she'd thought he would never want her again, had thought she would never have him again, and it had been such a long time…such a lonely time…

His hold on her relaxed, then he released her wrists and restrained her in a much more sensual manner—with caresses so gentle, so expert. He stroked her face, her breasts, her ribs, underneath the elastic waist of her shorts, over her belly. He suckled her nipples, made her muscles quiver, her skin ripple, and sent her temperature sky-high. It was so familiar—she swore her body remembered the shape of his fingers, the pressure of his touches, recognized the makeup of his very cells—so gentle, so sweet.

It made her cry.

She tried to be quiet, but a sound that was a cross between a hiccup and a sob escaped her. His caresses stopped, and he wrapped his arms around her, kissed away her tears, patted her awkwardly. "It's okay," he said, his words slurring as exhaustion caught up with drunkenness. "Don't cry, baby. I won't let anything happen to you. I'll keep you safe. I swear I will."

Within moments, he was snoring softly, oblivious to the world. Feeling heartsick and blue, Neely eased out of his embrace, stood, then gazed at him. *I'll keep you safe,* he'd promised.

But who would keep her safe from him?

Some mornings it didn't pay to be alive, and today was one of them.

Reese made that realization, along with several others, the instant he tried to roll over. That he was suffering the hangover from hell. That he'd slept sideways on the bed. And that someone's shirt was wrapped around his hand.

Neely's.

In spite of the pain, he lifted his head to squint around the room. Judging by the light outside, he was several hours late for work, and judging by the odors that came from both him and the bedcovers, he'd spent much of last night in a bar. But nothing offered a clue as to how he'd wound up with Neely's nightshirt knotted around his hand.

Unsure whether the queasiness in his stomach came from the hangover or the ugly suspicions her thin little top roused, he worked his way to his feet, swayed unsteadily, then made it to the bathroom in time to empty his stomach. He tried to not look at himself in the mirror while he brushed his teeth because the image was more than a little scary—hair standing on end, badly in need of a shave, bloodshot eyes filled with guilt and fear. If he'd hurt her...

Grimly, he pulled on jeans and a clean shirt and went looking for her. He found her in one of the rockers on the front porch, feet drawn into the seat, skirt tucked around her legs, an afghan from the couch wrapped around her shoulders like a shawl. She looked troubled.

Wounded.

The fear in his gut knotted. Taking the ragged breaths that were all he could manage, he crouched in front of her and off to the side, careful not to block her in.

She looked at him and smiled distantly. "Good morning."

He couldn't repeat such a benign greeting when he might have... "About...about last night..."

The distance moved from her smile to her eyes. "Don't worry about it."

He watched her fingers tighten around the afghan until her knuckles turned white and felt a corresponding tightening in his jaw, his chest, his own muscles. "I *am* worried. You—I—" Taking a breath, he blurted out the worst question he could ever imagine asking. "Did I rape you?"

For an instant, she looked as shocked as he felt, then immediately she shook her head. "*No!* Of course not."

"Did I hurt you?"

"No." Her smile was tinged with regret. "You didn't even have sex with me."

"Then why did I wake up with the shirt you sleep in in my hand?"

"I didn't say we didn't *start* to have sex. But you'd had a lot to drink, and you were tired."

"When we...*started* to have sex...were you willing, or did I force you?"

For a long moment she simply looked at him, then she smiled that innocent, wicked smile. "When have I ever been unwilling with you?"

He leaned back against the railing and studied her. He would bet his life that she was being truthful...but he would also bet that she was keeping something back. Something he'd done or said last night, or maybe something she'd said.

As a stiff breeze rustled through the blackjacks, bringing with it the smell of rain, he said, "I'm sorry."

"For what? Starting something you couldn't finish?"

"Drinking too much. Being too tired. Not remembering. I'm sorry about the argument with my father and going off the way I did." He managed a poor imitation of a grin. "I'm *very* sorry I don't remember seeing you without that shirt last night."

She smiled, then gazed past him. "It's hard to believe it was ninety-some degrees yesterday and cool enough for a jacket today."

"You know what they say about Oklahoma weather. If you don't like it, wait five minutes. It'll change."

"I thought they said that about Texas."

"They probably say it about most places, but according to popular myth, Will Rogers said it about Oklahoma first. Of course, that myth can't be proven as fact." With the muscles in his thighs starting to cramp, he stood, pulled the other rocker close and sat beside her, propping his feet on the railing. "I acted like a jerk yesterday, didn't I?"

"Not really. Your father dropped a pretty big surprise on you. You weren't prepared for it."

He gave a dismayed shake of his head at the memory of seeing his mother for the first time in twenty years. "Lena was in and out of our lives from the time I was a baby. She wouldn't stay, and she wouldn't stay away. I don't know how many times she broke his heart…but I can tell you exactly how many times she broke mine. Do you know how it feels to know your mother doesn't want you? I called her by her name because she didn't want to be anyone's mom. She treated me like a nephew or the child of a friend—someone she had a connection to, but nothing really significant. She was hardly ever around when I was growing up and needed a mother, and when she was around, it was for him, not me. And now she thinks she can come back and like that—" he snapped his fingers "—we can be a *family?*"

"You don't have to be a part of her family," Neely said

quietly. "I don't think anyone would expect that of you, certainly not right away. You may never be able to have that sort of relationship with her. But you do have to show her the respect your father's wife is entitled to."

"Or I could just pretend she doesn't exist." That was what he'd done with Neely all those years, and he'd gotten by all right...sort of. More or less.

"You could," she agreed with a tight, melancholy smile.

Troubled by that smile, Reese freed her hand from the afghan's folds and wrapped his fingers tightly around hers. "What did I do that makes you so blue?"

Her laughter sounded forced. "You think I don't have enough reasons to be blue without throwing you into the mix?"

"Look at me and swear I didn't do anything to hurt you last night."

Piercing him with a sharp, defensive gaze, she quietly said, "You didn't hurt me. You were persuasive. Gentle. You touched me the way you used to touch me. You kissed me the way you used to. You did damn near everything just like you used to."

"And this is a problem because...?"

She pulled away from him—not with anger or frustration, but merely eased her fingers out of his grip—and stood, letting the afghan puddle in the rocker seat. "Because you used to make love to me, and last night was just about sex, and you know what? I couldn't tell the difference."

Reese's throat went dry. He lowered his feet to the floor and slowly stood. They faced each other as the rain started falling in big fat drops that plopped and splattered. "Are you suggesting that I'm still in love with you?"

"No." Her voice quavered, and her eyes turned liquid. "I'm suggesting that you never were."

For a long moment they stared at each other. Part of him wanted to argue, to swear on his life that he'd loved her desperately all those years ago. But if that was true—and it was—and if what she said was true... Could he have fallen in love with her again? Was it possible he'd never stopped loving her in the first place?

Anything was possible. Shay had never stopped loving Easy in the eight years they'd been apart. Apparently his father had never gotten over Lena. And he...he certainly still felt *something* for Neely. He couldn't say it was love—he'd been too angry for too long to even consider the possibility so easily— but it was stronger than the best emotions he'd been able to summon for all the women since her combined.

Surprisingly his hand was steady when he raised it. Not much else about him was. He brushed his fingers gently across her cheek. "Neely..."

For one brief moment she leaned into his touch. Then she took a deep breath, wiped her eyes and stepped back. "I'm sorry. I'm not usually so emotional. It's just..."

"Your life has been turned upside down—again." His hand tingled where it had touched her, and he wanted nothing more than to pull her close and touch her again. Hold her, kiss her, do all the things they'd done last night and more. By the time they were finished, she wouldn't have the energy to wonder whether they'd made love or had sex. He wouldn't have the energy to care that it was probably both.

"I seem to have a knack for making things go wrong," she remarked with a feeble smile.

"You have a knack for pissing off the bad guys—which means you're doing your job right."

"Doing it right isn't such a great thing. It's cost me way too much."

Instinctively he knew she was talking about him. It said something for her that she could regret that after all he'd put her through. "You couldn't do it any other way. It's not who you are." After a moment of watching her watch the rain, he impulsively said, "Let's go somewhere."

"Don't you have to work?"

"I'm already four hours late. I'll call in."

"Where would we go?"

"Tulsa. Have lunch. See a movie. Go to the zoo."

"The zoo?" Her smile started weakly but turned into pure delight. "I haven't been to the zoo in years. But...are you sure it's safe?"

"You have no ties to Tulsa. Neither does Eddie Forbes. And Mohawk Zoo isn't the sort of place drug dealers and hit men hang out. But if you'd feel more comfortable, we can catch a movie. We'll sit in the darkest corner where no one can come up behind us, and we can neck in the boring parts." Or they could skip the movie, the zoo and Tulsa altogether and go straight to the necking. He couldn't think of a better way to spend a cool, rainy June day than naked in bed with Neely.

"Sounds wonderful," she agreed.

He ushered her inside, called his office and listened to the dispatcher's complaints about his no-show, answering his phone and personal responsibility before he finally got Brady on the phone. Reese gave him the vaguest of explanations, then took a quick shower and dressed.

They were at the garage door, ready to walk out, when Neely asked, "Aren't you forgetting something?"

His wallet was in his hip pocket, along with his sheriff's commission, his pistol was tucked under his shirt at the small of his back, his keys were in his left hand and his cell phone was in the right. "I don't think so."

She pointed downward and, when his gaze followed, wiggled her toes. "I admit, I've never been to Tulsa, but I understand most people there wear shoes."

He got a pair of thick-soled sandals for her, watched while she somehow managed to gracefully put them on with nothing more than the wall for support, then followed her to his truck.

"You're lucky you didn't kill yourself or someone else driving home last night," she remarked as he backed out of the garage.

"I didn't drive. I called two of my deputies. One drove me home in my truck and the other followed in his car so my driver would have a ride back to the station."

"Good, because driving in your condition would have been just plain stupid."

"But leaving you alone all evening was none too bright."

"I'm as safe alone at night as I am during the day."

"Actually, I was thinking about your...willingness last night and where it could have led if I'd been sober."

"If you'd been sober, you probably wouldn't even have started it."

He glanced at her, sitting with her hands folded primly in her lap. In her pastel summer dress, she looked like a watercolor painting come to life—beautiful, soft, exquisite. Just looking at her made his chest tighten and a lump form in his throat.

Directing his gaze back to the street, he murmured, "If I'd been sober, darlin', I would have started it...and I damn well would have finished it.

"Eventually."

She gave him a measuring look, but said nothing. When she did finally speak, she turned the conversation to nothing important—music, movies, food. He already knew she liked rock and jazz, comedies and love stories with happy endings, Mexican food and thick, juicy rare steaks, while he preferred country music, adventure movies and...well, thick, juicy rare steaks. He knew her better than anyone else in his life. In one short year, she'd become the better part of him.

And yet she doubted whether he'd ever really loved her.

"Oklahoma's a pretty place," she remarked as they crossed Lake Keystone. "I like all the trees and hills."

"So do I. It's a good place to live. A good place to raise a family."

"Your father seems to agree. He's anxious for grandkids."

Reese grinned. "He's spent half my life extolling the virtues of birth control and safe sex. Now, suddenly, his 'grandfather' clock is ticking, and he can't wait for me to throw the condoms in the trash."

"So why are you making him wait? He's not getting any younger, you know."

"You don't have kids with just anyone." Not all women were mother material. He and Lena were living proof of that.

Of course, he was fully capable of raising a child alone, but having grown up without a mother himself, he'd rather not put his own child through that.

"So you're being terribly romantic and conventional by looking for that special someone you can fall in love with," she teased.

A flush heated his face. "All my kids are going to have the same mother—one who lives in the same house with us and gets them up in the morning and tucks them in bed with kisses at night. That means I'm getting married only once. And that means I've got to get it right the first time."

But he'd already blown the first time. As Shay had pointed out, second chances didn't come along every day. He had to get it right this time.

Or he would regret it forever.

Neely had had far more sophisticated outings—fabulous food in legendary restaurants, cream-of-the-social-crop fund-raisers, evenings at the symphony, the ballet, the theater—but she had never enjoyed any of them as much as she enjoyed her afternoon in Tulsa.

For lunch Reese had introduced her to the best burgers in town, and they'd agreed on an adventure for their movie. True to his word, they'd sat in the darkest corner of the stadium-style theater.

But there weren't any boring parts in the movie to neck through. Darn.

Now, as the lights came up in the cavernous room, she stretched. "I really needed this—to just feel normal for a while."

Reese gave her a lazy, relaxed look, as if he'd needed it, too. "Once this is over and Jace has Forbes locked away, you'll wonder how in hell you're going to adjust to things being normal all the time—at least, until the next time."

When he stood, so did she, but she let him go down the stairs first. "There won't be a next time. I told you, I'm getting out of the lawyering business."

"And what will you do instead?"

"I don't know. I could go someplace that has Medieval fairs and be a kissing wench." When he snorted, she slapped his shoulder. "It's a real job. I knew a girl in college who did it during the summer. Or I could sell real estate. Misrepresenting property can't be too different from misrepresenting people, except the properties don't get hurt. Or maybe I'll start a family and be a full-time mom."

He stopped so abruptly that she ran into him, then stumbled back. She was about to sit on the steps—hard, she feared—when he caught a handful of her dress and hauled her upright again. "And just where do you expect to find the father for these kids?"

She smiled sweetly and pretended innocence. "You can't have kids with just anyone, you know...though I've always thought baby boys with Jace's black hair and big dark eyes would be so adorable."

Scowling at her, Reese muttered, "If I thought for a moment you were serious..."

"Yes?"

The scowl faded and turned into his smuggest grin. What should have been arrogant and cocky was, instead, charming and sexy as hell. "But I don't. Come on."

They left the theater by the side exit, stepping out of air-conditioned comfort into a literal steam bath. The rain had stopped, leaving puddles here and there and little wisps of steam rising from the sun-baked parking lot. Neely caught her breath as every pore on her body gasped at the temperature change. "This is a good day for lying naked beside a pool or under an air-conditioning vent on full-blast."

"Damn. I knew I should have gone ahead and had the pool put in before the construction was finished."

Smiling up at him, she fumbled in her purse for her sunglasses. Just as they reached the curb, she found them and started to put them on while waiting for a car to pass. The driver, slowing for a speed bump, looked at her, then did a double take—brows raised, eyes big, mouth opened wide—

that would have been comical if it hadn't been so damned serious.

An impatient driver honked, and the man looked behind him, then drove on, but he didn't go far—only to the next row of parked cars. As he turned onto that row, she fumbled blindly for Reese at her side, clutching his arm, managing little more than a frightened whisper. "That man! Reese, I think that man—"

She hit the hot sidewalk with enough force to knock the breath from her lungs and to tear raw patches on her palms and knees. As shots sounded—innocuous little sounds for something so potentially deadly—she realized Reese had pushed her down, and in the direction of a concrete planter filled with dirt. She crawled in that direction, ignoring the sting from her scrapes, not bothering to look behind her to check on him, since his hand was at her waist, hurrying her along.

When she reached the security of the planter, she glanced around. Reese was directly behind her, his body pressing her close to the concrete. Farther back, other movie patrons were screaming, seeking their own cover. She saw two on cell phones—calling the police, she hoped. Probably the local news hotline, she figured.

"Are you okay?" Reese demanded.

"Yes. You?"

"Yeah. You know that guy?"

"Never saw him before." She cringed as the man opened fire on the planter with what surely must be a semiautomatic weapon. Mouthing the best prayer she was capable of at the moment, she made herself as small as possible and held tightly to Reese's arm where it circled her. She didn't want to die, but God help her, she didn't want anyone else to die because of her, especially Reese. *Please, please, please...*

Dirt and bits of concrete and leaf rained down on them as the last spray of gunfire ended. A car door slammed, then tires screeched as the man sped away. For an instant everything seemed unnaturally quiet, though from somewhere nearby Neely could hear soft crying and vicious cursing. She couldn't decide whether she wanted to join in on one or the other, or whether she should stand and apologize to everyone for bringing such violence into their lazy afternoon. But with Reese wedging her into the tiniest of spaces, she couldn't do anything but tremble and think, with great sorrow, how close she'd come to causing another innocent person's death.

In the distance came the sound of a siren, joined almost immediately by a second, then a third. They spurred Reese into action. Standing, he extended his left hand and pulled her to her feet. His expression was harsh, unforgiving, and his words were clipped. "Let's get out of here."

"But the police—"

He slid his arm around her waist and propelled her along—across the traffic lanes, into the parking lot, on a rushed, weaving journey to his truck. When she would have pulled loose to get in on the passenger side, he held her tighter. "You're gonna have to drive."

"But, Reese—" Her gaze dropped from his face to the stain spreading across the right shoulder of his T-shirt, turning the dark fabric a few shades deeper. When she touched it, her fingers came away wet with blood and her stomach heaved violently.

As she swayed, he gave her a shake. "Help me into the truck and get me back to Heartbreak, okay?"

"Oh, my God... Oh, my God, Reese, you've been..."

He shook her again. "Suck it up, Neely. I'm not going to die. You didn't, did you? Now get us out of here."

She dug into his jeans' pocket for the keys, unlocked the door and helped him climb inside, then ran to the driver's side. The sirens were closer now, enough of them to make her quake inside and out. She got out of the parking lot in record time and said a prayer of thanks for the snarl of traffic at the intersection behind them that had slowed the police's arrival.

At the first stoplight, she adjusted the seat and mirrors, leaned across and fastened Reese's seat belt, then did the same with her own. "Where's the nearest hospital?"

He didn't even lift his head. "No hospital. Heartbreak."

"Reese, you've been shot!"

"You think I don't know it?"

"You need a doctor! You need to go to the emergency room!"

"If I go to the hospital, they're gonna report it to the police. They'll make reports, and the media will get hold of them. It'll be too damn easy for Forbes's man to get my name and address. Too damn easy for him to not miss you next time."

Of course he was right. But she knew from experience that he was in great pain, and the bleeding didn't seem to be slowing yet. If the bullet was still in his shoulder, he would need surgery. Even if it had exited, he still needed immediate medical attention.

"You can give a fake name," she said stubbornly. "So can I. We can lie about everything—"

"Damn it, Neely, take me to Heartbreak!" Shouting at her left him drained and pale. He was angry, and she couldn't blame him. She'd almost gotten him killed, all because she'd been a little down and wanted to do something besides hide in his house. Obviously, he blamed her—and how could he not? She blamed herself.

"I don't know how to get back to Heartbreak," she said in a small voice, feeling guilty that she hadn't paid more attention on the drive over.

"We'll take the long way—make certain no one's following." He did look up then, and gestured. "Turn right here and get on the expressway."

She followed his directions from expressway to turnpike to highway until they reached the small town of Sapulpa. There she turned into the parking lot of the first grocery store they came to. Reese glared at her, but she pretended not to notice. "You need a bandage on that."

"I'm okay."

To her dismay, she burst into tears. "You're not okay! You've been shot, and I'm sorry, I'm so sorry! I never meant— Oh, God, I never meant for this to happen! You have to believe me! I never—"

With a rustle, a twenty-dollar bill appeared in front of her face. "Is that enough?"

The lack of emotion in his voice and his refusal to offer even the slightest comfort hurt more than she could say. She forced back a sob so quickly that she hiccuped instead and turned away from him to dry her cheeks, find a tissue in her purse to blow her nose and check her reflection in the mirror on the visor. She didn't look too bad, considering that she felt as if she might shatter into a thousand pieces, and she wasn't likely—please, God—to run into anyone who knew her there.

But that was what Reese had said about Tulsa.

Feeling fragile, she got out of the truck, then turned back to take the money. Before she could pull back her hand, though, he caught her wrist. "Don't make me come in there looking for you, and don't leave me sitting here while you take off out the back." His expression was impossible to read, but his voice wasn't. It was hard, cold, sharp with loathing.

Great, she thought as she slammed the door with all the force she could muster. Now she felt fragile *and* wounded. She just might find a quiet corner in the store's stockroom and scream out her frustration until her throat was as raw as the rest of her felt. Of course, then he would come looking for her, and he would probably pass out from the loss of blood and crack open that hard head of his, and he would blame her for that, too.

How could he believe she would leave him there, wounded from saving her life? How could the thought even cross his mind? She had never run out on anyone who needed her— *never*—and he had no business thinking he might be the first!

But he did think it.

And that told her a lot about what he thought of her.

She made her purchases quickly, then hustled back to the truck. After moving to an isolated parking space around the corner of the store, she dumped everything into Reese's lap, then walked around to his side. He was pale and sweaty, and his right arm hung useless at his side. The pain etched lines around his mouth and at the corners of his eyes, and she hoped it was also responsible for the taut clench of his jaw, and not his disgust with her.

With the scissors she'd just bought, she cut off his T-shirt and discarded it on the floor. The wound was high in the right side of his chest, and the bullet had gone in at enough of an angle that it had exited through his upper arm, tearing a ragged path along its way.

"So what do you think, doc?" he asked sarcastically.

"I've seen worse." Bitterly, she added, "I've *had* worse."

Letting his head fall back against the headrest, he closed his eyes and turned his face away from her. He didn't want to watch? Fine. He didn't want to look at her? That was fine, too. Maybe now he'd be willing to send her back to Jace. That was all she'd wanted, ever since she'd climbed out of Jace's car in Killdeer and recognized Reese as her prison guard.

Well…that, and him.

She bandaged both wounds with gauze pads, cotton pads and adhesive tape, securing them as tightly as she could to apply pressure and hopefully stop or at least slow the bleeding. Once she was finished, she leaned across him to fasten the seat belt. She had trouble fitting the two ends together from her awkward position and was more than a bit distracted by her proximity to him, by the faint, familiar scent of him and all that warm brown skin—clammy brown skin—and his gentle touch…

She became still, unsure whether he'd actually touched her hair or she'd merely imagined it. Once the seat belt finally clicked together, she raised her head but couldn't read anything on his face but pain. Surely she'd imagined it. Why would he stroke her hair so tenderly when he was angry with her for getting him shot? Probably the only way he wanted to touch her was to wrap his hands around her throat and squeeze.

Once she was back behind the wheel, he gave her directions out of Sapulpa and north to Sand Springs, where they picked up the expressway they'd used to travel into Tulsa. She set the cruise control for the maximum speed, then spent her time dividing her attention between the highway and him.

She estimated they were more than halfway to Heartbreak when he reclined his seat a few inches and awkwardly brought his right hand up to rest on his stomach. She'd never seen him so pale, and had seen him so distant only once—when the tables had been turned and she'd been the one with the bullet in her chest.

He'd blamed her then, too.

"Is there a doctor in Heartbreak?" she asked, in great need of something to break the silence.

"Yeah, Doc Hanson. If he's not around, Callie'll take care of it."

"Who is she?"

"Callie Sellers. Nurse-midwife…works with him." With some effort, he managed to pull his cell phone from his jeans' pocket, found the number he wanted in its phone book and dialed. He was silent for a moment, then with a grimace and a muttered curse, he disconnected, then looked up another number. "Callie…hey, it's Reese. Can you meet me at Doc's clinic—" he broke off to catch his breath and made an effort to not sound so weak "—in about fifteen minutes? It's kind of an emergency…Thanks."

He made one last call—to someone named Brady, asking him to meet them at the clinic—then let his hand fall heavily, and the cell phone slid free. Neely caught it, disconnected the call, then laid it on the console. "You should have gone to the hospital in Tulsa."

"Yeah, and it probably would have gotten you killed."

"Would that be such a loss?" she asked bitterly. No one would care but her mother and her sisters—none of whom she had contacted, even though he'd said she could, as long as he listened in. They would be angry that she'd gotten herself in trouble again and hadn't told them again. If she survived this, they would never have to worry again, because she was never, ever again doing anything that might cause problems for anyone.

Reese didn't respond to her self-pitying question, which made her feel even sorrier for herself. She tightened her fingers around the wheel, clenched her teeth and focused intently on driving and nothing else.

He'd estimated the time perfectly. Exactly fifteen minutes after he'd called the nurse-midwife, they were pulling into the tiny parking lot behind the clinic in downtown Heartbreak. Another car was parked in a space marked Reserved, and a gorgeous redhead was waiting at the door. Her bright, practiced smile faded when Neely climbed out of the truck, and it disappeared completely when she helped Reese out. The woman none too politely moved Neely aside, draped his left arm over her shoulder and snapped at Neely to hold the door for them.

She did so, then let it close again—with her on the outside. She had Reese's keys and his truck. If she wanted to escape, this was her chance. She could go to his house, get her clothes, her credit cards and her cash, and she could be well on her way out of the state before gorgeous Callie was finished patching him up. He would be glad to see her go—glad to have her out of his life. He would recover from getting shot, no doubt with plenty of help from Red, and he would go back to life as normal, working days and romancing half the women in the county by night. And she…she would be all right. She was a survivor, remember?

She was standing there, keys clutched in one hand, other hand wrapped around the door handle, trying to decide, when the decision was taken away from her. A black-and-white Blazer bearing the insignia of the Canyon County Sheriff's Department pulled into the parking lot, blocking the truck.

The man who climbed out was tall and handsome, with eyes as remote as any she'd ever seen. He moved with the sort of masculine grace inherent in men who knew who they were and what their place in life was. His hair was black, his face as lean and hard as his body, his eyes surprisingly blue and his mustache wicked. He didn't need the badge on his shirt or the gun on his belt to intimidate anyone. She was unnerved by his mere presence.

"Is Reese inside?" he asked in a throaty voice custom-made for whispering sweet nothings…or deadly threats. When she nodded, he gestured for her to precede him through the door. "Callie?" he called.

"We're in here, Brady."

Neely followed the voice to the nearest treatment room. Inside she found Reese propped up on a gurney with a woman on either side—the redhead on his left, a blonde on his right. The blonde was working on him, and the redhead was…providing comfort, Neely decided uncharitably. She was clasping his left hand to her chest, stroking his face with her other hand and murmuring soft words in a familiar, sexy, sultry voice.

The redhead wasn't Callie the midwife, as Neely had assumed. No, Callie was the blond woman and she looked the way a midwife should—like some sort of earth mother. Though pretty, she had such an air of nurturing about her that Neely couldn't imagine being jealous of her. But her friend, pretty Isabella, *ride-me-cowboy* Isabella…

Neely disliked her tremendously.

Chapter 10

Reese felt like hell, and little of it could be blamed on the gunshot wound. In fact, with the medicine Callie had put in his IV, he wasn't even totally sure he still felt the gunshot wound. Too bad it couldn't work the same magic on all his other problems.

It took two or three tugs, but he managed to free his hand from Isabella's and catch hold of Callie's. "I need to talk to Brady alone."

"And I need to clean this wound, debride the damaged muscle and the surrounding tissue, insert a couple of drains and—"

"Before I get any woozier," he interrupted, and after a moment, she nodded.

"We womenfolk will wait in the hall," Callie said with a touch of sarcasm. "Sheesh, man gets himself shot, comes in here asking me to break the law and treat him, then throws me out of my own treatment room—" The closing door cut off the rest of her words.

Brady came closer to the bed. "What happened? Who shot you?"

Reese ignored his questions. "That woman is Neely Madison, a…a former prosecutor in Kansas City. A drug dealer she sent to prison has put a price on her head, and some lucky bastard damn near cashed in on it this afternoon. She's…she's staying at my house. I need…" He blinked a few times, tried to shake off the effects of the sedative. "I know it's way outside your job description, but I don't know…if I'll be…be able…"

"I can spend the night there, and tomorrow if necessary."

Reese nodded, or thought he did. His vision was blurring, and he was so tired. "Don't let her run…run away. Thinks…she'll protect ever'one if she goes alone…Got to keep her…"

With a sigh, he let his eyes close. He needed a minute's rest…just a few minutes'. When he opened his eyes again, he felt less tired, but not any better. His head ached, he was a little queasy, and the throb in his right shoulder increased with each passing moment. Once his vision cleared, he glanced around the room. Apparently he'd rested for more than a few minutes. His shoulder and arm were bandaged, and the IV bag was almost empty. Brady stood at the door, seemingly oblivious to everyone in the place. Callie and Isabella were talking quietly at the foot of the bed, and Neely was staring out a window that looked on a brick wall a foot away. She had that lost look again, as if her troubles were about to beat her down again.

She could have died today, and it was his fault. He'd kept repeating that to himself on the long drive home, but it still hadn't completely sunk in. He truly couldn't comprehend that he had put her life in danger. He could have caused her death. She'd asked him if going to Tulsa was safe, and he'd stupidly assured her it was, all because he'd wanted to do something to brighten her mood.

He felt the same sick fear that had swept over him when he'd seen the man's reaction to her outside the theater. The guy had looked like a grossly exaggerated example of surprise, like a cartoon character whose eyes popped out of his head as his jaw hit the ground. He'd thought fate had dropped a jackpot right into his lap, and it was only by the grace of God that he hadn't been able to cash it in. Reese hadn't deterred him. He hadn't done a damn thing, except get her shot at.

He started to sit up, not easy with his arm in a sling and protesting every tiny movement, but with a groan, he managed. Callie and Isabella came to stand beside him as he swung his legs over the side of the gurney. Neely did nothing more than glance over one shoulder.

"How do you feel?" Callie asked.

"Like I've been shot and treated by a midwife."

"You should probably spend the night here. I'll bunk out in Doc's room."

"I'll be more comfortable at home. And you'll be more comfortable at your home." He started to breathe deeply, then winced.

"You really shouldn't be alone tonight, Reese," Isabella said, stroking his hair back from his forehead.

"He won't be." That came from Brady. "Neely and I will be with him."

That drew her attention. She turned to look at Brady, then her glance skimmed over Reese, avoiding his face, before she silently nodded.

"Well...all right." Callie picked up two bottles from the counter. "These are antibiotics. Take two every six hours until they're all gone. Don't miss one. And this bottle is painkillers. Only as needed—but for God's sake, Barnett, if you need one, take one."

He nodded, though he had no intention of taking anything that might affect his judgment or his ability to protect Neely...such as it was.

She handed the bottles to Neely, then summoned Brady with a wave. "Let's get him in the wheelchair. The best thing for him now is sleep. If he gets hungry enough to eat, let him. No booze if he's taking the painkillers. Keep him in bed for a few days, and keep his arm in the sling anytime he's sitting up or is out of bed. If he starts running a fever, let me or Doc Hanson know immediately. I'll come by tomorrow to change the dressing, and I'll show you how—''

"I know how," Neely abruptly interrupted. "I changed my own dressings when I got shot." Carrying the pill bottles, she crossed to the door, then coolly looked back at Isabella. "Why don't you hold the door? I'll get the other one."

There was a moment of silence when the door closed behind her, then Callie gestured for Reese to scoot forward. "Who *is* she?"

He eased off the table, leaning heavily on Brady, then maneuvered into the wheelchair. There, he considered all the possible answers he could give before settling on one. "Someone I'm trying to keep—" He was about to say *safe*, but, while true, it was only part of the answer. He'd already told them all they needed to know, but with a weary smile he repeated it. "Just someone I'm trying to keep. Thanks, Callie."

"We'll check on you in a day or so. Take care of yourself."

Isabella held the door while Brady pushed the wheelchair. Neely was waiting at the other door, her features set in a hard mask. Seeing her brought a knot of regret to his chest that made the gunshot wounds feel like scratches. How many times had he let her down? How many times had she needed him but he wasn't there, or he turned away, or he couldn't do anything to help? Too many, and all of them unforgivable.

Brady helped him into the truck as Neely started the engine. The deputy went to his own truck while Isabella fastened Reese's seat belt, then brushed her fingers tantalizingly over his arm. "Take care of yourself, cowboy," she murmured before closing the door and stepping away.

"She would be happy to come over and stay with you," Neely remarked without emotion as she watched the rearview mirror.

"I don't want her there."

When Brady was clear, she shifted into reverse, then carefully backed out of the narrow space. "I told you she had a thing for you."

Deliberately he returned to a conversation they'd had before the day had gone to hell. "Hmm. How do you think little baby girls with her red hair would look?"

"Like clowns."

Her answer came so quickly, so dryly, that he couldn't help but chuckle—at least, until the first shock of pain spread through him. Gritting his teeth through it, he gave a small, contained sigh. "I don't know exactly what Isabella wants, feels or thinks, but whatever it is, Neely, it's not reciprocated."

When she didn't reply, he fell silent for the short drive home. He was tired and couldn't think of much more comforting than his bed...except his bed with Neely in it. He wouldn't be able to take full advantage of her, of course, but he was pretty sure he'd sleep better if she were beside him, if he could reach out and touch her and know she was all right.

But she didn't look too touchable as she pulled into the garage beside his sheriff's truck and shut off the engine. She didn't unfasten his seat belt or come around to help him out. She waited until Brady was inside, then closed the garage door and unlocked the door into the house.

Reese was navigating under his own power—well, with a little support from the wall—and on his way to the bedroom when abruptly he turned back to face Neely. "Give Brady the keys."

Wordlessly she handed them over.

"And the cell phone."

She pulled it from the deep pocket of her dress and gave it over, too.

"And give me the pills."

Taking them from the other pocket, she moved close enough to put them in his outstretched hand, and then she cut through the living room to reach her bedroom. He heard the door close and imagined he even heard the click of the lock. Wearily, he continued his laborious trip to the bedroom.

"If you need to go to your place to pick up anything, go ahead," he told Brady once he was settled in bed. "But if you go, take her with you—and keep a close watch on her. She's tried to escape before. If you need to go outside, she knows the code for the alarm. Make certain she resets it. Anything else...?"

Brady went into the bathroom and returned with a paper cup of water, then removed three pills from the bottles. "Take these."

"Not the pain pill. I don't need it."

"If you could see the way you look, you wouldn't say that. Take it. I'll keep an eye on Neely."

Because he knew he couldn't possibly look as bad as he felt, Reese took the pills, then lay back. "Let me see the cell phone, will you? I've got to call Jace before I go to sleep."

He waited until Brady left, leaving the door mostly closed behind him, before dialing Jace's cell phone number. When his cousin answered, he wasted no time telling him in the bluntest terms possible what had happened.

Jace let loose with a string of curses. "You're supposed to be keeping her safe, out of sight, not parading her around Tulsa! Which part of your body did you use to make this brilliant decision?"

"I know it was stupid, and I'm sorry. It's just been hard, her being here, and I thought—"

"You didn't think at all! Jeez, Reese, I took her to you because I thought you had better sense! I thought you would protect her and instead you do something idiotic like take her out on a freaking date?"

"I never wanted her here in the first place, Jace!" he said defensively. "You think you can do so damn much better, come and get her!"

The instant the words were out, something—instinct, intuition, sixth sense—drew his attention to the door, where Neely was standing, looking as if she were the one who'd been shot and he'd done it. "Aw, hell, let me call you back, Jace," he muttered. He laid the phone aside, threw back the covers and started to swing his feet to the floor.

"Don't bother getting up." Finally she moved, but not to run back to her room and lock the door, as he expected. She came into the room, around the bed and sat on the window seat. "I just wanted to see if you needed anything. I didn't mean to interrupt your call."

"What I said…" He started to rub his shoulder, in a way he'd seen her do a dozen times, but the first touch convinced him it was far too tender. "Jace was yelling at me like he did when we were kids. He's two months older, and he always acted like that meant he was twenty years smarter. I didn't mean…"

"You made no secret of the fact that you didn't want me here." She said it calmly, reasonably, but her gaze was locked on the rug beside the bed.

"Well, you know…things change."

Looking unconvinced, she nodded once, then stood again. "You want a drink? The ceiling fan turned on? The light turned off?"

He grinned weakly. "You know, just a little physical contact can go a long way toward providing comfort. A pat or two, a warm hand, a warm body."

The bleakness in her expression intensified. "Yes, it can." Then she walked out of the room.

Reese scowled at the ceiling. It was pretty clear that she'd been thinking about that when she'd gotten shot, when he wasn't there to offer her comfort, help or assurance at all. When she'd lain in a hospital bed and no one had cared enough to visit. When people who'd once been friends had forgotten her name or, worse, had become bitter enemies. Of everyone who'd treated her unfairly, he was the guiltiest, and neither of them could forget it.

He was almost grateful for the telephone's ring. He answered with a distracted hello.

"Is Neely all right?" Jace demanded.

"Yeah. She's just shaken up a bit." And remembering bad memories, reliving bad times.

"Tell me everything."

Reese gave him a blow-by-blow account leading up to, during and following the shooting. He described every detail of the man, his car and the partial license tag number he'd gotten, identified the weapon, estimated the number of shots fired. "It'll be in the Tulsa paper and on their news. You can find out what the P.D. there has to say."

"What about you? Are you all right?"

"I'm fine. Doc Hanson's nurse fixed me up."

"I'll come get her tomorrow—"

"Like hell you will."

"I thought you didn't want—"

"She's my responsibility, and she's safe here. No one at the theater knew us. No one followed us. My best deputy is staying here with us, and if worse comes to worst, there's always the safe room." He tried to swallow back a big yawn but with little success. "She's not going anywhere, Jace. Not now." Maybe not ever.

"I don't know…"

His cousin's lack of confidence stung. "I made a mistake. It won't happen again. I'll keep her safe or die trying."

"Oh, yeah, that's just what she needs on her conscience," Jace said sarcastically. "I'll leave her there for now. But don't do anything else stupid. Don't make me come down there and knock some sense into you."

Reese agreed, hung up and gingerly resettled in the bed. He'd screwed up big time today, but it wouldn't happen again.

He swore on his life it wouldn't.

"Want to go for a ride?"

Neely looked up from the magazine she'd been trying to read for the past two hours to find Brady Marshall standing a half dozen feet in front of her. She'd offered him breakfast this Thursday morning, but he'd taken only a cup of coffee. He'd sat in the living room, watching the news, while she'd

fed Reese his breakfast and had asked one simple question—
How is he?—when she'd returned with the empty dishes.

Reese had been tired, weak, unable to use his right arm at
all and unable to remember that. He'd spoken only when he
couldn't avoid it and then in a sullen, cranky voice. She'd
tried, in her awkward suddenly-an-outsider way, to assure him
that he had nothing to worry about. He would heal just fine,
with no residual problems. He wasn't about to lose another
career he loved because of a stupid injury.

He'd looked at her as if she'd abruptly started speaking
Aunt Rozena's tribal language instead of English, and then,
finally, silently, had looked away.

Pushing the incident out of her mind, she directed her attention back to Brady. "I'd rather not."

"I have to go to my house to pick up some things, and
Reese said to take you with me."

"And what if he needs me—" Her face flushed hot, and a
hard, frustrated knot formed in her stomach. He didn't need
her. He wouldn't even look at her when she went into his
room. "What if he needs something?"

"We won't be gone more than an hour. He'll probably
sleep. Come on."

She had no choice, but it made her feel better to pretend
she did. "Sure. Why not? Let me get my shoes. Oh, and if
you have a bullet-proof vest, you might want to put it on.
People tend to get shot around me."

She got her shoes and her floppy-brimmed straw hat, then
went to his truck with him. When they'd driven halfway to
Buffalo Plains without a word from him, she said,
"So…Deputy Marshall. Do people tease you about that name?
Point out that if you'd joined the marshal's service, you'd be
Deputy Marshal Marshall?"

"It's Undersheriff Marshall," he corrected her, then asked,
"Do I look like the sort of person people tease?"

She glanced at him, though it wasn't necessary. He looked
like the sort of man women fantasized about, but given the
chance to make those fantasies come true, they would be way

too afraid. He looked dark, wicked, threatening. He looked like a man who could keep a woman safe…if he didn't scare her to death in the process. "No," she admitted. "You don't. So you're the strong, silent type."

"Hmm. I'd been thinking the same thing about you…until now."

"I'm not strong, and I'm rarely silent."

This time *he* gave *her* a measuring look. "Most women who'd been through what you went through yesterday would still be in need of sedation."

For the first time in hours she smiled. "That's me—Neely Madison, attorney-at-law, bad luck personified, cool in a crisis, leader of a life of chaos. After you get shot at a time or two or fifty, it loses its impact."

"You're not kidding, are you?"

"Do I look like the type to kid?"

After another mile or two of silence, he asked, "How long have you and Reese been involved?"

She didn't ask whether he was guessing or Reese had told him. Quiet, intense people like him tended to pick up information out of thin air. It made them good cops—and better criminals. "It started ten years ago." She smiled blandly. "It ended a year later."

"It's not ended yet."

Twenty-four hours ago she would have agreed with him. Now she wasn't so sure. Some things were pretty hard to overlook, and she suspected that nearly dying because of someone else was one of them.

"I take it you're not married," she said, making no effort to disguise her change of subject.

"Nope."

"Have a steady girl?"

"No."

That suggested the women of Buffalo Plains understood the difference between the appeal of a dangerous man and the reality of a relationship with him. "You don't sound like you're from around here."

"No."

Strong and silent, she reminded herself. She let him remain that way until they reached the apartment complex where he lived. In keeping with what she'd seen of Buffalo Plains, it was nothing fancy—a half-dozen two-story brick buildings, with an office, pool and laundry room in the center. His apartment was on the second floor, with a tiny balcony that overlooked the pool.

"How long have you lived here?" Neely asked, pitching her voice loud enough to be heard in the bedroom.

"Six years."

She gave a shake of her head. It looked as if *no one* lived there. The furniture was standard, cheap apartment furniture—ditto the wall art—and everything was spotlessly clean. There were no books, newspapers or magazines. No shoes kicked under the couch. No dirty dishes in the sink. Not a speck of grease on the stovetop. A small corkboard on a kitchen wall held nothing but a short list of phone numbers—the rental office, a pizza delivery place, Reese's home number and, at the bottom, another number, complete with area code but missing any identifying information. Neely would give a lot to commit it to memory and call it later, but of course she didn't try.

Brady came out of the bedroom, wearing jeans and a red shirt, carrying a small duffel bag, with his gun in a holster above his right hip.

"Either you're the neatest person I've ever met, or you don't actually live here at all," she remarked.

He glanced around. "Don't you take care of your belongings?"

"I try. But my car still wound up in…oh, about two thousand pieces a few weeks ago."

"It was just a car. It can be replaced."

The seemingly contradictory remarks kept her puzzling over them for a good part of the return trip to Heartbreak. When she did finally speak, her voice was serious. "I suppose it would be pointless to ask you to give me the keys to Reese's truck."

"I suppose so."

"If he'd let me go when I asked before, he never would have been shot."

"No, but you might have been, and that would be a lot harder for him to deal with."

"Don't be too sure of that," she said dryly.

"Seems like I'm the only one who can be sure of anything. You and Reese are both too busy feeling guilty and worrying about each other."

"What does he have to feel guilty about?"

"Gee, I don't know. Taking someone he's supposed to be protecting into a crowded city where someone else can try to kill her?"

"It wasn't— He said— I was making us both crazy."

Underneath the neat black mustache, Brady's mouth spread in a surprisingly appealing grin. She would have bet he wasn't capable of it. "You can make him crazy without being in the same state with him. That wasn't why he took you to Tulsa. He was trying to score some points with you."

Neely scowled at him. "You're wrong."

"I'm many things, Ms. Madison, but 'wrong' is rarely one of them."

Was it possible that Reese was blaming himself instead of her for what had happened? Could that be the reason for his hard looks and harder words? But he *wasn't* responsible. It was just sheer luck that the shooter had recognized her. A tremendous coincidence, so unlikely that the odds were probably impossible to calculate. And coincidences happened. No one could predict them.

If anyone was to blame, it was her. And the man with the gun. And Eddie Forbes.

When they got home a few minutes later, Reese was asleep. Neely sat on the window seat, just watching him, until the aromas of cooking drew her to the kitchen. Brady had discovered the stash of goodies in the freezer and was heating one in the oven.

"Pot roast," he said when he saw her. "It'll be ready in a few minutes. You want to see if Reese feels like getting up, or would you rather feed him in bed?"

"I'll let him choose." She returned quietly to the bedroom, only to discover that Reese was awake, and looking guilty. Had he merely been pretending to sleep while she was there, so he could avoid having to talk to her? Apparently so.

Doing a little pretending of her own—that she wasn't hurt— she said, "Lunch is ready. Do you feel like coming to the table, or do you want me to bring your plate in here?"

"I'll go in there." As he sat up, she started to pull back the covers, but he shoved them aside first. When she reached for the sling, he took it away from her with a gruff, "I can do that." She watched him struggle with it, watched him wince and turn a shade paler before he got it in place, and then she reached for his antibiotics. He clumsily grabbed the bottle first.

He was a man, she counseled herself as she followed his slow progress to the kitchen, and men reacted in one of two ways to being incapacitated. They were childish, cranky and wanted to be pampered, or they felt emasculated and wanted to do everything themselves. Fine. Not a problem. She could accept that.

Brady had the table set, drinks beside the plates and was taking a foil pan from the oven. She took her usual seat, and Reese pulled out the chair to her right, hesitated, then moved to the one across from her. Any assistance he needed would have to come from Brady and not her. Great.

Lunch was awful. Brady, she'd already learned, wasn't very talkative. Reese was lousy at using his left hand and lousier at accepting help. Even the little things she did naturally, such as offering to refill his glass when she got up to refill her own, were met with hostility.

She ate quickly, rinsed her dishes and loaded them in the

dishwasher, then headed for the back door, when finally he voluntarily spoke to her.

"Where do you think you're going?"

"Outside." Her smile was saccharine-sweet and phony as all get-out. "I'm allowed, remember?"

"You *were* allowed. Not anymore."

"Why not?"

"Someone tried to kill you yesterday!"

"So what? They've tried before, and they'll try again. I'm not going to cower in the corner and wait for it to happen."

He clumsily got to his feet and carried his dishes to the sink, where they landed with a clatter. "I don't care whether you cower, but you're for damn sure staying inside. You're not dying on my watch."

"The depth of your concern for my safety overwhelms me. Go back to bed where you belong and leave me alone." She turned toward the door again, but didn't get even the third number of the four-digit code entered before Brady firmly pulled her away.

When she glared at him, he shrugged. "He pays my salary. And he happens to be right. You guys took a chance yesterday, and he's paying for it. No more chances, Neely, because sooner or later, your luck's going to run out."

"And I'm supposed to care about that?"

"You don't have to. But other people do."

She wasn't sure why her eyes suddenly filled with tears. She only knew she needed privacy before they spilled over. With as much dignity as she could muster, she squared her shoulders, freed her arm from Brady's grip and held her head high. "I'm going to my room to read. I don't want to be disturbed."

She made a perfect exit, only to hear Reese's murmur as she reached the bedroom door. "Her books and her glasses are on the coffee table."

Reversing direction, she detoured through the living room, then returned to the bedroom, where she closed and locked the door. Sure, she'd had better days, she thought as she threw herself across the bed, but she'd also had worse. She was sure of it.

She just couldn't remember when.

The clock on the nightstand showed a few minutes after midnight when Reese slowly sat up. For a moment or two he sat on the side of the bed, rubbing his neck, watching the occasional flashes of lightning that filtered through the closed window blinds. He hadn't spent so much time in bed in longer than he could remember, and it seemed his entire body ached from it.

Or maybe he ached because of Neely. She was hurt and upset, and he didn't know how to make her feel better. Hell, he didn't have a clue how to make himself feel better, either. The guilt and the regret were eating him alive, and he couldn't stop them.

He eased from the bed and made his way through familiar darkness into the living room. The computer was unplugged, all the lights turned off, the house silent. Neely, he assumed, was asleep in the guest room, and Brady was bunked out in the front bedroom that doubled as a storeroom. But he wasn't asleep. Reese heard the creak of the door only seconds before he spoke.

"Having trouble sleeping?"

Reese glanced over his shoulder at the tall, lean shadow that was approaching. "Too much on my mind."

"Anything you want to talk about?"

He started to shake his head, then stopped. If there was one person in the entire county he could count on to keep secrets, it was Brady. He was more closemouthed than any priest or psychiatrist ever thought of being.

Reese carefully lowered himself into one of the chairs in front of the window, and after a moment Brady sat in the other. "Neely and I used to be…together."

Brady didn't appear surprised. In the dim illumination provided by the lightning, he didn't show any reaction at all.

"Back then I was a deputy with the Keegan County Sheriff's Department. Neely and I had been together about a year when…'' He watched the wind whip through the trees and heard the crack of a falling limb. ''It's a long, ugly story that I'd rather not tell. The bottom line is, she got shot by another deputy, and I—I walked away from her. I left her lying on the sidewalk, bleeding, not knowing how badly she was hurt. A couple days later I came back home to Oklahoma, and I never saw her again until Jace asked for my help in protecting her. All those years I'd convinced myself I was right in leaving her, in blaming her for everything that went wrong. All those years I'd lied to myself.''

Raindrops rattled on the tin roof as a particularly loud crash of thunder vibrated through the house. ''I let her down so many times,'' he went on. ''Yesterday I almost got her killed. I promised her that trip to Tulsa would be safe, and I was wrong. She could have died because I was wrong.''

''So you made a bad decision. How does that justify the way you're treating her?''

It was something of a relief, Reese realized, that Brady didn't argue or try to absolve him of guilt. Of course, Jace hadn't argued, either. He'd been more than willing to put the blame squarely where it belonged. ''It doesn't. It's just…I keep remembering that when she got shot, she didn't have anyone to drive her home from the hospital. There wasn't anyone to fix her meals, change her dressing or make sure she took her medication on schedule. She was totally alone—had to cope completely by herself because it was my job, my responsibility, and I wasn't there.'' He rubbed his good hand over his eyes and his voice grew unsteady. ''I can hardly bear having her do things for me now when I was too selfish and stupid and judgmental to do the same for her then. It makes me feel so guilty.''

''Everybody makes mistakes. Everyone does things they later regret. The key is to accept the responsibility, make amends and get on with life.''

''And how do I make amends for walking away from her when she'd been shot? How in hell do I make amends for almost getting her killed yesterday? Both times she was counting on me, trusting me, and both times I let her down. How do I make up for that?''

''You start by saying 'I'm sorry.' By asking her to forgive you. Then you spend whatever time and effort it takes to let her know that she can count on you and trust you and you won't let her down again.''

''You make it sound so easy.''

''It's not. Asking someone to forgive you can be the hardest thing you've ever done. And if she refuses, it can be the most painful thing you've ever done.''

He spoke as if from experience, Reese thought, and wondered when and with whom. What had he done that couldn't be forgiven, and was that what had brought him from wherever to Oklahoma?

I'm sorry. Please forgive me. Difficult words to say, a difficult risk to face. But he owed them to Neely. Even if she never forgave him, she deserved the words, and every bit of the sincerity behind them. And if she chose to throw them back in his face…it was no more than he deserved.

He wished she was awake at that moment. Talking to her in the dark of night would be easier than in the bright, unforgiving light of day. Honesty came a little simpler under cover of darkness, and hurt was a little less hard to bear. But he couldn't wake her from a badly needed rest just to ease his conscience. That would be selfish, and he'd been too selfish already.

''At Doc's office yesterday, you said she was a former prosecutor. She doesn't do that anymore?''

''No. She swears she's giving up her law practice.'' Reese paused to let a rumble of thunder play itself out. ''There was a time when that was all I wanted—for her to quit defending criminals, stay home and raise our kids. But she's a damn good lawyer. The kind of lawyer that, when the opposing counsel hears who they're up against, their first response is, 'Let's make a deal.' She's too good to give it up and stay home changing diapers.'' Or waiting tables, selling real estate or kissing strange men at Medieval fairs or anywhere else.

''You didn't opt for an easy relationship, did you?'' Brady asked. ''A deputy and a defense attorney. Most people in that situation never would have gotten close enough to start anything.''

''I had 'easy' when I was playing ball. I could walk into any bar across the country and walk out fifteen minutes later with the best-looking woman in the place. In the beginning it was gratifying to my ego, but it got old real fast.'' He glanced at the other man. ''Was yours easy?''

Brady was so still that he could have been carved from granite. That was probably the first personal question Reese had asked him in all the years they'd worked together. Everyone in the department had learned early on that Brady had little or nothing to say about home, his family, his upbringing or anything else the least bit private. Anyone who did ask a personal question got a simple yes or no if they got any answer at all. He was more likely to give them a chilling look, then turn away.

But maybe because talking *was* easier in the dark of night, he gave a little more of an answer than usual. ''No. It wasn't easy at all. Which is why I'm here and she's…not.''

That was how he and Neely had spent practically the entire time they'd known each other—one of them here, the other there. Unless she was more forgiving than he had any right to expect, that might also be how they spent the rest of it. He wasn't sure he could bear that.

''My dad's getting married again,'' he said as the rain started in earnest. ''This is number four—and the last one, he says. Of course, he also said that about numbers two and three, but I think he really means it this time. I never minded all the women he brought temporarily into our family, but every time he brought a new one home, I reminded myself that I wasn't going to be like him. I was going to fall in love one time, get married one time, and that was it. But I never considered what I would do if the one woman I wanted wouldn't marry me.

That was what happened with him. He fell hard for Lena nearly forty years ago. They slept together, lived together for a few weeks one year, a few months the next, and they had a kid together...but for every month they spent together, they spent a year apart. So far, I'm turning out just like him. Neely and I were together twelve months, and we've been apart nine years. I don't want to spend the next thirty years without her."

There came a sudden lull in the storm—one of those stillnesses before a particularly powerful bolt of lightning or a clap of thunder that would rattle the house down to its very foundation. The wind stopped tearing through the trees and the rain eased to a sprinkle, as the storm seemed to catch its breath and decide what havoc to wreak next. And into that stillness, from somewhere close behind him, came the sweet, quiet voice that had haunted him since the first time he'd ever heard it, and it offered a challenge.

"So do something about it, Sheriff. Say the magic words. Make everything all right."

Chapter 11

The floorboards vibrated underneath Neely's feet as the storm returned with a vengeance. The rain that had beaten the tin roof for the past twenty minutes was joined by hail, the chunks of ice clanging on the metal. The wind was rattling the windowpanes, sending small branches with leaves still attached tumbling across the yard, skidding the rockers across the porch until they hit the wall, and the lightning was everywhere, brightening the sky in jagged sheets and striking the earth in brilliant forks. Such tremendous power and fury outside the log house…yet inside she felt calmer, more serene, than she had since first setting foot there.

Brady touched her lightly on the shoulder as he passed on his way to his room, and she smiled. He was an interesting man who deserved much closer scrutiny…but not tonight. Reese required all her attention tonight.

He was sitting in the leather chair, looking at her, but with the lightning at his back, she couldn't make out his expression. That was all right. She'd heard most of his conversation with Brady. She hadn't meant to eavesdrop. She'd gotten up to make certain he'd taken his antibiotics and as soon as she'd stepped into the kitchen she'd heard their voices. She'd merely waited for an opportune moment to interrupt, and it had taken its time presenting itself.

Her nightgown brushed the tops of her feet as she crossed the room to the chair where Brady had sat. Normally she slept in a T-shirt and shorts, but once in a while she indulged her taste for the fussy, frilly, unbearably feminine and romantic instead. Because she'd gone to bed tonight feeling bruised and battered and just possibly beyond surviving, she'd chosen the white cotton gown, with its ruffles, ribbons and lace. Its fitted top was tied with pink satin ribbons and dotted around the demure neckline with pink rosettes, and it fell in a long skirt that ended in an elaborate deep ruffle.

She sat primly, legs crossed, arms resting on the chair arms. "How's your shoulder?"

Reese stared at her. "F-fine. How—how's yours?"

Her first impulse was to touch the scar, hidden under the thin cotton, but she resisted, instead pressing her fingertips tightly against the cold leather. "It's a lot finer than yours is." Then, after a moment, she prompted him. "Well?"

His smile was heavy with regret. "I don't know any magic words."

"Sure, you do. You're a smart man. You know me well. You know which words hurt, and you know which words heal."

"I don't know words to make right everything I've done wrong."

"How do you know until you try?"

He looked outside again, and the lightning showed the range of emotions that weighted his expression—anger, great remorse, greater guilt and sorrow. "Some things can't be made right. Some things are unforgivable."

"You're right. Cold-blooded murder, hurting a child—those things would be impossible for most of us to forgive. But we haven't done either of those things, Reese." Shivering in the cool air, she leaned forward, resting her arms on her knees and hugging herself. "You blamed me for Judy Miller's death, and for a long time I blamed myself. I also blamed those deputies for tainting Leon's confession, and the justice system for letting him go time after time. I blamed his parents because too often, that's where an abuser learns to abuse, and I blamed Judy herself, for not getting that gun first and blowing *him* away. But, you know, Reese, the bottom line is Leon killed Judy. We were all a part of it, every one of us involved in arresting, prosecuting, defending and punishing him, but *he* made the decision to kill her. *He* had the gun available. *He* chose to point it at her and pull the trigger. Those deputies and Judy's family and everyone else can wish eternal damnation on me, but *I* know it wasn't my fault.

"Just as my getting shot, and everything that followed, wasn't your fault, and your getting shot wasn't my fault. It was *because* of me, and I regret that more than I can say, but that man made the choice to shoot, and you made the choice to push me out of the way, to save my life." She smiled faintly. "I haven't thanked you for that yet, have I?"

"You don't owe me any gratitude. If I hadn't taken you there in the first place—"

She slid soundlessly from the leather to the floor, kneeling in front of him. "Reese, we could play If-only until the sun comes up and manage to blame virtually everyone we've ever known. If only you hadn't taken me there, if only Jace hadn't brought me here, if only the jury hadn't convicted Forbes... Hell, if only my father's boss hadn't murdered his partner and framed my dad for it, I doubt I ever would have even considered becoming a lawyer, so that makes it *his* fault. But it's not *his* fault, or yours or Jace's or mine. Eddie Forbes offered a great sum of money to anybody who could kill me. *He's* responsible. The man who fired the shots is responsible. Not you, and not me."

He raised his left hand to her hair, slid his fingertips along her jaw. "But I feel so damn guilty."

"So feel guilty. Admit that maybe going to Tulsa wasn't

the smartest thing we could have done. We both knew it, and we went anyway. And then forget it.''

His laughter was choked and scornful. ''Forget it?''

''We're human, Reese. We make mistakes. We learn from them and move on, or we let them drag us down.'' Resting her arms on his legs, she found his skin as cool as hers. They needed to shut off the air-conditioning, put on some clothes or continue this conversation someplace a tad cozier. She intended to vote for someplace cozier. ''It's funny… We're so good at remorse and guilt. But the people who are really responsible for the bad things in our lives don't feel either one. Leon was sorry that his beating Judy landed him in jail, but he was never truly sorry for doing it. Dave Dugan regretted that his aim was off when he shot me, but he never regretted trying to kill me. And Eddie…to him killing people is just part of doing business. Someone interferes with your income, your control, your freedom, you kill him. Problem solved. What's to feel guilty about?''

''But—''

She laid her fingers across his mouth. ''Feeling guilty is good, because it means you've got a conscience. It means you're a decent, honorable person. But then you deal with it, and you move on. And that's what we're going to do.''

Rising to her feet, she took his left hand and tugged until he stood, too. She led him across the room to the side hall, then into his bedroom, where the lights were off, the covers rumpled from his restlessness. He sat on the bed, pillows at his back cushioning the headboard. She raised the blinds to let the storm in, got a cup of water from the bathroom, then sat facing him. After shaking the two pills from the bottle into his palm, she handed him the water, watched while he swallowed it down, then continued to watch. Considering that he'd been shot yesterday, he looked good—handsome, rested, vital. He also looked, at that moment, serious and intent.

''Neely…'' He threaded his fingers tightly through hers. ''I am so sorry. I don't know if you can forgive me, but if you'll try, I'll do my best to deserve it.''

Simple and to the point. So was her response. "I forgive you. If you'll try to do the same for me, I'll do my best, too."

"There's nothing to forgive. You never let me down. You never walked away. You never broke my heart. Those are all my failings."

Her smile came slowly. "Then I must be almost perfect. Hmm...I've never been almost perfect before. I think I like that." Leaning forward, she brought her mouth into contact with his for a gentle, innocent kiss. But when he released her hand and slid his fingers into her hair to pull her closer, when he thrust his tongue into her mouth and sent incredible heat and need shuddering through her body, gentle and innocent fled her mind in favor of fierce, raw hunger.

When finally he ended the kiss, he took a ragged breath. "Sweet hell, Neely, I want you, but I can't... My shoulder..."

She leaned forward and tenderly kissed a patch of warm skin between the two dressings. "You want me to go back to my room and let you sleep?" she murmured, though she had no intention of going anywhere.

He responded with an obscenity that suggested he shared her intentions. "What I want you to do is take pity on me and come over here and torment me a little more."

"Oh, good. That's exactly what I wanted to do." She turned to kneel on the bed, lifting one leg over his, sliding bit by bit until she was exactly where she wanted to be, until he was almost where she needed him. "Does that hurt?"

"No."

She slid along the length of him, then back again. "How about that? Did it hurt?"

"No." This time he ground out the word in a harsh voice. With his left hand, he caught hold of her, held her tightly, stopped her from moving again. "You're a generous woman."

"This?" She smiled seductively as she managed, in spite of his grip, to send sensation rocketing through him. "This is the height of selfishness. I need this. I've waited for it, for you, so long...I've been so lost without you." With the last words she brushed her mouth over his, and he opened to her, welcoming her tongue inside, accepting her kiss as if he needed it, too, as if he'd waited forever.

She savored the taste of him, the familiar, dark flavor that was embedded in her memory, in her soul. She thought she would recognize that taste, that texture and intensity, blindfolded—would be able to pick him out of a hundred men because he was a part of her.

Though his right hand was useless, he didn't sit idly while they kissed. With his left hand, he loosened the ribbons that held the front of her gown together, pushed it aside and treated her breasts to gentle, fleeting caresses. He stroked and rubbed and made her groan, pinched her nipples and took advantage of her gasp to take control of their kiss. He made her shiver and heated her body, raised goose bumps on her flesh, then chased them away with tantalizing caresses, claimed her mouth and promised to claim her body soon…but not soon enough.

When he began pulling at her gown, she helped him remove it, though she did most of the work while he played. When she removed the gym shorts that were all he wore, she repaid him in full, taking forever to do a task he would have accomplished in seconds, drawing the most interesting responses from him, from erotic groans to savage curses.

He was pulling her back into place astride his hips when she held herself back. "What about a condom?"

Lightning illuminated his face, features taut with arousal, eyes clear and sober. "In the drawer…if you want one."

She couldn't pull her gaze from his while she considered it. If she opted for protection, he wouldn't say anything, but he would be a little disappointed, she thought, and so would she. The chances of her getting pregnant tonight were minuscule—but the chances of Forbes's man finding her in Tulsa yesterday had gone way beyond that. But if she did get pregnant… She couldn't imagine anything better.

She settled herself over his hips, and he filled her slowly, sweetly, making her eyes close and her breath catch and her chest tighten with emotion. When she'd taken all of him, moisture filled her eyes and turned her smile bittersweet. "Do you remember the first time…?"

Sliding his fingers into her hair, he pulled her close, until they were practically nose to nose. "Every detail," he growled as if offended at the implication that he might have forgotten.

"You slid inside me, and it was so tight and full and incredible, and you said—"

"'I've been looking my whole life for the place where I belong, and here you are.'"

"And here you are," she echoed softly. Bracing her hands on the headboard, she began moving slowly, ever so gently, gliding easily along the length of him, gloving him tighter to provide friction for the return. She set a gentle pace, letting the pressure build slowly, taking her own sweet time, ignoring Reese when he silently urged her to move faster.

"Did I mention I've waited a really long time for this?" he asked, his voice raw, his breathing uneven.

"You told me to torment you." Her voice wasn't much smoother.

"You're doing a damn fine job…but you're killing me."

She tried to stop, but he refused to let her. "Your shoulder—"

"What shoulder? This— I need— I need to—" A great groan escaped him as he filled her, and she matched him pretty well with her own cries. Shudders racked her, and her lungs grew too tight to allow any but the smallest of breaths as sensation after sensation swelled over her. She collapsed against him, her head on his uninjured shoulder, and held tightly as the same shudders rocketed through him.

Minutes passed before they both became still, before she was able to once again fill her lungs with air that smelled of him, her, them, before she found the energy to lift her head. She gazed at him a moment before he raised his head and opened his eyes to look back. "And here you are," she murmured.

He kissed her gently before correcting her. "Here *we* are."

* * *

Thanks to his wound, Reese could lie only on his back, but he didn't mind, since Neely was stretched out full-length beside him. For a time she'd lain on her side facing him, before turning her back to him. His arm was still around her, though, and she still held tightly to him, even in sleep.

He'd dozed awhile, then decided he could sleep anytime. Right then he'd rather watch her and the storm. So that was what he'd done for the past hour, alternating between wondering if the storm system was ever going to clear the area and whether she would stay with him forever.

There was a rap at the open bedroom door, then Brady's voice broke the quiet. "Reese, Neely, either of you awake?"

"I am. What's up?"

"I just got a call from the office. That area off Chicken Farm Road is flooded again, and this time the bridge washed out. We've got some people stranded out there. You want to let me out or tell me the code or…?"

"It's ten-twenty-three."

"Ten-twenty-three," Brady repeated. "The code for arrived at the scene. Anyone ever suggest you need a vacation, Sheriff?"

"Aw, heck, why would I want a vacation from police work?"

"The best reason's lying there beside you." Brady took a step away, then turned back. "You have a gun handy?"

"On the nightstand."

"How do you score with your off hand?"

"I may not be able to use a fork with it, but I can hit a target with my .45 at twenty-five yards."

"Then I'll be outta here."

"Thanks, Brady, for everything. And be careful." Reese listened to the sounds of him leaving, then made sure his pistol was still on the night table. He was glad to be alone with Neely, but he had to admit, there was a part of him that had been more than happy to share the protection detail with Brady. He'd known she was safer, and that had made him feel safer.

"Is he gone?" Neely's voice was husky, as if she'd just awakened, and throaty, as if he needed arousing again.

"Hmm."

She wriggled out of his embrace. "Let me doublecheck the alarm, then close the blinds so we don't fall asleep and wake up in the morning exposed to the world."

"Darlin', it *is* morning, or just about. It's after six. It's just the storm clouds that make it seem earlier." He watched her hurry down the hall to the garage door, then come back, her body pale in the dim light. She closed the blinds, leaving the room a few shades darker, then snuggled under the covers with him again. "The alarm was set, wasn't it? Brady doesn't get sloppy."

"He's got a lot of secrets."

"Yeah." And Reese had learned one last night. Not that it had really been a secret. He had supposed all along that a woman was somehow involved in Brady's past. Maybe a fellow sufferer couldn't help but recognize the symptoms.

"Do you really have a road in the county called Chicken Farm Road?"

"Yeah. It's outside Buffalo Plains."

"And let me guess—it got its name from all the chicken farms located along it."

"Actually, I don't recall there ever being any chicken farms out there. I imagine some of the folks raise their own chickens, but mostly it's just regular farms."

"Those poor people. I hope they don't lose anything."

"You're softhearted."

"You just think I'm all sorts of things, don't you?" she teased, then suddenly turned serious. "Last night you told Brady I was a damn good lawyer—too good to give it up. Did you mean that?"

"Of course. You've always known—"

"No. The closest you ever came to saying I was good was when you said I was too good to be wasting my talents defending the scum you were arresting. But you would have thought a chimpanzee was too good to defend them."

He thought about it, but knew she was right. Raising her hand to his mouth, he pressed a kiss to the palm. "I apologize for that. I've always admired your intelligence, your understanding of the law, your talents and your skills. I just thought your choice of clients sucked. But every deputy in Keegan County knew that if I ever got into any sort of trouble, you were the only one I'd want to represent me."

"Thank you. That means a lot." She rolled onto her stomach, leaning on her elbows to study him.

He used the time to recommit a few things to memory, like the straight line of her nose, the delicate shape of her features, how kissable her mouth was, how long and pale her throat was, the location of each of her scars. The entry wound was below the right shoulder, lower than his own, low enough to get into dangerous territory. The surgical scar was straight, neatly cut and neatly sutured, as was the third scar, not visible now.

He ran his fingertip over the entry wound, round with irregular edges, thickened. "It doesn't count for much, but...walking away from you that day was the hardest thing I'd ever done. There was a part of me that knew it was wrong, that wanted to hold you and protect you and never leave you, but I...couldn't. I had Judy's blood all over me—she'd just died in my arms—and I couldn't..."

Catching his hand, she kissed the palm, then the callused skin at the base of his finger, then dragged his fingertip into her mouth for a sensual bite. Too soon her play stopped and she clasped his hand in both of hers. "I went into surgery as soon as I got to the hospital that afternoon. They removed the bullet, and I had a pneumothorax, so they put a chest tube in—that's the smaller scar under my breast. That night I was pretty heavily drugged, and I dreamed you were there. It was odd. Even while I was dreaming, I knew it was a dream. I knew it was over between us." There at the end her voice quavered, and she lowered her head so he couldn't see her eyes. "I'd never thought that day would come. I'd thought we would be together forever. We fitted each other so perfectly...except for my job, and your...dislike for it. Not having you in my life was inconceivable. It took weeks to get past the certainty that it was all just a terrible misunderstanding."

"Weeks? Try months. Something would happen at work, and I'd think, Neely will get a kick out of that, then remember that you were gone. I'd wake up in the middle of the night and I could smell you on the sheets and on my skin, as if you'd just gotten up a minute earlier. The first few times it happened, I actually got up and checked the apartment, because I was so sure..."

In an obvious attempt to lighten the conversation, she leaned over him and sniffed. "Do you smell like me now? Because if you don't, I haven't done my job properly."

"Maybe you'd better do it again just for good measure."

In a surprisingly obedient mood, she kissed him, teased him, pleased him. Her talented, slender fingers touched him everywhere, bringing heat, and her talented, kissable mouth followed, promising so much more. He was hard, his skin glistening with sweat, his muscles quivering with sensation, and yet she continued to play, to stroke, to kiss, to arouse. When he'd endured about all he could, he pulled her away from her intimate kisses and lifted her over him.

"Not yet," she chastened, but he maneuvered her into place and filled her with one long thrust that made them both groan.

"Not yet?" he echoed when he could speak. "Another five seconds of what you were doing, and it was gonna be over for me, darlin'."

"This time, maybe. But there's always next time." Smiling self-assuredly, she sat straight, raised her arms high above her head and arched her back in a full body stretch. The action lifted her small, perfect breasts, made her narrow waist seem narrower and delivered a potent surge of pleasure where her body sheltered his deep inside.

"Next time?" He stroked her breast, then watched her nipple pucker and swell. "You have great faith in your ability to arouse me."

"Do that again," she commanded breathlessly, then halt-ingly replied. "I have great faith in...in your ability to...be...aroused. Oh, yes, exactly like that," she whispered as he kneaded her nipple between his fingers.

"I have great faith in us both." He'd barely ground out the last word when she began moving in long, slow, sensuous strokes that threatened every bit of self-control he'd ever pos-sessed. Every part of him ached to roll her over and make love to her fast, hard and fierce, to thrust into her deeper than she'd ever taken him, to fill her more incredibly, to ruthlessly claim her for his own and never let her go, but that would have to wait. This stormy morning *she* was doing the thrusting, the taking, the claiming, and he was glad to be claimed.

He came in an explosion of brutal need and raw satisfaction, emptying into her, and felt her body clenching and trembling with her own approaching finish. Her gasps turned to breath-less cries, then dissolved into helpless whimpers, as he held her, stroked her, whispered quiet words. As her tremors faded and the tension that tightened her body eased, as she sank limply against him, clinging to him the way she had nine years ago, he again remembered their very first time.

I've been looking my whole life for the place where I be-long, he'd told her. Neely was that place. He'd found her, lost her and found her again, and this time, he swore, he wasn't letting her go. He was her place, and she was his.

And nothing—please, God—would change that ever again.

The first thing Neely noticed after her shower was that the kitchen phone was back in its place, plugged in and apparently functional. She went to Reese, making sandwiches at the kitchen counter, and slid her arms around him from behind. "Gee, give a man a couple of great climaxes, and he'll give you anything in return," she gently teased.

"Like a couple of great climaxes of your own."

"Or a telephone."

"That you can use only for emergencies." He turned to face her, to let her know how serious he was. "I'll do my best to keep you from getting bored—'' his charming grin flashed, then disappeared ''—but you have to swear to me you won't call anyone just to let them know you're all right.''

She solemnly raised her right hand. ''I swear.'' Automatically she reached for the knife he held, then caught herself and pulled back. ''Need any help?''

He eyed her wryly for a moment, then handed the knife over. ''Our hands aren't so different, you know—five pairs of fingers, each in the same place on its hand, perfectly matched. The fingers on the left hand work the same way they do on the right, and the grip works the same. But it's amazing the things you can do with one hand that you can't manage with the other, like slicing a tomato or using a razor.''

''Oh, but think of the amazing things you can do just as well,'' she said slyly, seductively, bringing a smoky look to his eyes. Frankly, she hadn't missed his right hand at all, not one of the several times they'd made love.

When they were seated at the table a few minutes later, she ate part of her sandwich before laying it aside to somberly face Reese. ''How long can this go on with Forbes? If Jace can't get enough evidence to charge him, do I go back to Kansas City and wait for him to try again? Do I sell my house and close up my practice and never go back there again?''

''You can't go back to Kansas City. You can't make it easy for him, Neely.''

''So I let him scare me away from home for good? I go into hiding for the rest of his life or mine, whichever ends first?''

''No. You can't do that, either.'' After a moment he asked, ''What do you want to do?'' The question was unemotional, the tone noncommittal, as if the answer didn't matter to him one way or the other. She knew it did. She just didn't know how much.

She wanted to stay right there in Heartbreak with him. She wanted to live out the life they'd talked about ten years ago— marriage, kids, the works. She wanted to get to know Shay better, and Brady and Callie, and she wanted to meet everyone else Reese considered a friend. She wanted babies and bar-becues and riding lessons—both with horses and without, she thought with a faint smile—and small-town life and friends and a father-in-law and a mother-in-law, or two or three.

She wanted the happily-ever-after.

"I don't want to live the rest of my life looking over my shoulder. I don't want to worry every time I go out that some innocent person might die for no reason except that he was standing too close to me. I don't want Eddie Forbes to believe he can get away with what he's done." She'd surrendered to the bad guys once before, when she'd run away from Thom-asville without a whimper, and she wasn't doing it again. "I want to be free to live my life, to love someone, to have babies, without putting them in danger."

He pushed his own plate aside with an unsteady hand. In-side the sling, his right hand was curled into a fist, and his face was unusually pale, his expression unusually hard. "There's a way you can do that, but it's dangerous. It involves using you as bait to draw Forbes out. Would you be willing to risk it?"

Cold inside, Neely stared at him. Suddenly the idea of spending the next forty years in hiding didn't seem so bad. Sure, it would cramp her lifestyle a bit, but at least she would *have* a life. But to deliberately face the man who'd sworn to kill her…

She'd faced worse and survived. She'd lived through losing Reese.

She nodded several times before she managed to get any words out. "All right."

He held out his hand, and she moved without hesitation to sit on his lap. He wrapped his arm around her and held her close, resting his cheek against her hair. His voice was grim, his embrace secure, when he reluctantly responded.

"Then I'll talk to Jace."

It took about three minutes of listening to Jace's ranting for Neely to figure out that he didn't like their idea—and she wasn't the one on the phone. She was a fair distance away, but didn't miss a thing. He used every swearword she'd ever heard and came up with a few combinations she wasn't familiar with before finally stopping for a breath.

"Jace, it's been nearly three weeks since he first moved on her. She can't go on like this indefinitely."

"Why not? She's safe."

Neely hid a smile at his belligerent tone. "Believe it or not, Detective Barnett, she's got a life, and it doesn't allow for hiding behind locked doors twenty-four hours a day," she said, raising her voice so he could hear.

"You weren't behind locked doors Wednesday, were you? And look what happened. Jeez, Reese, you discussed this with her? Can't you two find something better to do with your time than coming up with stupid plans to get one or both of you killed?"

She took the phone from Reese, but held it where he could hear. "And what would you suggest?"

"Hell, I don't know. Wild sex?"

She responded to his sarcasm with flippancy. "Been there, done that, enjoyed it tremendously. But you've got to come up for air sometime, you know."

"With the hours I've been putting in on your case, no, I wouldn't know. Bottom line, Neely—you're not setting yourself up as a target for a cold-blooded killer."

"Jace, I'm already a target. I just want to bring it to an end."

"Are you so anxious to die?"

"No." She looked at Reese and felt a sharp ache in her chest. "I'm anxious to live. Please think about it, Jace."

He said he would and would call them back. They watched a little television. They lay together on the sofa and talked about interesting cases. Brady called to check on them and to report on the flood damage. Callie came by to check up on Reese—without Isabella, Neely was happy to see. So much as one *cowboy* or semi-sultry look in his direction, and pretty

Isabella would have left minus a handful of that lovely red hair.

Shay called to see if she could persuade Reese to take Neely to their ranch for dinner, but he said they already had plans, then made good on his lie by making love to her again with his hands, his mouth, his body, and leaving her too weak to do more than sigh delightedly when it was over.

She was lying on her back across the bed, and Reese was stretched out beside her, watching her with a smug grin. "I may never move again," she murmured in a ragged voice. "I've got tingling in places I didn't know existed."

"Thank you."

"Oh, no. Thank you." Behind her closed eyes, she could make out the shadows caused by the ceiling fan blades as they whirred, the breeze they created drying the sheen that covered her body from head to toe. Her entire body felt satiated and achy and thoroughly well used, and her heart felt... The way it always had with Reese—swollen to near bursting with love. "You are too good, Sheriff."

"Thank you, ma'am," he said in a lazy drawl. "I'm sworn to protect and service."

The ring of the telephone startled her eyes open, and she rolled over onto her stomach. She hadn't realized that he'd hooked up the phone in the bedroom, too. Of course, she'd been more than a little preoccupied when they'd come in.

Reese sat up without too much difficulty and hit the speaker button, then offered a curt hello.

"Hey, bubba. Is Neely around? I need to ask her something."

"I'm right here," she replied. "What do you want to know?"

"In your office at home, you had a picture frame on your desk—silver, with lots of curlicues and stuff."

She smiled. "You need a little culture in your life, Jace. It's called filigree. What about it?"

"What was the picture in it?"

"It's a handsome pitcher before the game that ended what would have been one of baseball's most stellar careers. Why?"

"Would he be easily identifiable?"

Looking at the duplicate on the opposite nightstand, Reese said, "I'm standing on the field in Kauffman Stadium, wearing a Royals uniform. Uh, yeah, I'd say every sports bar in the city has at least one trivia buff who would be able to identify me. If not, there are the media guys, or the clip files at the libraries or, hell, just go to the Royals and ask."

Judging from his grim tone, Neely realized she was missing something. "What does it matter? The picture's in my office...locked...up... They *broke* into my house?"

"I guess they thought they might find something there when your office came up empty."

"They broke into my *office?*" she shrieked. "*When?* Why didn't you tell me?"

"I told Reese," Jace said defensively, and she turned her scowl on him.

"We had other things on our minds, babe. You can yell at me later. Let's get back to the subject. When was the house broken into?"

"Don't know for sure. Best guess is sometime between yesterday morning and this afternoon. Neighbor noticed the blinds were closed differently or something and called us. The place was ransacked, but the only thing that's obviously missing is the picture. They left the frame on the desk and the broken glass on the floor. My theory is the man who winged you, bubba, was either involved or gave 'em a real good description of you. Someone recognized you in the picture and was smart enough to realize they could get a name from it."

And with a name, it wouldn't be difficult at all to get a town, Neely acknowledged. Anyone with a smidge of motivation could easily find a dozen sources that gave Heartbreak as Reese's hometown. It had been common knowledge when he'd retired from baseball that he was going into law enforcement. Every soul in Thomasville knew he'd gone back home

when he'd left there, and not a soul in Heartbreak would thin
twice about giving a stranger directions to the sheriff's house

"So chances are better than good that Forbes's people ar
on their way here, if not already here." Reese sounded calm
serious, but not overly worried. When he caught her watchin
him, he winked, then wrapped his fingers around hers.

"That'd be my guess. Can you get her to the county jail?'
Jace asked.

"I don't think that would be our best move. You know th
road from here to Buffalo Plains. I've only got one good arm
and while Neely could put the fear of God into just abou
anyone with her driving, she doesn't have any training in eva
sive or defensive techniques. I'll call Brady, my undersheriff
and see if he can help us out, and I believe she'll be movin,
from the guest room to the safe room this evening."

"So…" She cleared her throat and tried to make her voic
steady. "I guess our stupid plan is no longer necessary. Instea
of facing Forbes on our own terms, we get to wait for his guy
to come after us like sitting ducks."

"I'm sorry, Neely," Jace said.

"Please, no more apologies and no more talk about blam
or fault. We're not the bad guys here." Tugging free of Reese
she sat up, located her clothes where he'd scattered them, an
quickly got dressed. "Wish us luck, Jace."

"Listen, I've got a buddy with his own plane that I'm gonn
track down. I'll get there as quick as I can. Until then…yo
guys take care of yourselves. You know I love you both."

She glanced at Reese, feeling suddenly shy, then replied
"We love you, too." As he disconnected the call, she took
deep breath. "This sounds serious."

"You'll be okay."

"*We'll* be okay." Though she tried to sound confident, sh
knew she barely managed hopeful and came too close for com
fort to pleading.

"Help me with my jeans—and no fondling," he warne
when a smile curved her lips. After she obediently helped hir
with the snug-fitting denims without any untoward touches, h

kissed her forehead. "Stay here. Don't leave this room for anything."

"Where are you going?"

With the pistol gripped firmly in his left hand, he gazed back at her on his way out. "To get ready. We're gonna stop these creeps, babe, once and for all."

Chapter 12

While talking to Brady on the cell phone, Reese made the rounds of the house, checking locks, closing blinds and drapes. He moved his truck out of the garage so Brady could pull in when he arrived, got his department-issue shotgun from the sheriff's vehicle, then returned to the bedroom. Neely was sitting exactly where he'd left her, looking pensive.

"I bet you wish I'd destroyed that picture," she murmured. "I've managed to lead them right to us."

"Actually, I'm flattered that you kept it." He laid the shotgun and the cell phone on the bed, then opened the nightstand drawer where his own photographs stayed. She didn't smile but she did look a little less troubled.

"Brady's on his way over. He's going to have a look around before he comes to the house. He'll be armed for bear. You're sleeping in the safe room tonight. Except for going to the bathroom, I don't want you farther than ten feet away from it. These guys could already be set down out there in the woods, just waiting for us to go to bed, or they may still be in Kansas City. You hear a sound, get your butt in there and lock the door. Don't worry about what's going on out here, and don't come out for anyone you don't know.''

"I have a better idea. Why don't you, and Brady when he gets here, go in the safe room with me? After a while, they'll get tired of shooting at what's basically a bulletproof room and they'll go away."

"But they won't go far. It ends here, darlin'."

"Forbes probably won't be with them."

"Probably not. But at best we'll be able to tie him to them. At worst, we'll put the word out that trying to cash in on his contract is a good way to wind up in jail or dead." While they were talking, he'd been making trips back and forth from the closet to the bed. After the last one, he surveyed his cache. One .45, one .38 revolver, two shotguns, one single-shot rifle, one semiautomatic rifle, and nowhere near enough ammunition. He wasn't a hunter, so the only shooting he did was at the range, and since that was for the job, he picked up ammo at work.

If he survived this, he would add both weapons and ammunition to his arsenal. With Neely's knack for pissing off criminals, he would probably need them.

"What do you need from the guest room?" he asked, then went on before she could reply. "Never mind. I'll get everything. You're not sleeping in there again."

"You're awfully bossy."

"I'm just looking out for your welfare, darlin'." And his future. Their future.

He moved through the quiet house, wondering what, if anything, was going on outside. They were fortunate in that there weren't a lot of places to hide out there—just the barn out back and the woods out front—and there weren't any neighbors close enough to get caught in any cross fire.

Assuming there was cross fire. They'd tried using a bomb the first time and a semi-automatic weapon the second. It was anyone's guess what their next weapon of choice would be.

Neely had finally unpacked, he found out when he picked up her suitcase from the corner. He refilled it hastily with soft dresses and silky, satiny lingerie, tossed in her books, glasses and chocolate kisses, then got her shampoo and stuff from the bathroom. Carrying the unzipped suitcase with one arm was awkward, but he made it back to his room and the bed before dropping it. While she watched, he put the bathroom stuff in *his* bathroom, and the clothes in his closet. The lingerie went into a drawer with his briefs, until he had time to clear out a drawer for her, though he stopped with the last matching set. Peach satin that was incredibly soft, little pieces that couldn't possibly cover more than the bare essentials, tiny lacy panties, barely-there bra. Designed for form rather than function.

"I never understood why clothing people make something so pretty just so it can be hidden under T-shirts and jeans."

"I offered to model those for you on the deck last Saturday, but you said if I took my clothes off, you'd have to arrest me for indecent exposure." She smiled. "Of course, you pulled a peeping Tom later, anyway."

He could too easily imagine her long, slender body lying in the sun, all creamy skin and pale peach scraps. He would have been a goner, then and there.

Swallowing hard, he dropped the garments in the drawer and bumped it shut with his hip, then turned to face her. "That pretty much takes care of everything."

"So what do we do now?"

"We wait."

It sounded so easy. Do nothing and wait for Brady to arrive, for Jace and for Forbes's men. Wait for them to make another attempt on Neely's life. Wait for some criminal to decide that this was a good time to kill her.

It was going to be one of the hardest things he'd ever done.

Brady showed up first, more than an hour after Reese had called him. He called on the cell phone to let them know it was him pulling into the driveway, and Reese went to meet him in the garage. He'd brought enough ammunition to hold off a small army, along with good news. "I parked down the street and came up through the woods and checked the barn. There's no one around, no strange cars parked anywhere, no one in town looking like they don't belong. Everything's quiet. I guess now we wait.''

Neely waved one slender hand in the air to get their attention. ''I have a suggestion. Why don't we wait…oh, gee, how about in Dallas? I could introduce you to my sister, Kylie. She's the pretty one, Brady. You'd like her.''

''I thought you were the pretty one,'' Reese teased as he sat beside her on the bed with a pair of socks and running shoes. ''Can you help me with these?''

She slid to her knees on the floor as if she'd helped dress him a hundred times. ''Kylie's the pretty one, Hallie's the popular one, Bailey's the smart one, and I'm the…'' For a moment, she became still, a distant look creeping across her face, until he touched her hair, pulling her back. ''I'm the determined one,'' she finished. ''The one who doesn't give up.''

But there was a difference, Neely thought as she quickly finished the task, between being determined and being courageous. In spite of her suggestions that they put off this fight for another day, she knew the confrontation was inevitable, but she couldn't find it in her to face it bravely. She couldn't help but dread the knowledge that Reese and Brady—and maybe Jace—were risking their lives for her. She couldn't face the possibility that she might die so soon after resolving the past with Reese, without resolving the future.

She couldn't stop being afraid.

''Do you remember how to use this?''

She blinked, then focused on the gun Reese was holding. It was a revolver, fairly small and rather cute, as well as quite deadly. He'd used it to teach her how to shoot in Thomasville—primarily as an excuse to get his arms around her, she'd teased him. Because, he'd responded, considering the scum she defended, she never knew when it might come in handy.

When she nodded, he asked, ''When is the last time you shot one?''

''Three months ago. When we found out Forbes was being paroled. Jace thought I needed a refresher.'' She took the gun, tested its weight in her palm, wrapped her fingers around the grips, then offered it back.

"Keep it with you all the time. Sleep with it under your pillow. Have it on you when you're awake. We'll try to make sure you don't have to use it, but just in case…"

In case she had no one left to rely on but herself. In case he and Brady were wounded…or worse. Feeling sick deep inside, she slid the gun into the roomy pocket of her dress and felt its weight acutely, as if it weighed a ton instead of a few pounds.

"It's ten-fifteen," Brady said from the doorway. "Why don't we turn the lights off? I'll watch out the back, and you can take the front."

Neely watched them divide the weapons and ammunition. When Brady started to turn away, she scrambled to her feet and circled the bed. "Last chance, Undersheriff Marshall," she said, forcing a lightness she didn't feel into her voice. "Take my word for it—Kylie's blond, beautiful and has a fine appreciation for dark, dangerous men. We could be on the road to Texas in three minutes tops, if you'll vote with me."

Underneath the mustache, his mouth curved into the coolest of smiles. "You can introduce us when she comes for the wedding."

"What—" She glanced from him to Reese, checking his guns and paying little attention to them. She didn't know whether he'd thought that far ahead, but she had. She intended to marry him and live happily ever after. If it took some convincing…she was up to the challenge.

Rising onto her toes, she kissed Brady's cheek. "Thank you."

His cheeks turned bronze. "Just doing my job."

"Right. Be careful."

He took a few steps into the hallway before pausing. "I'll shut off the lights out there. Wait a minute or two, then turn off the ones in here."

She nodded and, with an apprehensive shudder, watched him go. The TV they'd left on in the living room went silent, then the lights were turned off. A moment later the faint glow from the light over the kitchen sink went dark, too. She watched Reese, who'd laid out his weapons on the window seat and was arranging the ammunition nearby.

He looked up and smiled. "We'll be all right."

"Sure."

"Aw, come on. You've got the damnedest luck of anyone I know. Bullets bounce off you. Bombs can't touch you."

Not all bullets bounced. She carried the scars to prove it. Soon, as the healing process continued, he would have his own scars.

She turned off the bathroom light, lingered a moment, then shut off the bedside lamp. The bedsprings creaked as she sat, and thin light filtered into the room as Reese opened the blinds just enough to see out. She settled on his side of the bed, hugging his pillow to her chest, and he settled on the window seat, back against the wall, legs stretched out in front of him.

"Do you have other deputies out there, keeping an eye on us?"

"No. Brady and I decided to keep it between us. You have to understand, law enforcement in Canyon County is pretty minor stuff—traffic violations, break-ins, burglaries, bar fights. We've had only three homicides in nine years, and only a handful of shootings. Other than maybe the new one, my deputies haven't been shot at, haven't shot at anyone else or even drawn their guns on someone. Armed and scared, they're likely to be as dangerous to us as to the bad guys."

His voice was quiet, reassuring even if his words weren't. She rested her chin on his pillow and breathed deeply of his scent. "Do you think they'll come tonight?"

"They have to assume that the break-in at your house will be discovered before long and that someone will know who was in the photograph they took. They already know you're with me. They just have to find out who I am. That'll tell them where I am—and the fact that I have the same last name as the detective handling your case won't go unnoticed. They have to consider that the police already know all that and, as soon as they find out about the break-in, they're going to warn us and, most likely, move you someplace else immediately. Their only chance is to get to us first, before Jace can put together a move to a new location.

"That's the long answer," he said, and she could hear the smile in his voice. "The short answer is yes. I think they'll come tonight."

The seconds dragged by, each lasting an hour, or so it seemed. Neely watched Reese's shadowy form as he watched the scene outside, and she listened—to the air-conditioning cycling on and off, the distant chirrup of tree frogs, the quiet hoot of an owl—until every sound was magnified in her ears. She wanted to hide her head under the pillows to block out the noises, but then she would hear the uneven thud of her own heart and the shallow breathing that was all she could manage. She wanted to talk but didn't have a clue what she could say—wanted to run away but knew there was no place to run.

"Neely. Why don't you go in the safe room and sleep a bit?"

"I can't."

He chuckled. "Sorry to break this to you, darlin', but you've been snoring into my pillow for about five minutes— delicately, of course."

Pushing the pillow aside, she stood, rubbed her eyes, then stretched. "Remember the scene in *Close Encounters of the Third Kind* where all the people are waiting for the alien ships to return?"

"Or the takeoff on it in *Airplane!* where they're lined up waiting for the plane to land?"

She sounded edgy and afraid. He sounded amused. Though it was wasted, she frowned at him. "Everything's so quiet and still and normal, and yet there's this air of anticipation, and then suddenly… I hate waiting," she said petulantly. "There's a part of me that wants to go out in the front yard and yell, 'Here I am! If you're going to do something, for God's sake, do it!'"

"You'd have to get past me, darlin'."

"You only have one good arm."

"Yeah, but I could still haul you into the safe room like a sack of grain. When this is over, I'll prove it to you, only I'll settle for hauling you into bed for a week or two."

"Promises, promises." She knelt beside the window seat, laying her head on his thigh. "I don't mean to whine."

"This is whining? Darlin', you need some lessons. My aunt Rozena can whine—make you sound like a songbird in comparison. She can teach you the finer points, and anything she misses, Lena can fill in."

"Are you any happier about her and your dad getting married?"

He was silent for a moment, then he shrugged. "We may never have much of a mother-son relationship, but I can show her the respect my father's wife deserves." He stroked her cheek. "That's advice from the best damn lawyer I know, so I think I'd better take it."

"I think you probably—"

"Get in the safe room," he said abruptly, pushing her away and getting to his feet. "Brady, I've got flashlights out in the woods—at least three of 'em. Neely, get in the safe room and lock the door!"

He yanked her to her feet and shoved her in that direction, sending her stumbling across the threshold. Before she could catch her balance, he'd slammed the door and was harshly commanding her to lock it. Rising from the bed where she'd landed, she felt her way in the pitch black until she ran into the wall, then fumbled around to the door. After securing both locks, she took another blind plunge and located a flashlight on the shelf.

The twin bed was the only furniture in the room. She pulled it away from the wall and onto its side, folded the mattress in half, then wedged it and herself into the corner behind the frame. She huddled there, flashlight unsteady in one hand, pistol shaky in the other, and trembled while mouthing silent prayers.

Though the temperature in the room was comfortably cool, sweat dotted her forehead, and though the oxygen supply was way beyond adequate, she couldn't squeeze enough air into her lungs. Oh, God, she was afraid! She just wanted to live—wanted to live the rest of her life with Reese, wanted Brady to be around, too. She would give up the law completely and concentrate on being the best wife and mother of his children Reese could ever ask for, or she would go back to the law, if that was what it took, and devote every working hour to pro bono cases or putting away criminals or any other kind of legal work God wanted her to do. She would pay whatever price He set, if only she survived, if only they all survived.

Please, God, let us live.

Reese stood to the side of the bedroom window, lifting the blinds slightly with the barrel of the semiautomatic rifle. There were five lights in the woods now, huddled together, making no effort to hide themselves. Were they unaware of how easily the lights showed up in the dark night? Or did they figure there was no reason to hide when there would be no survivors to identify them?

As he watched, he felt as if his heart had lodged in his throat, tightening his chest and making his breathing ragged. He should have taken Neely someplace else—to the Raffertys' place or the Harrises'. Nearly ten miles out of town, both ranches would have been as safe as if they were in another state. Even Ethan and Grace James's house, just a few miles away, would have been better than keeping her here.

But it was too late for regrets. All he could do now was to try his best to stop the bad guys before they stopped him, and pray that if he and Brady failed, the safe room would do its job until reinforcements arrived to rescue her.

After a few moments in the huddle, the lights separated. Two went to the left, two to the right, and the fifth came straight toward the house. Reese's stomach knotted as he called in a low voice, "They're moving, Brady. We've got one from the front and at least two from each side."

"Not a problem." Brady sounded so cool and relaxed, as if he'd gone through this plenty of times and had no doubt he would win.

Reese was neither so calm nor so confident. Of course, he didn't have much more experience at dangerous situations than the deputies he'd judged too green to be of any help to them, and he had a lot more to lose tonight than Brady did.

The figure approaching the front of the house stopped some twenty feet back. He was a cocky bastard, standing there as if he had no concern for his own safety. Reese's finger tightened fractionally on the rifle trigger as the man reached into his pocket and pulled out an item too compact for a gun. The question of what it was was answered seconds later when the telephone on the nightstand rang.

Reese left his post only long enough to grab the phone. When he answered bluntly, the man came a few feet closer. "Sheriff Barnett, this is Eddie Forbes. I regret we have to meet this way—actually, I'd probably regret meeting you under any circumstances—but we have to make the best of the situation. You know why I'm here?"

"Because you've got some guy working for you who's the luckiest bastard in the world."

"You mean Kenny. Spotting Neely in the theater parking lot was an amazing stroke of luck, wasn't it?"

"Amazing."

"Why don't you save me the hassle of coming in after Neely and hand her over? That way your house doesn't get shot up, you don't risk getting hurt, and your neighbors' sleep won't be disturbed."

"Gee, I don't think so. I kinda like hassling people like you." To say nothing of the fact that if he were coward enough to turn her over, he would still die right alongside her. No witnesses, no evidence, no impending arrest.

"Don't think I was stupid enough to come alone."

"I didn't think that for a minute, Ed—though I do think you're stupid."

"The odds are in my favor, you know. I'm repaying my

debt to Neely tonight, and there's no way you're going to stop me, Sheriff."

"I don't know. I figure it would take…oh, probably about five of you to equal one of me. Seems fair enough."

From Brady in the kitchen came a low warning whistle, then, farther away, Reese heard the muted sound of breaking glass. The guest room or the front bedroom, he guessed. About the same time, another tinkle of glass came from the laundry room. He tossed the phone onto the bed, traded the rifle for the shotgun, stuck the .45 in his waistband, along with two extra clips of ammo, then eased into the hallway. Sounds of a scuffle came from the other side of the house, followed by a substantial thud and another of Brady's whistles. One down, soon to be two, and three to go.

Provided they were right in assuming five lights meant only five men.

The laundry room door creaked as it was slowly opened, then a light appeared—a flashlight taped to the barrel of a gun. The beam moved across the kitchen, then down the hall. An instant before it reached him, Reese fired. The flashlight, along with the gun, fell to the kitchen floor, illuminating the blood splatter from the other room.

His ears ringing from the shotgun blast, and his stomach roiling from the knowledge that he'd just killed his first person, Reese heard sounds from Brady's side of the house—shots, a shouted curse, more shots—along with a commotion out front. He was turning toward the living room when a spray of bullets disintegrated the window, shredding the drapes, shattering lamps and tearing through furniture before hitting the log wall opposite. He dropped to the floor, rolled into the doorway and fired once, then rolled back onto his feet and headed for the kitchen.

His shoulder was burning like fire, and his arm was damn near useless, but he ignored it. As long as he could pull the trigger, he was okay, and as long as there was breath in his body, he would find some way to pull that trigger. He wasn't letting Neely down this time. Not on his life.

Strange voices—three, or was it four?—came from the living room and the beams of powerful flashlights swept across the room and through the doorways. He pressed himself flat against the wall, breathing deeply, quietly, straining to hear anything that might tell him where the next gunman would appear, where Brady was or what the hell was going on. The lights strengthened from two directions at the same time—the hallway leading to his bedroom and through the broad doorway into the living room. He eased into the corner behind the dining-room table and held himself utterly still, not even breathing. The men came through the two doorways, hesitated when they saw each other, then continued their slow, cautious path.

"Damn, here's Kenny," one said as he glanced in the laundry room door, then he shrugged, checked behind the door, then came into the kitchen. Their lights hit the back door at the same time, which was standing wide open. *Good thinking, Brady.* "You think…?"

The other man made a gesture, and the first stealthily left the house about three seconds before the second saw Reese. Blinded by the flashlight's beam, Reese fired instinctively, used the shotgun's weight to chamber another round, pointed in what he hoped was the direction of the French doors and shot again before lunging into the darker shadows of the hallway. Tightly hugging the wall again, he blinked to clear the stars from his eyes. Every breath he took smelled of sweat and fear—his own—and blood and death, and every beat of his heart thudded painfully in his chest.

This nightmare would end tonight, he'd promised Neely. It was time to make good on that promise. He inched down the hall toward the living room door, flexed his right hand to make certain it was still working, then stepped into the doorway— and the barrel of a large-caliber handgun.

"Sheriff Barnett, I presume," Eddie Forbes said silkily.

Reese had only a moment to notice that the bastard was cool and steady, the gun not wavering from the underside of his jaw one bit, before someone else came up behind him and disarmed him. The man shoved him to the living room floor, sending another hot flash of pain through his shoulder.

"On your knees," Forbes ordered.

Ignoring the bits of glass that covered the floor, Reese obeyed. He'd barely made it onto his knees when his arms were forced behind his back and secured with handcuffs. He bit back a groan at the pressure the position put on his wound. "What're you gonna do, Ed?" he asked as if he weren't scared for his life and Neely's. "You gonna kill me?"

"Yes, I believe I am."

"You know Jace Barnett? Detective Barnett, who's already working to put your ass back in prison? We're family. He won't settle for prison after this. He'll kill you."

"He may try. Other people have. Obviously, no one's succeeded."

The sounds of battle at the other end of the house came to an abrupt end. Reese hoped Brady had killed his man, but the hope faded when his undersheriff was brought into the room at gunpoint. They put him on his knees, too, and cuffed his wrists behind his back, then Forbes took a seat a safe distance in front of them while sending the two men to find Neely. When they returned empty-handed, Forbes asked, "Where is she?"

"If this is an example of the way you run your illegal enterprises, you can't blame her for your going to prison," Reese said. "You planned and carried out this entire raid without making certain that the person you were looking for was even here? Jeez, Ed, how stupid can you be?"

The flashlights that provided their only illumination showed the anger that flashed across Forbes's face. "Where is Ms. Madison?"

"You've got the wrong Barnett. You need to talk to the detective, not the sheriff."

"There's a locked closet in his bedroom," one of the men said. "Maybe she's in there."

Forbes turned his anger on the man. "You think?" he sneered sarcastically. "Where's the key, Sheriff?"

"Don't have one."

He gestured, and the man behind Reese grasped his shoulder, right over the dressings, and squeezed brutally. For a moment Reese saw stars again and wasn't sure whether he was going to throw up or pass out, or maybe do both and die. When the pressure eased, he gasped heavily, praying for the waves of pain and nausea to pass, then he managed a shrug. "You can do that all night," he said, his voice ragged, little more than a groan, "but it's not going to change the fact that I don't have a key to that closet."

Forbes motioned again, and the agony started again. Sweat popped out on Reese's skin, his vision went blurry, and every nerve in his shoulder cried out for mercy. "I don't...have... a—a key. S-sor...sorry."

For a moment Forbes studied him, then he stood. "Let's go in the bedroom—all of us." There he turned on a bedside lamp, then gave the safe room door the same study he'd subjected Reese to. "Open it."

The command was directed to his men, who took up position a dozen feet back and opened fire. Wood, wallboard and concrete splintered under the fully-automatic assault, but the room, true to its promise, remained impenetrable.

After a hundred rounds or so, Forbes stopped them. "This is one of those safe rooms, isn't it? So the only way to get to Neely is to get her to open the door. And I'd bet the only way to get her to open the door is for you to tell her to. Am I right, Sheriff?"

Reese's shoulder started throbbing and sweat formed on his forehead in anticipation of the pain. He could bear it, he assured himself. He could keep his mouth shut long enough to pass out, and Neely would be safe for a while longer.

But when Forbes reached a decision about how to proceed, it didn't involve Reese, not directly. "On the floor," he commanded Brady. "Take out your .45, Troy, and place it at the back of the gentleman's head. If Sheriff Barnett doesn't tell Neely to open the door...oh, by the time I count to five, blow his brains out. One."

Reese went cold inside. Brady was facing him, his features hard and expressionless, his eyes harder and cold. If he was afraid, Reese could find no sign of it, and that was fine, because he was afraid enough for both of them.

"Two."

Obviously Brady had no intention of pleading for his life with either Reese or Forbes. He was willing to die to keep Neely safe…but it was a waste when she would probably die anyway. If Reese remained silent and they killed Brady, Forbes would try again, except it would be Reese with the gun to his head and Neely with a decision to make.

There was no doubt what that decision would be.

"Three."

But how could he sacrifice Neely to save Brady, just so they could all die together? It was a lose-lose situation. None of them was walking out of there unless…

Neely had the .38. If he could somehow warn her, let her know that she had to be ready to shoot…

"Four."

Reese took a deep breath. "All right."

"No," Brady said sharply.

"I'll get her to open the door."

Troy, holding the gun to Brady's head, looked disappointed as Forbes told him to lower the weapon. Brady looked disappointed, too.

Reese walked to the safe room door, acutely aware of Forbes directly behind him, of Troy a few feet farther back and the third man, standing on the other side of the bed. He focused his gaze on the damaged steel door and called, "Ms. Madison… It's Sheriff Barnett. Can you hear me?"

Neely's voice came through the door, weak and thready as if from a great distance. "Y-yes."

"There are three people out here who would like to talk to you. How about opening the door?"

For a long moment there was nothing but silence, then finally came the familiar scrape of the bar being raised, followed by the twist of the lock. He shifted to the right as she slowly opened the door so that, for one instant, he was the only one who could see her. She was pale, frightened, shaky, but also grimly determined. He wished he could tell her how sorry he was and how much he loved her, but he had time to mouth only one word. *Gun?*

She nodded.

Forbes pushed him aside then and smiled warmly. "Ms. Madison. You're a difficult woman to find."

She smiled, too, a cool, deadly smile, then pulled her hand from her pocket and shot him, center-mass, at point-blank range.

Troy and his partner gaped in surprise, but before either of them could react, Brady rolled onto his back, sweeping Troy's feet out from under him, then delivering a kick that sent his pistol flying. As the other man took aim, Reese lunged, knocking Neely to the floor. He maneuvered her against the bed, then shielded her body with his own, but the next shot didn't come. What they did hear in the silence was a quiet, familiar voice.

"Hey, bud. Did you know it's impossible to miss your target at this close range?" Jace asked conversationally. "Why don't you take your finger off that trigger and give me the gun? 'Cause if you don't, I'm gonna have to pull this trigger, and there won't be enough left of your face for your mama to identify." Raising his voice, he went on. "Reese? Neely? You guys all right?"

"Yeah," Reese replied. "We're fine." He raised his head to find her staring at him. He'd expected tears, grief, overwhelming guilt. There was some regret, but mostly he saw relief. Tenderness. Love.

He eased off of her, tried to raise his hand to her face but couldn't, so settled for kissing her instead. "You're not going back to Kansas City."

"No," she agreed. "I'm staying here and spending the rest of my life with you whether you want me or not."

"I've always wanted you. I always will." He studied her intently. "Are you all right?"

She nodded. "Are you?"

He nodded, too. The pain, the sick feeling, the fear—they were all gone. There was only relief. Satisfaction. And love. "You gonna marry me?"

"Yes."

"You gonna tell me you love me?"

She smiled a slow, lazy, womanly smile. "As soon as we get someplace that's not all shot up, I'm gonna show you...over and over."

"Promises, promises," he murmured.

"The safe room's right here."

"And God bless it." He nuzzled her hair from her ear and was making her shiver when she said, "Hi, Jace."

Reese looked up to see his cousin standing over them. Behind him, Brady was on his feet, unhandcuffed, and standing guard over the remaining two thugs.

"Hey, darlin'," Jace said in response to Neely's greeting. "You do know how to stir up some excitement, don't you?"

"Hey, I didn't do any of this. I was cowering in the safe room until a few minutes ago."

"If Reese has any brains, he'll turn this whole house into a safe room. It seems the only way to keep you out of trouble."

"I only get into trouble because I do my job right. A very smart man told me so." She sat up, then helped Reese sit up. When Jace tossed her his keys, she caught them, then removed Reese's handcuffs before tossing them back. With a wicked smile, she closed both cuffs, then slid them into her pocket. "For later."

In spite of her apparently easy mood, Reese noticed when they got to their feet that she avoided looking at Forbes. He put his left arm around her—the right one was beyond using at the moment—and held her tight. "Damn, I love you," he murmured in her ear.

A shudder vibrated through her, then she lifted her head from his shoulder to look at him. Now the tears he'd expected earlier were in her eyes. "See?" she whispered. "I told you you knew the magic words. I love you, too, Reese."

His house had been shot up, at least five men lay dead or wounded on the floors, and he'd killed his share of them. His own wounds were bleeding again and hurt like the fires of Hades. Brady had come closer to dying than any man ever should, and with more courage than most men ever could. Hell, he and Neely had come close to dying.

But none of it seemed important at the moment, because she'd been right. He was a smart man, and he knew her well. He knew which words hurt, which ones healed and which ones made everything right.

He knew the magic words.

And so did she.

Epilogue

The Fourth of July was hot and humid, with a sun bright enough to blind the eyes and fry the brain, but no one at the second annual Harris celebration seemed to notice. There were burgers and hot dogs cooking on the grill, galvanized tubs filled with ice and pop, tables and chairs set up under tall shade trees, a couple of fans stretched out with extension cords to stir the heavy air, and enough good friendship to make anything bearable.

Neely was leaning against the board fence of the corral, waiting while Reese admired Guthrie Harris's new custom-made saddle in the tack room. It was the work of the newest business in Heartbreak, a saddle- and boot-maker who'd opened a shop downtown and lived up above, and was Olivia Harris's anniversary gift to her husband.

Maybe she would give Reese something similar for their first anniversary, Neely thought dreamily. Of course, they had to get married first, which would happen as soon as the repairs on the house were finished...and after Reese's parents had their chance to tie the knot...and presuming the trials of the surviving hit men didn't interfere. But when they married wasn't so important. Being together—that was what mattered.

"Hey, Miss Neely," the Harris twins greeted in unison. Elly climbed onto the fence, sitting astride the top rail. Emma wrinkled her nose and looked up. "I don't want to get my dress dirty or maybe tear it by climbing."

"Want me to lift you up?" Neely offered, then, when the girl nodded, did so.

Elly gave an ear-splitting whistle, then asked, "You seen my horse, Cherokee?"

"I think the horses decided it would be quieter behind the barn."

"Huh. I'll go see." She leaped to the ground inside the fence and tore off across the corral. Her twin watched her go, then gave a long-suffering sigh. "Elly can't sit still to save her life. Miss Mary calls her a critter. Daddy says she's just got lots of energy, and Mama says she's just bein' Elly and I'm just bein' Emma and that's all right."

"Just being Emma is better than all right. It's perfect," Neely said with a smile. Emma was the little girl most mothers dreamed of—well behaved, polite, demure, happier in frilly dresses, lacy socks and floppy hats than anything else. Elly called her prissy, and in her few weeks as part of Heartbreak's community, Neely had heard a remark or two about her timidity, but she thought Emma really was the perfect little girl.

Of course, so was Elly. And their cousin Annie Grace was the perfect baby, as was their brother, Taylor. These days, Neely thought all kids were wonderful. She could hardly wait for one of her own. She and Reese had been working on that quite a bit lately. She'd never had such fun.

"I like your hat, Miss Neely."

"I like yours, too, Miss Emma. We almost match, don't we?" They both wore sundresses in soft pastels, sandals, and straw hats tied around the brim with pastel ribbons.

"You could pass for mother and daughter," Reese said as he and Guthrie joined them.

"Hey, no one's claiming my daughter," Guthrie said,

swinging her onto his shoulders. "I worked too hard to get her, and I'm keeping her."

Neely listened to Emma's giggles as Guthrie carried her back to the celebration in the yard. No one would guess to see them together that they weren't related by blood, or that a year or so ago was the first time they'd laid eyes on each other. They were so perfect together.

"Having a good time?" Reese asked, leaning against the section of fence Emma had vacated.

"Hmm. You have good friends, Sheriff Barnett."

"*We* have good friends." He studied her, his gaze intent, for so long that she shifted uncomfortably, then laughed awkwardly, then finally leaned back against his chest so he couldn't see her face.

"Don't do that," she teased as he wrapped his arms around her. "I feel like a bug under a microscope."

"Sorry. Sometimes I just can't believe you're here, and that you're all right, and that we're all right."

He'd expected her last dealings with Forbes to cause some problems for her. Truthfully, so had she. She was so accustomed to accepting blame and guilt, and she had *killed* the man—had pointed a gun at him, deliberately pulled the trigger and ended his life.

But she'd grown up some, or developed more of a backbone, or gotten a more realistic take on life. The simple truth was she'd protected herself, the man she loved and another man willing to die for her. If she hadn't killed Eddie Forbes, he would have killed them. Kill or be killed. If faced with the same situation a hundred times over, she would do the same thing every time. She was sorry he'd forced her to make that choice, but she wasn't sorry she'd done it.

The final body count that night had been seven. The house had looked like a war zone, and Reese and Brady had looked as if they'd been put through the wringer, while she'd felt it. Only Jace had been cool and unruffled when it was all over. Of course, only Jace hadn't killed anyone, or faced anyone trying to kill him.

"I wish Brady had come today," she murmured. "I hate to think of him sitting home all alone on a holiday."

"You can't make the man be sociable. He's always been a loner. I imagine he always will be." He nuzzled her hair from her ear and made her shiver. "I'm sorry Hallie didn't make it."

"She probably met husband number four on her way to the airport and went off to Tahiti instead." Feeling a little blue about her recent divorce, Hallie had called two days ago to say she would be in town that morning to spend the Fourth with them, and if Buffalo Plains and Heartbreak weren't just too distressingly different from Los Angeles, she might stick around awhile and give Neely the benefit of her exquisite taste in finishing up Reese's house.

Neely had rolled her eyes and mouthed to Reese, *God save us.* Hallie's exquisite taste came with exquisite price tags and was better suited to Beverly Hills or Palm Beach than Heartbreak.

"But that's okay," she went on. "She'll show up for the wedding, dressed to dazzle all the local yokels. She might even break a heart or two before jetting off to London or Paris."

"You've already dazzled this local yokel so thoroughly he couldn't look at another woman if he wanted."

She turned in the circle of his arms and twined her arms around his neck. "Which, of course, he doesn't."

"For damn sure." He was bending his head to kiss her, his lips brushing tantalizingly over hers, when Jace spoke up from behind her.

"We've been looking all over for you guys, and here you are, making out like teenagers. Jeez, bubba, are you so grown-up that you've forgotten you're supposed to neck *behind* the barn, not out front where everyone can see?"

Ignoring him for the moment, Neely and Reese smiled tenderly at each other. She knew the words whispering in his mind as surely as if he'd spoken them out aloud…and one special time, he had. *I've been looking my whole life for the place where I belong, and here you are.*

He bent close again, kissed her sweetly, chastely, then murmured, for her ears only, "And here you are."

"And here we are," she gently corrected him before turning to greet Jace.

Together, alive, happy, whole and in love in Heartbreak. It was nothing less than magic.

*   *   *   *   *

INTIMATE MOMENTS™

presents a riveting 12-book continuity series:

A Year of loving dangerously

Where passion rules and nothing is what it seems...

When dishonor threatens a top-secret agency, the brave men and women of SPEAR are prepared to risk it all as they put their lives—and their hearts—on the line.

Available May 2001:

CINDERELLA'S SECRET AGENT
by Ingrid Weaver

As a sharpshooter for the SPEAR agency, Del Rogers was determined to capture an arch villain named Simon. Love and family did not factor into his mission. *Until* he found the Cinderella of his dreams in the form of a pretty, pregnant waitress. Helping to deliver Maggie Rice's baby girl was all in a day's work. But keeping his heart neutral was an entirely different matter. Did this chivalrous secret agent dare indulge in fantasies of happily ever after?

Available only from Silhouette Intimate Moments at your favorite retail outlet.

Where love comes alive™

Visit Silhouette at www.eHarlequin.com   SIMAYOLD12

Don't miss the reprisal of
Silhouette Romance's popular miniseries

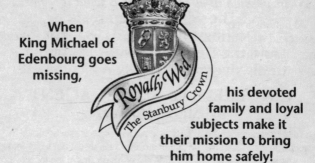

When
King Michael of
Edenbourg goes
missing,

Royally Wed
The Stanbury Crown

his devoted
family and loyal
subjects make it
their mission to bring
him home safely!

Their search begins March 2001 and continues through June 2001.

On sale March 2001: **THE EXPECTANT PRINCESS**
by bestselling author **Stella Bagwell** (SR #1504)

On sale April 2001: **THE BLACKSHEEP PRINCE'S BRIDE**
by rising star **Martha Shields** (SR #1510)

On sale May 2001: **CODE NAME: PRINCE**
by popular author **Valerie Parv** (SR #1516)

On sale June 2001: **AN OFFICER AND A PRINCESS**
by award-winning author **Carla Cassidy** (SR #1522)

Available at your favorite retail outlet.

Silhouette®
Where love comes alive™

Visit Silhouette at www.eHarlequin.com   SRRW3

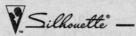